Royally Scandalized

KELLE Z. RILEY

Royally Scandalized

ISBN 978-1-7367811-1-1

Cover Artist (Illustrated Cover): Books Fluent
Cover Arist (Photographic Cover): Ronald J. Rice,
Novel Cover Designs by RJRice Photography

To Thomas Patrick Riley, husband, lover, best friend, and light of my life. In every book, you are the heart and soul of my heroes, and in this you get to be a prince!

Without your inspiration and support these books could not come to life. Thank you for inspiring me to write, and thank you for dragging me out of the writing cave and into the real world.

All my love, forever.

ACKNOWLEDGMENTS

Writing a novel is hard work. Publishing a novel is even harder work. Without my team of dedicated experts and tribe of writer friends, this work would not have been possible. Special thanks go to:

- Tina Winograd, editor extraordinaire. Your input always makes my work better!
- Connie Leap and Theresa Huber, proofreaders,. Thank you for catching errors and providing feedback. You comments challenged and inspired me.
- Katie Salidas , formatter. Thank you for taking on this task and turning my manuscript into a real book.
- Ron J. Rice, Novel Cover Designs by RJRice Photography, cover designer. Your clear eye and ability to turn my words into evocative images is second to none.
- Laurie White, PA. Thank you for helping me manage the social media aspects of the writer's life and countless other details. I'd be lost without you.
- Special thanks to my beta readers and writer friends, Susan Gibberman, Dyanne Davis, Denise Swanson, Frederica Meiners, and Cheryl Woodson. You are my writer tribe. You inspire, motivate, and help me find my way out of plot corners I've backed into. Thank you for the many helpful discussions and great plot twist ideas!
- Thanks to the rest of my writer tribe, members of CARA; Windy City RWA, GRW, TGN, CWG, KOD, and the Crazy Buffet Club Writers. You are a constant source of inspiration, prodding, and laughter.
- Thanks to my family, for standing by me and supporting me as I pursue my dreams.
- Finally, thanks again to Tom Riley, for knowing when to guard my writing time and energy, and knowing when to pull me away from the process. This one's for you.

All errors and omissions are mine alone.

TABLE OF CONTENTS

Chapter 1 1
Chapter 2 12
Chapter 3 23
Chapter 4 36
Chapter 5 48
Chapter 6 57
Chapter 7 63
Chapter 8 76
Chapter 9 86
Chapter 10 93
Chapter 11 101
Chapter 12 109
Chapter 13 121
Chapter 14 130
Chapter 15 142
Chapter 16 152
Chapter 17 164
Chapter 18 178
Chapter 19 190
Chapter 20 203
Chapter 21 210
Chapter 22 217
Chapter 23 223
Chapter 24 235
Chapter 25 244
Chapter 26 253
Chapter 27 262
Epilogue...271
Reluctantly Royal 276
Riches & Royals Excerpt..276

Chapter 1

Prince Constantine Phillippe Ramon D'Malia resisted the urge to pull his shoulders back with military precision. Instead, he slouched beneath his poorly tailored suit coat and ignored the brush of his longer-than-normal hair against his brow.

People saw what they expected to see. His disguise—thin as it was—had allowed him to pass for a tourist many times since he'd learned the trick from his friend Clayton McClaine.

Today, the disguise was critical to his mission. He reached into his suit pocket and pulled out the black-frame glasses his brother had given him as a joke. Well, why not? It always worked for Superman. He slipped them on.

At his side, his aide whistled softly, breaking his concentration. Constantine squinted through the clear lenses and followed the man's gaze to the tall, leggy brunette exiting a bank of elevators on the other side of the cavernous office building. Her tailored, red power suit revealed a generous portion of leg and more than a hint of tight, sculpted curves.

"Look at that one, Your Highness. A woman like that could make you forget this cold Chicago wind."

"Yes, she's a beautiful woman." Constantine watched her glide across the marble foyer, imagining everyone in the twenty floors of windowed offices flanking the foyer stopping to look down at her.

He turned to his friend and long-time confidante. "Remember, Edmund, don't address me as 'Your Highness' in public. Until we find the stolen Crown Jewels, I'm a low-level accountant here to audit the books and learn about our stake in the import business."

"That's a pity. A royal title could convince her to warm your bed within a week."

"You underestimate me. It's not the title that lures them to my bed. Or keeps them there."

"Maybe it's your fabulous wealth."

"It's neither." Constantine turned his full attention to the woman, who was almost within earshot.

"Care to make a wager on that?" Edmund's lilting Melesian dialect was no louder than a whisper. "A thousand U.S. dollars says you can't tempt her into your bed without resorting to either title or money."

"Interesting theory," he replied, switching to English as the lady came face-to-face with them. "Good morning, beautiful one," he said, deliberately letting a thick accent flavor his words. The smile she gave him didn't quite reach her eyes, but, like a poised diplomat, she didn't flinch at his greeting.

He took her hand offered for a cool American handshake, and raised it to his lips instead, lingering over the soft satin of her knuckles while he enjoyed the view. Her neck was slender, its elegance enhanced by a deceptively simple necklace nestled in the hollow of her throat.

His pulse quickened at the sight and all that it implied, confirming his suspicions about the woman. He shoved the thoughts aside and continued his perusal.

More soft, creamy skin was perfectly framed by her tightly buttoned suit coat. Its deep V neck covered just enough to be decent and exposed just enough to whet his imagination.

Black, he thought, momentarily distracted from his purpose. A woman like her would wear only black lace beneath that jacket. As if she could read his thoughts, a blush crept along her skin, delicate pink against the vibrant red silk. He lifted his head but kept her hand in his.

"I am Phillip Raymond, and this is my associate Edmund Russell. I believe you are expecting us."

"Yes, I…" she tugged her hand free. The slight breathlessness in her voice was at war with the frank, assessing look in her eyes. "I'm Jill Bradley. I'll be assisting you during your visit to McKinley and Company Imports. If you follow me, I'll introduce you to the staff and show you to your temporary offices."

She motioned to the elevators, her smile completely cool and professional. Only the pink flush peeking above her neckline and the fluttering pulse in her throat indicated she'd had any reaction to him at all.

But for Prince Constantine Phillippe Ramon D'Malia, second in line to the Melesian throne, and second-to-none in the art of seduction, it was enough.

The offices she led them to were adequate, and most importantly, private enough to conduct his investigations. An attempt at providing Melesian décor explained the royal green and gold furnishings and the potted palm tree withering in the chilly April sunshine that seeped through a lone window.

A portrait of his brother, posed in regal splendor against the backdrop of the Melesian flag, stared down at him from the wall facing the desk.

Constantine felt the involuntary clench of his jaw. Calling on years of royal discipline, he forced himself to relax. His half-brother, King Alexander Augustus Tyronne D'Malia, had been splendid on the day of his coronation five years ago. Now he was gaunt, crippled by disease and pain, his tragic legacy from the king before him.

I shall not fail you, brother. He executed the formal half bow to the portrait as he repeated his silent vow. Beside him, Edmund did the same. Jill stood to one side, respectfully quiet.

"Miss Bradley, I thank you for this touch of home. Your kindness is appreciated."

"Melesia is always in the heart," she said softly in his native tongue.

"You know our national motto? And in our own language? I'm impressed, Miss Bradley."

She shrugged, the self-deprecating gesture at odds with her power suit and its come-hither neckline. "I host all of the firm's international clients when they visit. I'm conversant in most European languages, and I speak three of the seven Melesian dialects."

"Three?" He didn't try to hide his admiration. "Most natives speak only one or two dialects—from the islands closest to their homes. And those outside of the islands rarely learn our language at all. You are, indeed, gifted."

"It's nothing special, really. Languages are easy for me." But despite her protest, a smile tugged at her lips and she glanced down, looking, for a moment, almost shy.

Constantine shrugged the image aside. He couldn't be distracted by the blushing schoolgirl act. Nor would he be seduced by the vixen in red. He studied her, slowly sweeping his gaze from her head to her toes and back again until it came to rest on the filigree necklace with its tiny diamond chip nestled in the hollow of her throat.

The necklace. His mission. It was almost too easy. This woman quite likely held the key to his country's future and stability. With luck, he could be on the way home within a matter of days.

Yes, Jill Bradley was more than she appeared. Yes, she was a woman with secrets. But he was a man with power and purpose. She'd already shown she wasn't immune to him. He would use his charm and any other weapon at his disposal, to uncover each of her secrets. Starting with why the filigree setting of her necklace had the royal insignia, forbidden by ancient law and modern tradition to all but members of the Melesian court, woven into its design.

Jill kicked off her shoes and wiggled her toes in the thick carpet in the lounge area of the private washroom. Almost as an afterthought, she locked the door. She padded to the sink and splashed cold water on her hands before collapsing in an upholstered chair.

Careful not to disturb her makeup, she dabbed her face with a cold, damp paper towel. Even after the icy dousing, she still felt the warm touch of Phillip Raymond's lips on her hand.

It had taken all of her will not to react to the sizzling representative of McKinley and Company's wealthiest client—the island nation of Melesia. Even from across the lobby, he'd drawn her attention.

Approaching him was like walking up to a poorly grounded electrical circuit—her skin tingled and prickled, the downy hair on her forearms lifting in a shiver of sensation. She was aware of her body, the shifting of her hips as she walked and the pull of her breasts beneath her jacket with each breath.

She was aware, too, of how her suit molded to her shape like a lover's caress. The image she'd so carefully cultivated felt tawdry, false. For the first time in years, she'd longed to smooth her jacket and tug at her skirt. The weight of his gaze rested on her until she struggled with every move, like a fish trying to swim in molasses.

He was the incarnation of a lustful dream, easily a head taller than his companion, with thick, dark hair and golden-bronze skin stretched over chiseled cheeks and jaw.

Up close, he was even more magnificent, his startling aqua-blue eyes both mesmerizing and melting, even behind the lenses of his glasses. Their sparking intelligence had shifted to a simmering, smoldering seduction the moment he'd taken her hand.

At the touch of his lips, an image flashed through her mind—him waking, his jaw covered in a faint morning beard, his sleep-rumpled hair sliding over her naked shoulder.

Her breath quickened. *Thoughts like that could only spell trouble.*

Not that Mr. McKinley would mind. He never minded her using the illusion of sex appeal to soothe an irate client or to entice a reluctant one. A potent smile, a hint of flirtation, and a gaze full of implied promises had eased many tense situations over the years.

But instinct warned her that Phillip Raymond wasn't easily manipulated. For reasons she didn't fully understand, Jill needed to keep the upper hand. She'd let charm and passion sweep her away once before, and it had brought her nothing but pain and loss.

Warmth spread through her as she pictured Phillip again in her mind. Like a recovering alcoholic savoring a sip of medicinal brandy, she knew she was in trouble.

Jill wadded up the paper towel and tossed it into the trash, forcing her thoughts back to the present. *Your family depends on you.* Four younger siblings and an overburdened stepmother were counting on her to provide a better future. *Don't let lust ruin their lives like it ruined yours.*

Every dollar she saved or sent home—for college funds or other expenses—made their lives easier. Her own comforts didn't matter. Her father would have been proud of her sacrifice.

She opened her purse to grab a tube of lipstick and instead pulled out the invitation to her high school reunion. Could she return home and face her broken dreams of a husband and family? Would her classmates pity her for still being single? Or envy her for her supposed glamorous life? Both options made her stomach knot. But she'd promised her family she'd visit. If for no other reason than to assure herself they were doing well.

And they were doing well, thanks to her job. A job she needed to get back to. Jill shoved the invitation and memories out of sight.

She stood and smoothed her jacket, trying to ignore the tiny whiff of Phillip Raymond's scent that clung to it. The tangy, spicy aroma carried a hint of exotic floral overtones that conjured up images of sun-drenched beaches and cool shaded palm groves. It was a complex scent, as rare and expensive as the imported Melesian perfumes that McKinley and Company traded.

The expensive cologne fit the man perfectly, but it was out of place with his unpretentious, off-the-rack suit and slightly scuffed shoes. Unease nudged at the back of her brain.

She pushed it aside, shifting her attention to the essentials: a fresh coat of lipstick, a spritz of perfume, and her job. Long hours and dedication weren't enough. She may have graduated near the bottom of her class, but she was smart enough to know what the boss valued her for: her eye appeal, not her mind.

At twenty-seven, it was getting harder and harder to maintain the image of perfection. *You're the pretty one, not the smart one.* Her stepmother's voice hadn't been unkind, just truthful. She'd loved all her children and taught them to use their natural strengths to overcome adversity.

If not for Jill's ability to mimic others and learn languages, she'd have flunked out of school. She knew her beautiful façade—not any unusual intelligence—was responsible for her successes. Once it slipped, she doubted she could provide for her siblings' futures. Ivy league tuition—or any tuition at all—for four didn't come cheap.

She focused on their hopes and dreams as she carefully applied the lipstick. But, despite her best intentions, she tucked the perfume away, unable, or unwilling, to douse his scent with her own.

"I tell you, Edmund, the woman is involved. I want her followed."

"You'll pardon me for saying so, Your—Phillip," Edmund glanced at the closed door before continuing, "but I don't think she's the brains behind an international smuggling ring. She's far too…"

"Too beautiful to be that corrupt? Or to be that smart?"

"Let's say I don't think she's Director of Client Relations because of her organizational skills."

"Nonsense. Our visit has been organized in meticulous detail. As for her intelligence, Melesian is one of the most difficult languages on earth to learn. If she's even half as competent as she claims, she's got a brilliant mind."

"So you truly think she's the mastermind behind the thefts?"

Constantine grinned at his friend's naiveté. For one who grew up inside the royal court and spent his days guarding a prince, he showed a remarkable innocence when it came to politics and intrigue.

"Edmund, I don't know who she is, but I know that her sex appeal is a smoke screen. Consider this. The design of the royal insignia is one of our most guarded secrets. Even the international press humors us by respecting our tradition. A replica like the one on her necklace couldn't have been created by chance."

He studied the painting of his brother. In the official coronation portrait, the artist had obscured the exact details of the insignia, as demanded by a centuries-old tradition. "The insignia is worn by none except the royal court."

"Or the intended bride of the monarch."

"That's nothing but a romantic legend. It may have been true in the days when our brides were married by proxy and shipped to the Caribbean from Greece. But in recent history, outsiders have not seen that specific design."

Constantine leaned back in his chair and stared at his longtime friend and bodyguard. "She's involved. And I intend to find out everything there is to know about her."

"As you wish. I'll set up a surveillance team immediately." He rose to leave.

"Edmund?"

He turned back, almost snapping to attention. "Yes?"

"Try to relax, or you'll accidentally reveal our identities before the week is out." Constantine hid his smile. Edmund wasn't cut out for subterfuge. "And leave the door open when you go. I want to pick up any stray gossip that might help us in our quest."

Taking on this mission himself was risky. Edmund's actions could easily unmask him. Unfortunately, intelligence reports had led him—and the king—to suspect that someone in the top ranks of government was also involved with the theft.

They'd decided not to trust the mission's leadership to anyone outside of the family. And to be honest with himself, he'd wanted one last adventure before he settled into his new role.

An hour later, Constantine scanned the piles of invoices on his desk. They were as empty of information as the hallway was empty of people. No gossip. No paper trails. No leads. He reached for another stack of invoices, but a quiet knock interrupted him.

Jill stood framed in the open door, her hand resting on the polished wood. "I brought you a list of local restaurants and attractions you might enjoy over the weekend." She placed a thick folder on his desk. "I see you're already reviewing the Melesian shipping manifests. Is everything in order?"

He waved his hand over the cluttered desk and grinned. "There's a lot to learn."

"This business can be overwhelming at first. I try to make things easier by at least keeping the office stocked with everything you need."

Constantine looked around the room, again taking in the details of the décor. Small Melesian artifacts and pictures of his island nation graced the bookshelves and credenza top. Even the chairs and the carpeting featured the green and gold of the Melesian flag. "Including the touches of home?"

She smiled and walked over to his bookshelf. "Each of our major clients has a guest office. The Melesian suite is my favorite." She picked up a mother-of-pearl vase and ran her slender fingers over the surface.

Constantine remembered the fragile feel of those fingers in his hand. He watched her circle the room, lightly touching the artifacts, pausing reverently in front of the portrait of his brother. How could one so in tune with the soul of his country steal its most important symbols?

"The office is beautiful," he said softly when she returned to his desk.

"Thank you." Her eyes glowed and a touch of pink colored her cheeks. "I try to make our visitors as comfortable as possible. Which brings me to the other reason I'm here. You must be hungry by now. There's a tea shop and deli on the second floor of the building that might interest you. They have a variety of sandwiches as well as some international specialties."

"More ways to cater to your international clients?" From the look in her eyes, he guessed she had a hand in the international offerings. "Miss Bradley, you are an amazing host. Since my associate has left me to visit with some acquaintances in the area, may I ask you to join me for some tea? You could explain how you process incoming shipments," he added before she could decline the offer.

"Of course."

As Jill transformed from shy into professional before his eyes, Constantine found he missed the young woman who lit up at his modest words of praise and who showed such fondness for his country.

But no matter which face she showed him, he was determined to get close enough to uncover her secrets. He watched the movement of her hips beneath the tight, short skirt as she led the way to the elevator. Either way, it promised to be a pleasure.

Chapter 2

Jill's heart beat a little faster, and her breath hitched as Phillip guided her to the back of the tearoom. His fingertips grazed her shoulder, and a jolt of heat shot down to her pedicured toes. She hadn't been this aware, this responsive to someone since…

Never. Not her first kiss behind the back row of lockers with Tommy Jacobs. Not the time they'd hidden beneath the bleachers at the homecoming game. Not the night of the party that changed her life forever. Not any of the bland, possessive kisses she'd pretended to enjoy since then. Never.

Jill slid into the chair he held for her and tried to regain her composure. But it didn't matter. Even with him settled across the table, his hands occupied with his lunch, waves of heat rippled through her body. She cleared her throat and tried to focus on something normal.

"How long have you been in the import business, Mr. Raymond?"

"Call me Phillip, please. And my involvement in the business is fairly recent." He shrugged as if it didn't matter. "You, on the other hand, seem well versed in imports. How long have you been with McKinley and Company?"

"I joined the company six years ago. They needed an administrative assistant; I needed a job. It was a perfect fit."

"Something tells me there's a lot more to the story than that. To rise from administrative assistant to Director of Client Relations in only six years takes something special." The look he sent her was hotter than her steaming cup of Ceylon black tea.

Jill touched the good luck charm at her throat then jerked her hand away, irritated that her nervous gesture brought attention to her plunging neckline. She fidgeted with her lemon knot cookie instead, shredding the shortbread between her fingers.

Phillip's eyes followed her movements. "Even though I know little of the import business, I'd find someone with your skills quite an asset."

A familiar tightness settled in her belly as she imagined what he saw in her—eye candy. "Exactly what skills did you have in mind?"

As soon as the words were out of her mouth, she regretted them. She'd been more professional with clients who talked only to her breasts. Phillip didn't deserve her condemnation. He hadn't shown any salacious interest. Those hot looks and searing touches were only in her imagination. "I'm sorry. I didn't mean to snap at you."

"I intended it as a compliment, Jill." He captured her hand, pulling it away from the shredded cookie crumbs, distracting her again. "Someone with your knowledge of languages and international cultures must be in high demand."

"It's nothing. I just have an ear for it, I guess."

His thumb slid over her knuckles sending tingling, peppermint-cool shivers across her skin. "You underestimate yourself," he said softly in Melesian. "You are a beautiful, desirable woman, and you think that is the reason for your success, do you not?"

"*Aaya,*" she whispered in reply, using his native language. *Yes.*

"Shall I tell you what I see when I look at you?"

"*Aaya.*" Did she really want to know? She braced herself for his judgment, curling her toes in a hidden display of tension that left her visible features unaffected.

"I see a woman with rare intelligence and exquisite beauty. Yet she does not know herself. I see an actor playing a role with great skill, yet hiding in the shadows off stage. I see someone who sparkles with as many facets as a diamond, who cannot see her own worth."

"I'm no diamond." She fingered the crumbs on her plate with her free hand. The tension seeped out of her toes. "Cut glass, maybe, but no diamond."

"Still, you sparkle. Like the sun on the sands of my homeland." He sighed. "I have been away from my home for only a day, and already I miss the sounds of my island. It is a pleasure to hear my own language from your beautiful lips."

He smiled and a twinkle popped into his ocean-blue eyes. Warmth replaced the tightness in her belly and spread throughout her body. Like a vacationer under a tropical sun, she relaxed in his presence, basking in his compliments, letting down her guard in a way she hadn't done for a long time.

"Jill, it's Friday night, and I'm alone in a strange city. May I take you to dinner?"

The music in his voice and the hunger in his eyes tempted her to think of her own desires first and her duty to her family second. His hand wrapped around hers in a beguiling invitation. Longing as tight as a vise squeezed her chest, forcing air from her lungs, making her head swim in a giddy haze of sunlit fantasies.

"Come with me," he repeated in Melesian.

"*Aay*—I, uh, I can't. I have a previous engagement."

"Cancel it."

She almost obeyed the hint of command in his voice. "I can't." She'd delayed tonight's confrontation for too long. Her attraction to Phillip only intensified her desire to get it over with.

She'd dated the wrong kind of men for too long, thinking they would help her provide for her family. Tonight she would put that option behind her. She didn't have to marry for money—at least not yet. With luck—never.

"Ah, well, maybe another time." Phillip's voice pulled her back to the tearoom. Regret darkened his eyes. He brushed a kiss across her knuckles and released her hand.

All she could do was stare, her heart and mind at war. The man tempted her to throw common sense to the wind. And she knew the disasters that could result from giving in to that kind of temptation.

She had to leave. With a mumbled excuse about a meeting with Mr. McKinley, she stood and hurried from the tea shop, away from Phillip Raymond, before her heart could overrule her mind.

Constantine stashed the glasses in his pocket as he watched Jill leave, more disappointed than angry at her refusal. He'd seen the desire in her eyes, soft and dreamy, as he seduced her with his native tongue.

He felt her shivering response to his touch. And he'd heard the breathless agreement in her voice until she'd covered her slip with a stammering excuse.

So, she had a previous engagement more important than him, did she? Constantine wondered who, or what, doused the light in her eyes and turned her *yes* into a *no*. Not someone who could coax that shy blush to her cheeks with a single compliment. Not someone who looked beyond the luscious curves and creamy skin, or she would have no reason to doubt herself.

The image of the unseen competitor formed in his mind, taunting him with each thought until a searing pain jerked Constantine's thoughts free. Hot tea splashed over the rim of his mangled paper cup onto his fisted hand.

He sopped up the puddle of tea with a napkin, angry at his lack of control. He was a prince on a mission, not a besotted suitor. He was after the Crown Jewels, not Jill. He'd find out where she was going and follow her—for the sake of his mission.

He wasn't interested in her. Her personal choices, no matter how unsuitable, were her own. And if they dimmed the light in her eyes and tinged her voice with resignation instead of joy, what was it to him?

Even though it shouldn't matter, it did. But when had anything ever come between him and his duty to his country? For the first time in many years, Prince Constantine Phillippe Ramon D'Malia of Melesia wished he was merely a man.

Jill tilted her head and pretended interest as Peter Michael Waring III, a man who'd turned his silver baby spoon into a gold-plated place setting for twelve, droned on about his latest coup in the stock market. Peter downed his second gin martini and signaled for another.

The restaurant's flickering candlelight thrust his sharp nose into prominence and hid his eyes in shadow. She glanced toward the window, but the darkened glass only reflected his blurred, wavering profile.

Rain splattered against the window, washing away ten years of detachment and denial, thrusting her mind back into her darkest memories.

She was seventeen again, sprawled in the rain-slick leaves amidst the wreckage of her father's ancient Oldsmobile. Numb from the October cold and dazed from a night of partying with too much spiked punch and too little adult supervision, she'd prayed for rescue, prayed for her father's life.

If only she hadn't called him in an alcoholic haze, begging him to take her home. And if she hadn't blurted out the story of her lost virginity, he might have seen the deer that darted across the car's path.

Instead he'd been looking at her, eyes full of shock and disappointment. His disappointment was the last thing she remembered before she woke up to the sight of vultures circling until the ambulance siren scattered them. Like Peter, they fed on weakness.

Jill pushed back a wave of nausea and turned from the window, blindly accepting a second glass of wine when the waiter offered it. She turned back to Peter, hoping he hadn't noticed her preoccupation or discomfort. As usual, he paid less attention to her than to the sound of his own voice.

She pasted a smile on her face and took a sip of the Cabernet. The mellow, fruity taste and smooth texture marked it as an expensive vintage. When its warmth spread through her, loosening the tension in her neck and shoulders, she didn't resist. It wouldn't hurt to relax a little, just this once.

Jill stifled a yawn and tried to focus on Peter but his face blurred again in the candlelight. This time a pleasant image replaced his fair hair and bland features. Phillip Raymond, his aqua-blue eyes and dark, mesmerizing looks filled her imagination. She could almost hear the music of his voice.

"Jill?" Peter's nasal tones grated on her ears, destroying her romantic memory. He looked at his empty glass and frowned, signaling the waiter for yet another while he popped the alcohol-soaked olive in his mouth.

"Darling, you look pale. Are you feeling poorly? I hope you're not coming down with something. I told Father and Mother that you'd join us for the annual spring cotillion at the club this weekend. It's very important that they get to know you before they give us their blessing."

"Blessing?" Jill stared at Peter. "Why do we need their blessing?"

"Don't worry, darling. They'll approve of you. They'll find your rural roots charming once they realize how sophisticated you've become. You're a perfect companion…"

For one horrible moment, she thought he was about to propose. With his wealth and connections, he was the answer to Mom Rose's prayers, but Jill's stomach clenched at the prospect of spending her life with him. Her stepmother's voice sounded in her head. *It's as easy to love a rich man as it is to love a poor man.*

She wondered if her own mother, who'd died when she was six, would've agreed with the woman who'd taken over the job of raising Jill. *It's as easy to love a rich man…*

Jill had tried. Heaven knew she'd tried to fall in love with Peter, but she couldn't. A loveless marriage to a wealthy predator—even to secure her siblings' futures—suddenly seemed as wrong as her high school indiscretion. Except this time, she'd be true to herself. She'd play it smart and leave before anyone got hurt.

After tonight, she'd never see Peter Waring again. She'd break it off and start fresh, not sacrificing love for money.

Besides fate had given her another way to support her family. With hard work and a little luck, she could help them without sacrificing herself. Her chance meeting with Mr. Dimas a few years ago had blossomed into a steady, growing income stream.

Next year, she could move her sister from the community college to a better school. Maybe not Ivy League, but better.

And in a few more years, the other sisters and brother could follow.

She grabbed at the excuse Peter had offered, claiming a migraine and saying she'd get her own cab home. When he nodded, accepting her ruse, she made her apologies and slipped from the restaurant. Maybe one day, he'd realize this was the night she'd slipped from his life, too. But for now, he had a fresh martini to keep him company.

Constantine sipped his aged single malt scotch and watched Jill leave the restaurant. Her posture and bearing were as regal and remote as any member of his court until she dabbed at her eyes with a handkerchief.

He rose from his seat, instinctively wanting to comfort her, then sat down again, remembering that he'd come to observe, not to be observed.

Her date threw a wad of bills on the table and headed for the bar. His gait had too much refinement to be called a swagger and too much arrogance to be anything else.

Like the bluebloods at home who questioned Constantine's legitimacy because of his heritage and the fact his mother wasn't of their rank, the man oozed privilege and disdain. Constantine saluted him with his glass and nodded in his direction.

"Hell of a night," the man said, accepting the invitation and plopping down on an empty bar stool.

"I'll bet. Your date was a real looker. Too bad she dumped you."

"Dumped me?" He signaled for a drink and grinned "No. She never leaves with me. Always meets me in public and takes her own cab home. She's one of those who thinks if she strings me along without putting out, I'll eventually ante up with a diamond ring. I've got someone on the side to warm my bed, anyway. Don't worry about her dumping me. She'll be back."

"For a man who's drinking alone, you seem sure of yourself."

"I know how to handle women. I'm sure you do too," he said downing his drink and ordering another. "Or maybe not."

The man looked him over and Constantine regretted not changing from the plain wool suit of his disguise into something befitting his station. He shrugged and offered his hand, relying on breeding and bearing to show what his clothing did not. "Phillip Raymond."

"Peter Waring the third." They shook hands.

"And the lovely woman who walked out on you?"

Waring downed his drink—Constantine had lost count of how many he'd had—and considered the question with a smirk. "Jill? She'll be back. She's smart enough to know who butters her bread. And I'm smart enough not to let her go. She's got everything I need in a wife. Poise. Polish. Small town, heartland roots. The perfect mate for a man in my position."

"What position is that?"

Waring hesitated, contemplating his empty glass. But the alcohol overruled common sense. "I don't like to say. But since you're obviously a foreigner, it won't hurt. I've got my eye on a couple of political appointments and eventually a bid for an elected position. I'm tired of just making money. I want to make a name for myself."

He signaled the waiter for another drink, then continued. "Jill is exactly the kind of woman I need. She looks like a model, she tugs at the American heart strings, and when I get bored with her, she'll pretend not to notice—for the right price."

"And the right price would be..." Constantine lifted an eyebrow, encouraging Waring to continue.

"Trinkets from Tiffany's." Waring tossed back another drink. "She's smart enough to know that I'm the best thing that ever happened to her."

A hot rage coiled in Constantine's gut, as sudden and forceful as the hurricane winds that assailed his island coast. How dare she wear the royal Melesian signet yet treat him with such cool dismissal? How dare she sell herself to this bigoted opportunist for a few jewels?

He didn't know which bothered him more—that she'd sell herself for money or that she'd sell herself to Waring while ignoring him. His rational mind protested that he was undercover. He had no claim on her—he'd offered her nothing more than an impromptu dinner. He was being foolish. But his anger was stronger than his rational mind.

Constantine rolled his glass between his hands watching the slow swirl of the amber liquid. He'd have his men do a little digging into Peter Waring III's background, but he already knew what he'd find. Old money and old connections. Jill set her sights high.

A thousand U.S. dollars says you can't tempt her into your bed without resorting to either title or money. Edmund's voice taunted him. He'd been so sure of himself until she turned him down. The yearning, the desire in her eyes had been as real as the desire pounding through his veins. Yet she'd chosen Peter Waring III and his trinkets instead.

No matter. Constantine reined in his anger and focused on the problem at hand. He was sure Jill held the key to finding the stolen Crown Jewels. He had to uncover her secrets. And where better to do that than in the intimacy of his bedchamber?

Yet even as he contemplated ways to seduce her, he knew he couldn't take the easy way out and use his title or money, as Edmund suggested. How likely was it for a jewel thief to confide in her victim? Especially one who could punish her for her crimes against his state?

No, he would earn her confidence and learn the depth of her involvement in his guise of Phillip Raymond. Then, if she was the jewel thief, he would extract justice as Crown Prince Constantine, future king of Melesia. And if Jill was the kind of woman who would sell herself to the highest bidder, it would make his duty easier to swallow.

At least that's what he told himself as he left the bar and walked out into the cold drizzle. But as he waited for the valet to bring his car around, he glanced toward the bus stop and saw her again. Shoulders slumped and head bowed, she barely resembled the woman he'd met earlier.

So, she hadn't taken a cab like she'd told Waring. Instead she'd chosen to wait in the rain for a bus. Like so many things about her, it didn't fit.

A car skidded to a stop, horn blaring as another car swerved out of its path in the intersection. Jill raised her head and flinched at the sound, the movement exaggerated enough for him to notice from half a block away.

The treacherous desire to comfort her warmed his heart again. Snatching the keys from the valet, he took a step in her direction, only to stop when the bus pulled up. It had been a bad idea, anyway.

He needed to watch and learn about her, not get sucked into whatever games she was playing. His common sense knew that, but as he watched her board the bus, another part of him warned that learning about Jill and completing his mission were not going to be easy.

Chapter 3

onstantine expected to use the Saturday morning quiet to investigate McKinley and Company's operations. He didn't expect to come face-to-face, or rather face-to-backside, with Jill.

She stood on a chair by the window, the succulent curves he remembered hidden beneath soft, faded jeans and a baggy sweatshirt. She stretched up on tiptoe, showing him the delicate arch of her bare foot. His eyes traced the high, soft curve down to her coral painted toenails.

An unbidden wave of protectiveness surged though him, stronger than the lust she'd inspired yesterday. He took a step forward, curious to know if her foot felt as soft and vulnerable as it looked. Foolish. A man of his reputation should be immune to the sight of a bare foot.

Then she moved, stretching her arms higher until her fingertips brushed the tendrils of ivy carved in the plaster molding near the ceiling. And exposing a sliver of bare back beneath the hem of her sweatshirt.

More private flesh, not intended to be seen, not consciously displayed. This time he was within an arm's length of touching what he wasn't meant to see.

At home—or on his public forays abroad—he could attract any woman he wanted with a single look of interest. Here, he was reduced to a voyeur spying on the desirable from afar. Yet the challenge of it aroused him in a way the easily offered delights of home did not.

She shifted and a whiff of vanilla teased his nostrils, the scent was warm, homey and in tune with this version of Jill. His body tightened with the need to touch her, to kiss the exposed small of her back and see if she tasted as sweet as she smelled.

Instead, he took the high road. "You look like you could use some help."

Jill whirled and shrieked, teetering on the chair. The whatever-it-was she'd been holding clattered to the floor seconds before she pitched forward, unbalanced.

He caught her and slid her down his body, bracing his hands against the firm length of her legs until the lush, unseen curves of her butt filled his grip. He pressed her close, not wanting or able to hide his arousal from her.

Despite two layers of denim between them, the warmth of her intimate curves cupped him in a perfect fit. Lowering her the rest of the way to the ground was an agonizing stroke of foreplay, the rasping of dry fabric replacing the slick glide of bare flesh he desired.

He slipped one hand beneath the hem of her sweatshirt, feeling the silk of her back. Her uneven breathing and the soft press of her chest against his made it clear that the only thing she wore under the sweatshirt was a splash of perfume.

"You startled me."

Her brown eyes were wide, her lips parted, soft and vulnerable.

"I'm sorry," he whispered into the void as he claimed her lips with his own.

He tasted the softness, gently caressing while she yielded. He stroked her lips, outlining them with his tongue, tempting and teasing until she opened completely to him.

Jill accepted the hot sweep of his tongue into her mouth without protest. She'd wanted this since the first moment she'd seen him, dreamed of it last night when sleep evaded her.

She twined her arms around his neck. His hair, cool and soft, brushed her knuckles, tickling them even as he tickled the roof of her mouth with his tongue. Shivers skittered down her spine where he soothed them with the burning stroke of his hand. And lower still, he held her, hip pressed to hip, his hard desire the only thing not held captive under his mastery.

Her heart still raced, no longer from his unexpected presence, but rather from his sensual possession. He was everywhere, surrounding her. His spicy, exotic scent, his heat, the wonderful careless abandon he inspired in her. She pressed closer, craving the heat, and the connection, more than she craved her next breath.

"Your—Phillip!"

Jill's attention flew toward the door. Out of the corner of her eye she saw his companion standing there, mouth agape. She tried to pull away, but Phillip refused to release her.

"Not now, Edmund." Phillip lifted his mouth from hers long enough to issue his terse command. Edmund slunk out of sight.

Phillip kissed her again, his lips working a gentle, slow rhythm against hers, but the moment had evaporated under Edmund's brief scrutiny. Jill wiggled away, feeling like a teenager caught making out on her parents' front porch.

Self-control was one of the few things she took pride in as an adult. She'd learned it over hard years of struggle and denial, atoning for her self-indulgent youth. Eventually, she'd mastered the art of adding just enough sex appeal to smooth a relationship without going too far. Of giving the illusion of intimacy without giving of herself. At least until she met Phillip.

"I need to finish," she turned to the window and tried to collect her jumbled thoughts.

Behind her, Phillip cleared his throat. "Yes. As I recall, I was offering my assistance before you took your tumble. What is it we were doing?"

We. His tone made the word intimate, comforting, like real cocoa on a cold, winter night. Jill wished there were a *we* in her life, but she'd been on her own, shouldering responsibility for her family for so long, she doubted it would ever be any other way.

"I was trying to hang this lamp."

"So that's what nearly bashed me on the head when you fell."

"Sorry about that," she mumbled, retrieving it so he wouldn't see how flushed the memory of that fall made her. Her body still tingled from the brief, intimate contact with his. Clutching the lamp, she turned to the chair. His warm hands at her waist stopped her.

"Let me." He moved with athletic grace and male confidence, not caring that his shoes could mar the upholstered fabric. Within seconds, he located the hook she'd been trying to reach and anchored the lamp.

"Good." She plugged it in and switched it on. "It has a flexible arm—can you adjust the angle a little?"

He twisted it so the light fell on her face, obscuring her view with its glare. "So tell me, Jill," his voice drifted to her from the darkness behind the glare, rich, regal, and slightly amused, "how long have you had this secret desire to be in the spotlight?"

"It's not for me. It's for the palm tree." She swatted him on the calf, breaking the spell. "Now, be helpful and give my tree the benefit of that artificial dose of sunshine."

"If you insist. But you are much prettier than that half dead excuse for a palm tree."

"It's not dead. It's just a little stressed because I transplanted it last week." She pulled a fertilizer solution from the basket next to the tree and doused its roots, then sprayed the fronds with a fine mist. "All it needs is sunshine, warmth, and a little attention."

He moved beside her and cocked his head, gazing first at the tree, then at her. His eyes locked on hers, darkening to a deep, stormy blue. Jill held her ground, resisting the urge to look away, though she sensed that he was assessing her, measuring her against some unseen standard.

When a smile replaced the turbulence in his eyes, she drew a deep, calming breath. Phillip brushed a strand of hair behind her ear. "Do you do this for all of your clients? Or am I special?"

"What do you mean?" Her mind filled with images of the kiss they'd shared.

"Surely you have better things to do on a Saturday morning than to fuss over a potted palm tree."

"And what about you? What are you doing hard at work on a weekend?"

He shrugged, the motion understated yet somehow elegant. Even wearing a simple, blue cotton sweater, he looked like a model. It was a shame that a man like him chose to bury himself in a dark room under shipping manifests and sales logs.

"My country expects a great deal of me." His gaze slid to the portrait dominating the wall.

"Giving your all for country and king?"

He nodded, turning more fully to the wall. As he executed the customary half bow in honor of the king, his eyes flashed, brief and stormy, before he hid his emotions.

"Have you ever met him?" Jill asked.

"Of course." He hesitated. "All of the students from the Royal Academy are introduced to the royal family. King Alexander is the sponsor of King's College at the Academy."

"Alexander Augustus Tyronne D'Malia, 38th reigning monarch of the Kingdom of Melesia," she said softly.

"Do I detect a hint of a royal watcher in you? Is that why you like our country? Admit it," he teased, "you're a sucker for a Cinderella story."

Jill felt her cheeks grow warm. "Prince Alexander and Lady Helena were the love story of my generation. All the television stations, radio channels, and newspapers in America carried coverage of the royal couple.

"He saw her walking along the beach, fell instantly in love, and proposed to her within the hour. You can't beat that for romance. I think every girl at the Clarkson Community College crammed into the student union to watch their wedding."

"American royal watcher to the core," he accused with a grin. "Who would have thought it from a sharp businesswoman like you?"

"Every woman fantasizes about the man who'll sweep her off her feet one day. We don't expect a literal prince. Just...love."

"Love and marriage are two separate things. Especially in royal families like the D'Malia family. Your romantic story is nothing more than a media invention. Let me tell you the facts."

His voice grew hard, and he held up a hand and ticked points off on his fingers with the precision of a teacher in a college lecture hall. "One. Helena was betrothed to Prince Alexander on her first birthday. Two. Their marriage cemented a political bond between the throne and a very influential old family. Everything else was fantasy."

"Don't you think they were in love?"

He stared at the portrait for a long time then finally shook his head. "It doesn't matter. Modern monarchies are about duty and power. And don't fool yourself into thinking that your political system is immune. People marry for all kinds of reasons. Love is the least of them."

"But…"

"No buts, Jill." He grasped her arms and turned her to face him. Though his hands were gentle, his eyes were hard and his jaw rigid. "Duty and power. Remember that."

"Duty and power," she echoed as she slid her gaze from his face to her still bare toes. "In other words, you won't find a Melesian girl with romantic dreams about Prince Charming."

"No."

"What kind of romantic dreams would she have?"

He loosened his grip and trailed his fingers along her arm until she looked up. His jaw relaxed as a slow, wicked grin replaced his frown. "Cowboys, ma'am. Rough and ready, ride-into-the-sunset American cowboys," he drawled.

"That fantasy is about as unrealistic as your cowboy accent, which, by the way, is the worst I've ever heard." She giggled, the tension between them finally broken. Laughter bubbled and fizzed through her system, making her giddy, like champagne drunk too fast.

Before she could get control of herself, he joined in, adding a rich baritone chuckle of his own. Jill couldn't stop. Years of bottling her emotions erupted in the laughter, making her feel free for once. She could barely gasp for breath as the laughter fed on itself making everything, from the lopsided palm tree to the dizzy way her heart raced around Phillip, seem funny.

At last she collapsed against the desk, ribs aching. Phillip leaned on the desk beside her, sliding his arm around her waist.

"So," he said reverting to his natural Melesian accent, "if you don't dream about princes or cowboys, what do you fantasize about?"

"I stopped dreaming a long time ago. Real life and my obligations to my family are the only things that concern me now."

"Me too."

Although he sat beside her, his hand warm and secure at her waist, his gaze was fixed on the portrait of King Alexander. From the stormy blue of his eyes and the frown tugging at his mouth, Jill understood, without knowing why, that his burdens were as heavy as her own.

Constantine ignored the thump of his heart and tried to control his breathing, resisting the urge to step away from the floor-to-ceiling windows as he pretended interest in the city below. Though he'd learned to mask the outward signs of panic, he'd never liked heights.

Crowds thronged around him—too close for comfort—a teeming reminder that today he was a tourist, not a royal dignitary. He mentally recited the words to the monarch's pledge as he envisioned his upcoming coronation, trying to forget he was 1,300 feet in the air in a steel and glass cage. The city blurred beneath him—not entirely due to the unfamiliar glasses of his disguise.

"From this side of the Willis Tower, you get a great view of the lake." Jill's voice broke through his self-imposed mantra and gave him something else to focus on. He followed the sweep of her arm as she pointed along the shoreline. "Those little star-like dots are marinas where the sailboats are anchored. Boating on the lake is a popular pastime in the summer."

"Sailing is popular in my home too." He would gladly trade the drunken sway of this tower for the rhythmic list of his sailboat. He understood, and respected, the forces of the wind and the shifting waves.

"On a clear day, you can see Wisconsin, Michigan, Indiana, and Illinois from the tower."

"On a clear day in Melesia, you can see the sea, glistening in the sun and stretching to the horizon."

"Is Melesia as beautiful as it looks in the photographs?"

"You've never visited our archipelago?"

"I've never been anywhere." A wistful look crossed her face and for a moment, Constantine forgot his worries.

"We shall have to remedy that," he said softly. "Perhaps one day, sooner than you think, you will visit my country."

"Perhaps." She smiled, hiding the longing in her eyes. "But for now, you are our guest, and I'd like to show you the rest of Chicago."

There was one advantage to crowds, Constantine thought as he endured the crush of tourists in the elevator. Jill stood in front of him, the warm curve of her buttocks pressed against his hips in a way that made the ride memorable. Even on the street, the constant brush of humanity made it seem only natural for him to walk close to her.

When they paused at an intersection, reflex made him grasp her elbow to assist her across. Something else made him trail his hand down her sweatshirt sleeve until he entwined her fingers in his own.

He heard her sharp intake of breath, but she didn't pull away. Instead, she covered her gasp with a small, unconvincing cough.

"The Chicago River is a man-made marvel of engineering," Jill began, her voice as bland as if her hand wasn't cradled in his. As if the morning's sizzling kiss hadn't stirred her passions. Constantine knew better.

"Tell me about you."

"What?"

"The river is nothing but water, the city nothing but buildings. I can read its history in a book or find dozens of descriptions on the internet. I want to know about you." He squeezed her hand gently. "You said you've never been anywhere before. Were you born here?"

"No. I was born in a small town in Ohio. I grew up on a farm and went to the community college. Then, after college, Mr. McKinley offered me a job, and I moved to Chicago. This was the first big city I'd ever seen."

He hid his surprise as they passed into the shade of a skyscraper. The cool darkness, broken by occasional strips of sunlight, was as foreign to him as Jill was.

"Chicago is a long way from your home." He let the words hang, waiting for her to fill the silence and satisfy his curiosity.

"I wanted to see at least some of the world before I settled down."

"Why not all of the world?"

"Maybe someday." Jill shrugged. "For now, I have to focus on my job."

"Is it not strange to work for an import house and yet never travel outside of Chicago?"

"I'm just a glorified errand girl. I don't have any special skills. Mr. McKinley doesn't need me to travel."

"No special skills?" He almost laughed, surely, she was jesting, until he saw her look of utter seriousness. He softened his tone. "Jill, did you not tell me that you spoke most of the European languages and three Melesian dialects?"

She nodded.

"Your proficiency with language is a very special skill."

"It's mostly just a hobby." She dismissed his interest with a delicate movement of her shoulders that was almost lost beneath the baggy gray sweatshirt.

"I enjoyed Spanish, French, and German in college, so I convinced Mr. McKinley to pay my tuition and I enrolled in language immersion courses. I manage to squeeze in about one course a year. It's useful when we have foreign visitors. McKinley and Company has a brisk international business, so I get plenty of practice even without leaving home."

"And Melesian? Did you learn that in an immersion course too?"

Jill ignored his question and pulled him out of the shadows into a sunlit plaza dominated by a huge twisted piece of steel.

"This," she said, pointing to the towering piece, "is one of our best-known landmarks. It's a sculpture by Picasso. You'll get a better view from the front."

She pulled him around, circling the sculpture for the perspective she wanted. A sphinx-like face emerged from the chaos.

"So it is a work of art after all," he mused, teasing her. "And I thought you were showing off a piece of wreckage from the Chicago fire."

"No, the fire was much earlier. In fact, everything east of Michigan Avenue was created from landfill as a result of the fire. It—"

"Jill," he interrupted her tour-guide routine and looked down into her face. "I know. I read it in a guidebook. Why did you bring me here?"

"It's part of our heritage. I always bring guests to see the Chicago highlights."

"Am I just a guest to you, then?"

"No, I…" She paused, her eyes glazed as if searching for the right words.

Constantine turned her to face the sculpture, his hands resting lightly on her shoulders as he stood behind her. "Tell me why you like the sculpture—or if you do. Tell me about the city as only you can. Let me see it through your eyes, not through the text of a guidebook."

Jill intrigued him—first giving him a glimpse of vulnerability then quickly hiding behind her detached, professional persona. Which was the real Jill?

For a moment, she stared straight ahead at the sculpture. Then, instead of pulling away as he'd feared, she leaned back, relaxing against him. He released her shoulders and took her hands instead.

In a fluid, gentle move he wrapped his arms, still twined in hers, around her middle, hugging her close. The warmth between them built until at last, she spoke.

"I first saw the Picasso when I used to walk up here for lunch. I came in the way we just did—from the side. It didn't look like anything to me at first, but one day, I walked around and studied it. That was when I saw the face. Everything is a matter of perspective." She eased free of his grip and faced him "Sometimes what you see at first isn't the real thing at all."

Constantine studied her. Her wide brown eyes filled with a vulnerability and softness. A breeze tugged at the wisps of hair that framed her face. He leaned close, ready to kiss away the haunted look.

His gaze slipped lower and caught a glint of silver beneath the baggy sweatshirt she wore.

The necklace.

How could he have forgotten his mission, even for an hour? The real question wasn't whether or not Jill was involved with the stolen gems. The necklace alone proved she was. But nothing else about her was easy to read. What had she just said? *Sometimes what you see at first isn't the real thing at all.*

What was real about Jill? Was she the savvy, sexy businesswoman of yesterday, or the wide-eyed waif in front of him today? Was she a knowing participant in the theft and disposal of the gems? Or an unwitting pawn?

Chapter 4

Jill stared at Phillip, watching his eyes change from aqua-blue to a deeper hue and back again. Why had she spouted that foolishness? *What you see at first isn't the real thing.* Her words reverberated in the silence between them. She didn't really want him to look beneath the surface, did she?

As his gaze flitted over her face, she wondered what he *would* see if he looked past her carefully constructed image. The headstrong homecoming queen who hadn't thought beyond her own popularity until the accident that took her father's life? The determined daughter struggling to ease the life of her step-mother and four younger siblings? The cold imposter who used the illusion of sex to keep people at a distance? Or would he see something else entirely?

Jill shivered, feeling naked under that gaze, despite the comforting warmth of her father's baggy varsity sweatshirt. She closed her eyes, not wanting to let him look into her soul. Not wanting to know what Phillip Raymond would see if he pierced her defenses.

The soft press of his lips to her temple stirred something inside her, a longing she'd pushed aside for too many years. Just once, she wanted to be carefree again. To feel alive. More than that, she wanted someone to hold her, comfort her, give her a sense—however fleeting or false—of belonging.

Why not? Phillip Raymond would be out of her life before spring turned to summer, and she would go back to being the responsible, dependable support for her family. After ten years of propriety, she deserved one little fling. Even a single night of warmth and caring.

But listening to her own desires had only brought heartache. Most girls fought with their parents during the turbulent teenage years. Most moved beyond that stage to be loving, warm families. But Jill's rebellion had led to her father's death.

She'd almost lost the rest of her family that night too. Her once adoring younger sister turned away and locked herself behind a mountain of books. Her other sisters and brother clung to their mother. And Jill withdrew, trying to make amends in the only way she knew how. By giving them the financial support her father no longer could.

If her teenaged desires had cost so much, what would giving in to her adult desire for Phillip cost her?

She didn't dare risk it. She dragged herself away from his lips, his embrace, and stiffened her spine. Distance. If she could create the distance between them that she'd kept between herself and all her other clients, they'd both be safe.

Jill grabbed Phillip's hand and pulled him away from the sculpture. "If you want to see Chicago through my eyes, we'd better start with lunch—I'm starving."

After several breathless blocks, she turned along Chicago River and led him down a flight of stairs to the streets below the main city. An inexpensive pizzeria—one of her favorite haunts—lay hidden between grimy storefronts.

Beside her, Phillip drew in a sharp breath. His hand tightened on hers as he looked about the stuffy, exhaust-scented shadows.

"This way." Jill tugged him toward the restaurant. Phillip walked ahead of her and opened the door.

Beside the stoop leading to the pizzeria, a thin, unkept man huddled into a dirty blanket. Jill fished a wad of crumpled bills and some coins out of her pocket and dropped them into his cup before entering the tiny grotto where the smell of garlic and tomato hung in the air. She moved past the counter and headed to a booth in the back.

"That man," Phillip said behind her, "should we not notify the authorities? He needs assistance."

Jill shook her head. Maybe Melesia didn't have poor crowding the streets. Or graft and corruption. Or maybe Phillip was as sheltered and naïve as she'd once been. "The police would only chase him away. Come night, he'll find a shelter. Or he'll go home to his house in the suburbs and deposit today's take in the bank."

She signaled for a waiter. "It's like I said before. Not everything is as it seems. Some of the panhandlers you find on the streets are actually con artists living off the charity of gullible tourists."

"If they are con artists, should you not be wary of giving them money?" His brow creased in a frown.

Jill reached for her glass of water and took a sip to hide her smile, amazed at how a simple step off the beaten tourist path shook his self-assurance.

"I'd rather fall for a scam than pass up a case of real need," she said. "Besides, this area isn't known for waves of tourists. You did say you wanted to see Chicago through my eyes, didn't you?"

Phillip nodded, encouraging her to talk. Half an hour later, when the waiter served their food, she'd given him a crash course on street smarts that took her two years to learn.

"Anyway," Jill chattered as she served him a slice of cheesy deep-dish pizza, "the trick is to do what you can. If I emptied my wallet every day, the hungry would still be there. Instead,

I talked Mr. McKinley into making a sizable donation to the shelters."

"You are both generous and wise. I hope you will tell me how I can make a donation as well. A personal donation, that is. I also have some influence with my government. Perhaps our embassy could arrange a gift." He took the pizza, lifting the plate to observe, then sniff the cheesy concoction, like a gourmet approaching a new dish.

"You look like you've never had pizza before."

"Pizza, in my experience, is flat. I…have not had anything quite like this before." He cut off a cautious bite and chewed, his face an impartial mask. After a few seconds, a smile replaced the stoic look. "But I will definitely have it again."

Jill watched as he ate in silence, his brow creased in thought. His gaze peeled away her defenses, leaving her raw, exposed without her business suit or tourist guide patter to hide behind. Was this the price of giving in to her desires? She resisted the urge to squirm in her seat.

Bringing him here was a mistake. She should have stuck to the tourist routine. It was a mistake to come out with him at all. She glanced down at her clothes, ashamed of their ragged comfort. She didn't like being stripped of her defenses, nor the vulnerable feelings Phillip awakened in her. He shouldn't have been at the office today, intruding on her privacy, tempting her into an unfamiliar world filled with emotional landmines.

Yet after the searing kiss and that moment of understanding that passed between them, how could she have abandoned him for the day? Besides, what harm was there is letting her image slip a little? She'd never see Mr. Phillip Raymond again after he concluded his Chicago business. The junior executives rarely returned to McKinley and Company. She could afford a day, or a week, of happiness before she stepped back on the treadmill of responsibility.

"So, Jill, you never told me where you studied the Melesian language." His smile tempted her to forget responsibility.

"You'll laugh."

"Try me."

"Well, it all goes back to the marriage of Prince Alexander and Lady Helena. Everyone at school gobbled up the details of the courtship and whirlwind romance. It was so popular, my French teacher, Miss Foster, offered to teach a semester class on Melesian culture.

"She'd studied on the islands, so she contacted friends at your Royal Academy for materials. I checked out the language CDs every chance I could. I fell asleep listening to those CDs so many times, that I'm sure I dreamed in Melesian."

"You learned the entire language from CDs? Including the dialects?"

Jill laughed at his incredulous look. "Of course not. Miss Foster tutored me in the Royal Melesian and Main Island dialects. I picked the other up later. So, you see, the romantic fantasy of Prince Alexander and Lady Helena did have some practical value."

"Indeed. I shall have to remember to thank them when I get home."

"Yes," Jill said, switching from English to Melesian. "Please thank Their Majesties for me as well. Without their love story, I would have missed the opportunity to learn of your home."

"And what else do you know of my home?"

"I know that you're not likely to drop by the palace for tea, even though part of the grounds have been turned into a high-class resort for the international elite. The king and queen are reported to be very private."

"Do you know what it is like to be constantly on display, Jill? To be hounded by the press and mobbed by the curious?" His jaw tightened, and his eyes darkened to a stormy hue before fixing on a point just beyond her shoulder.

The sudden, wary look in his eyes and the hard edge to his tone was out of place with their casual conversation. Like the expensive cologne that contrasted with his simple clothes, something about Phillip's demeanor puzzled her. She chose her next words carefully.

"I understand a little of what that's like." A familiar coldness settled in Jill's stomach as she recalled the appraising looks her clients gave her, as if she could be bartered and sold like the rest of the imports. The administrative assistants resented her. Peter treated her like a prized possession to be displayed or stored away at will. Yes, she knew the sacrifices of living life under the eyes of others.

"Basically, I know anything you can learn from a book," she said, pushing the uncomfortable thoughts away. "Culture. History. Legend."

"Ah. History and legend. Over the years the two have become so entwined that it is hard to separate one from the other." His teasing tone was back. The tension between them faded and Jill leaned against the booth, tightness seeping from her bunched shoulders.

"Legend says the first monarch was an exiled nobleman from Greece. Other theories say he was a thief." She smiled and skewered him with a look. "Which theory do you believe?"

"I would not dare call him a thief in the presence of the king. Besides, once one is a monarch, does it matter what he was before?" He smiled, his blue eyes alight with a twinkle that lit up the dim interior of the pizza shop.

"What about the royal insignia?" Jill gave free rein to her curiosity. "Legend has it that only the royal family is allowed to wear it. When the royal wedding was broadcast, the insignia was obscured by one of those blurry squares. You know, the kind they use to hide body parts when someone appears nude on camera."

"Ahh. And are you an expert on such things, Jill?" A tingle crept down her spine at his devilish grin.

"No, and no. I'm not an expert on nude films, and I'm not an expert on the royal insignia. Is it true that it's worn only by the royal family?"

"The royal family and, once upon a time, the intended bride of the monarch. Or so the legend says." He took another slice of pizza. "Speaking of designs, that's an interesting necklace you're wearing. You wore it yesterday too, didn't you?"

Jill fingered the piece, pulling it out from behind her sweatshirt. "It's kind of a good luck charm. I've worn it for years."

"Tell me more." The words, although softly spoken, were more forceful than a request, yet stopped short of being an outright demand. Something in his voice, his look, compelled her to answer.

"A few years ago, McKinley & Company was approached by a Melesian expatriate, Mr. Dimas. His nephew, an island artist, wanted to export some of his wares. Pottery mostly."

"Mr. Dimas?" Phillip frowned. "What business was he in?"

"He was retired. His goal was to travel the world, but I believe he lived somewhere in Florida. Anyway, as a favor to his nephew, and a way to earn a little on his travels, he offered to sell the pottery while he traveled."

Phillip leaned back against the cracked, red vinyl of the booth and waited. A hint of a smile curved on his lips, but his eyes turned cool. Assessing her. Or her story. Jill clamped her mouth shut, irritated by his demeanor until the weight of the silence between them compelled her to continue. Damn. She'd never been good at negotiations. Silence unnerved her.

"The account was too small for the firm to handle, but Mr. McKinley encouraged me to work with it on my own time. He said it would help me understand the business.

"So I taught Mr. Dimas about the paperwork and regulations and found some local art fairs and shops to sell his wares.

We became partners. I handle the sales and split the revenue with him." She fiddled with her necklace, the insecurities that had always plagued her coming to the fore. "He's far too generous with me. My commission feels excessive."

"How does that relate to your necklace? Did he sell jewelry as well as pottery?"

"No. The necklace belonged to his mother." Jill fingered the piece remembering the sad tone of Mr. Dimas's voice when he spoke of his mother. "He told me if he had a daughter, he'd have passed it on to her. Instead, he gave it to me as a good luck charm and a symbol of his faith in me. I've worn it ever since."

"And did it bring you luck?"

Jill didn't believe in luck, but the association had changed her fortunes. "Let's just say it opened my eyes to a new path. I've gained a lot of experience by working with Mr. Dimas. I owe him more than I can repay."

"I'm told Melesian art pieces bring a good price in the U.S."

Something about his tone made her uneasy, as if the conversation had turned into an interrogation about her finances. A rush of anger washed over Jill, leaving her light-headed.

"Are you interested in art? Or do you have something you want to sell?" She heard the tension in her voice and instantly regretted her lack of control, but her personal struggles and modest financial successes were more than she cared to reveal—even to a man as attractive and tempting as Phillip Raymond.

He chuckled, apparently unaffected by her reaction. "Jill, I apologize if I sounded harsh. It was not my intention. And, no, I have nothing to sell. I do, however, appreciate art. Although I am still undecided on the Picasso sculpture." He offered her a smile that reached his eyes this time.

"Fair enough." Some of the tension left her shoulders. "In that case, let's finish the pizza and continue our tour."

"I'd like that. And afterward, perhaps you would allow me to escort you to an evening of dinner and dancing."

"I don't think it would be a good idea for us to—"

"Please," he interrupted her. "I have offended you. You must allow me to atone for my offense by spending the evening dedicated to your pleasure. It is my humble duty as a guest of your country."

His thick accent and the dramatic sweep of his hand to his chest contrasted with the mischievous sparkle in his eyes. He inclined his head slightly and a rogue lock of dark hair tumbled over his left eye.

Jill bit the inside of her lip to keep from smiling. Her doubts shrank to a manageable size. "If I agree to go out with you, will you stop acting like a wounded Romeo?"

"Your wish will be my command."

"Somehow, I doubt that. The posture of humble, pleading suitor doesn't fit you."

"But you will accept my invitation?" he pressed, the mischief in his eyes fading to an intense scrutiny.

"*Aaya*," she whispered, "yes, I will accept."

He reached across the table and caressed her hand, his thumb rubbing lightly along her knuckles. She didn't pull away. His simple touch ignited a need in her, a hunger for companionship, connection, and intimacy she'd denied herself far too long. Even as he drew away, the imprint of his hand burned on hers, a tangible reminder of all she could have, if only she would let herself.

"Well, then, shall we go?" She paid the waiter and gathered her purse.

"I am delighted to see the fine city of Chicago—through the expressive eyes of Jill Bradley."

"Careful, Phillip. You're slipping back into Romeo again." This time she gave in to the urge to laugh. After all, she'd already shown him a part of her soul—romantic fantasies, business ambitions and all. What harm could there be in showing him a little more?

And what harm was there in learning more about him? Six foot, three inches of dark-haired, blue-eyed temptation sat across the table—hers for the taking. And if she followed where temptation led, what harm could come to her?

Edmund slapped another folder onto the desk in front of Constantine. He reached for it, annoyed that the call from his security team had forced him to postpone his evening with Jill. But he'd come here for the investigations, not the woman. He slid the file closer and listened to Edmund.

"These are the results of our investigation based on the information you gave us earlier today, Your Highness. There is no Hector Dimas from Melesia that fits the age and description the girl gives. And none who traveled abroad during the times she indicated."

"Of course not." Constantine studied the three members of the security corps standing at attention behind Edmund. Twilight filtered through the ornate windows of the Melesian Consulate in Chicago, but the men showed no sign of fatigue. Every member of the royal security team was hand-picked for his loyalty, trustworthiness, and expertise. "Were you able to substantiate the claim of the nephew—or any small business who created pottery for export?"

"No, sir. We're still working on those leads."

Constantine nodded. "While you're at it, look into expatriates living in the Chicago area as well as anyone—native or foreign—who may have an extensive collection of Melesian art. Meanwhile, gentlemen, have a seat while I review this set of findings. Edmund, send for coffee and refreshments."

Constantine settled back and flipped through the documents. He dismissed the lists of tourists who had visited the U.S. only once during the times in question. Travelers from various businesses with ties to the U.S. made up the bulk of the files.

He knew detailed investigations were underway for each of them. Diplomatic visits and good will tours made by various members of the royal family made up the remaining trips.

The final file, slim compared to the others stacked on the desk, contained information on Jill Bradley. Address. Employment history. Family background.

The statistics in front of him revealed a small-town girl living on her own in Chicago, making an average wage. Nothing unexpected. Nothing Jill herself hadn't already told him. The tense muscles in his neck eased, and he relaxed in his chair. He didn't know till that moment how much he'd wanted to discover Jill was exactly what she appeared to be.

He flipped a page. Financial information. The tension rushed back, gripping the base of his skull in a vice. Four accounts, each containing a sizable amount of cash, and a fifth, smaller, account were listed under her name.

The headache lacerated his skull with icepick-sharp shards of pain. The tally of her income versus savings sent a clear message.

Unless Jill was scraping by on breadcrumbs and water, she couldn't have saved that amount. And Jill, despite the pleasant simplicity she'd shown him today, wasn't a bread-and-water kind of woman.

The luscious, creamy softness of her skin, the subtle, teasing whiff of her perfume and the perfect cut of her designer suits pointed to a champagne-and-caviar woman. A woman whose suitors wooed her with trinkets from Tiffany's.

Constantine massaged his forehead and studied the file a moment longer while a staff member brought in the refreshments he'd requested. Then, gathering the duty and the reserve that were as much a part of his royal heritage as the Crown and Scepter, he moved to the security officers who awaited him in the formal sitting area.

"Gentlemen, we have a thief to catch."

Jill hovered in the doorway to the office. Phillip sat absorbed in a file he was reading, his jacket slung across the chair back and his shirt sleeves rolled up, exposing summer brown skin. His brow wrinkled in a frown as he scribbled notations in the margin. Despite his intense concentration, his hair was barely tousled.

Jill wondered if he ever raked his hands through those thick locks. He might not, but her palms itched, and she wanted to feel that dark silk against her fingertips.

He turned to the office landline, giving her a glimpse of his strong, perfectly sculpted profile. It was as if he'd been genetically bred for good looks and sex appeal. She watched, entranced.

His simple act of picking up a receiver and punching numbers into the keypad awakened a yearning as intense as she'd ever known. He cradled the receiver in his palm. His fingers touched the keys with surety, grace, and a kind of masculine gentleness, not so much punching in the numbers as caressing the keys and coaxing a tone from them. The man could call her anytime, day or night.

She dragged her hand across her forehead. *This is ridiculous. Only an attention-starved idiot could get turned on by watching someone make a phone call.* But she couldn't deny the rapid beat of her pulse, the quivering in her belly and the slight shallowness to her breathing. She turned to leave, glad he hadn't heard her soft tap earlier.

"Jill, please." She turned back at the sound of his voice. "Come in. I won't be long." He motioned for her to enter with a casual wave of his hand. She could no more ignore his invitation than she could control her reaction to him.

Like a fish being reeled in on an invisible line, she moved into the office. His knowing smile and the smoky darkening of his eyes as she came near made her wonder if he was a mind reader.

The tension between them quivered, loosening and pulling, giving and taking, until it snapped as someone on the other end of the phone call demanded his attention.

Jill drew a breath and moved across the room toward her palm tree. The energy between them simmered in the cool office air. Neither the width of the office nor the presence of the invisible third person on the line diminished it.

She switched on the sun lamp, flooding the space with brightness, trying to ignore her tingling awareness of Phillip. As she checked the plant's soil and misted its fronds with nutrient water, she noticed how much stronger and more alive the tree looked—all because of the warmth of the light. Just like she felt more alive in the warmth of Phillip's presence.

Funny, she'd grown used to the cold, dead weight of conscience dragging her down since the accident. It was as if her spirit had been buried alive with her father. The Jill that walked away from the gravesite took on the image of Charles Bradley, the responsible, reliable family caretaker.

She'd locked away her romantic dreams and personal indulgences, considering them a waste of time and an unneeded distraction. She hadn't known how much she hungered for warmth and connection until now.

Until Phillip.

She craved the vibrancy he awakened in her. Life pulsed through her veins, fueling hungers she'd only imagined before.

As if he were called by her thoughts, Jill sensed him behind her. His hands settled on her shoulders, and she gave herself to the hunger inside, leaning against his solid chest and letting his warmth seep into the cold recesses that had been empty for so long.

"The palm loves water, but you don't have to drown it." His whisper was seductive and, for a moment, Jill couldn't assimilate the words with her actions. He reached for her hand and gently took the mister from her. How long had she been daydreaming?

"I guess I was lost in thought," she confessed.

"Pleasant thoughts?" He nuzzled the sensitive spot behind her ear, sending shivers down her spine.

"I can't think at all when you do that."

"Good." He chuckled. "It would be a terrible blow to my ego if you could concentrate when I was trying so hard to distract you."

"Your distraction technique is working." She could feel the roughness of his afternoon growth of beard, smell the peppermint on his breath as it fanned her cheek and increased the quivering in her belly. Her knees turned as soft as jelly, and she wanted to sink down to the ground with him.

Instead of a hard floor, her imagination made her think of the hot sands and cool ocean breezes of Melesia. What would it be like to travel to his homeland with him?

"Phillip, I think we'd better stop." She hauled in a breath and tried to steady her heartbeat. Even though she wore one of her professional suits—the uniform designed to keep people at a distance—he could still see beneath the surface, still make her long for more.

"We may stop for now, but I promise you, *Er'hona-mei*, we will continue this later."

Er'hona-mei. My desirable one. The Melesian endearment wove its way around her heart.

"Later," she echoed, stepping away from him and sinking to her knees by the palm tree. Despite her words, she felt a stab of disappointment when his embrace didn't tighten to hold her.

"What are you doing?" Phillip's voice drifted down to her sounding amused.

Jill grasped the heavy pot. "I need to turn the pot a bit every couple days so the tree grows straight. Either that or reposition the lamp."

"Ahh, the lamp." Phillip rested his fingers on her nape, reestablishing the connection she'd just broken. "I rather enjoyed helping you hang that lamp."

The memory of the way his body had crushed hers in their first kiss flooded her with a heat more intense than the sun lamp. Before she could recover from the image, he knelt on one knee beside her.

His hand splayed across the small of her back until she thought she would ignite from the heat of it. The length of his torso molded to her side, as close as two people could get while still clothed.

"Let me help you." He snaked one arm around her waist and grasped the rim of the pot, his hand close, but not quite touching hers. His other arm completed the circle. She was trapped but willingly so.

With an easy, smooth motion, he shifted the pot slightly. Jill watched the ripple of muscles in his forearms. Everything he did spoke of grace and ease. She wondered how those hands would feel on her body, if he would caress her with the same easy confidence and strength. Her skin prickled, damp and aching with sensations she'd long forgotten.

Stop fantasizing about his hands. Don't think of his elegant fingers caressing the keys of the phone. Ignore his broad, strong palms gripping the rim of the pot. And whatever you do, don't relax back into the circle of his arms. But her fantasies persisted, as real as the heat that simmered between their bodies. *Jill Bradley, you are a goner.*

"Jill?"

She looked up to see Phillip once again on his feet, his hand extended to her to help her rise. She placed her palm in his, aware for the first time of how small her hand felt, of how insignificant she felt next to him. With a tug, he helped her to her feet. The lazy, almost bored look in his eyes sent a frisson of unease across her skin. When he smiled, the unease fled as quickly as it came.

"Thank you for coming to my rescue again. Keep up the good deeds and you may become my own personal knight in shining armor."

"My pleasure." He bowed slightly to her, his stance formal, despite the playful smile tugging at his lips. "Since we were interrupted on Saturday, will you dine with me tonight? This humble knight-in-training would be most honored with your presence."

"There you go again, trying to be humble and failing miserably. You, sir, are a shameless flirt."

"Guilty as accused, beautiful lady. But the question remains: will you have dinner with me tonight?"

"*Aaya,*" she agreed, automatically switching to his romantic, island language. "Dinner would be lovely."

"Good. Then shall I pick you up at seven?"

Jill's heart thumped erratically. She'd never invited a man to her apartment. It was too shabby for entertaining and too much of a contrast with the polished, successful image she projected each day. Besides, she'd never allowed herself to get close enough to anyone to invite him over. *But this is Phillip. He's already seen through your disguise. Nothing ventured, nothing gained.* The homey platitude gave her courage.

"Seven o'clock would be fine. My address is—"

"Jill, there you are." Mr. McKinley strode into the office, a handful of files stuffed under one arm. "I trust she's helping you with everything you need, Mr. Raymond?"

"Jill has been most helpful."

"Good. Good. Jill's a marvel when it comes to hosting our international clients. Which is why I'm here." He turned to her. "I need your help. We've set up a teleconference with one of our new suppliers based out of Tokyo. They need to straighten out some shipping issues. Can you help? You're fluent in Japanese, aren't you?"

"Yes, of course, Mr. McKinley. I'd be glad to attend. When is it scheduled?"

"That's just the thing. You see, we've got a fourteen-hour time difference to deal with and they need to get the issue settled today. Or tomorrow, depending on what side of the International Date Line you're on. So we've set it up for eight o'clock tonight. We'll have an informal dinner at six. I'll brief you on the issues then."

"Tonight? But I…"

"Business before pleasure," Phillip murmured in Melesian. "We can meet another night."

"What's that, Mr. Raymond?" Mr. McKinley turned to him. "Jill is the language expert, not me."

"I was simply wishing her luck with the negotiations tonight."

"I see. Very well, then, if there's nothing else you need, I'll just steal Jill away from you for a while to discuss some other business." Mr. McKinley steered Jill into the hallway, talking nonstop. He passed her one file after another.

"I need you in early tomorrow, too, Jill. We have to contact a supplier in the Netherlands about a shipment of Delftware. And the Italian glass orders need to be processed. Next week you'll need to set up travel plans for the Swiss visitors.

"Oh, and contact the California customers who want Champagne. Find out the vintage and year they're looking for. Offer them the options of other sparkling wines, like our Spanish Cava, Italian Prosecco, or the new Cremant d'Alsace we just contracted for. Then get started planning the reception for our guests from Germany. Cocktails and dinner for forty, at last count."

As she hustled along behind Mr. McKinley, Jill cast a lingering glance back at Phillip, wondering if she'd been saved from the fire or denied the opportunity of a lifetime.

Constantine watched Jill walk away, the swish of her hips making a mockery of his decision to get to know her slowly. If McKinley hadn't interrupted, he was sure he'd have known her intimately by morning.

Although he knew her rather thoroughly already. He returned to the desk where information on Jill and the presumed thefts lay in neat piles. When he'd seen the first reports, just days ago, Jill had emerged as the prime suspect. Now, he wasn't so sure.

"Excuse me, sir." Edmund appeared at the door. "Have you seen the latest reports?"

"Yes." He motioned for Edmund to come in and close the door. "The situation appears more complex than we originally thought."

"If you'll pardon me for asking, has the situation changed, Your Highness, or is it your feelings that have changed?"

Constantine fought the urge to reprimand Edmund. No man should be punished for being perceptive. And Edmund, despite his suspicions, was a loyal, discreet friend. Constantine kept his voice, and his reply, mild.

"You know I would never jeopardize the honor of my country over a mere woman." *Not even a woman as enticing as Jill Bradley.* No matter what he wanted to believe, he was a prince first and a man second. "As it happens, the time I have spent with Jill—Miss Bradley—leads me to believe that she is not a thief or a knowing accomplice. Nevertheless, my belief is nothing without proof."

He gestured toward the documents before continuing. "We know from earlier reports that Miss Bradley's expenses were…unusual. At the time, I believed that no one could accrue the savings she had without either engaging in illegal activity, or extreme frugality."

Edmund nodded. "And those reports led you to believe the extreme frugality theory."

"Consider this. Jill's apartment is off the beaten track and, even by Chicago standards, small and inexpensive. Her credit reports show that she has a penchant for shopping at high-end stores, but each purchase is returned quickly."

"I understand this type of scam is not uncommon, Your Highness. Perhaps she purchased items for social occasions and then returned them, slightly used. Is this not considered deceptive?"

"Or perhaps she had second thoughts. There have never been any merchant complaints against her. She does not have a gym membership or records of paying a personal trainer, despite her excellent physical condition."

He pictured the way she moved with the grace of a dancer. And her smooth skin was taut in all the right places and rounded in all the pleasing ones. Maybe her idea of good exercise was a few laps around the bedroom. He frowned at the thought.

"Sir?" Edmund's voice broke into his thoughts. "You were briefing me on Miss Bradley's file."

"Yes. Thank you, Edmund." He owed the man for overlooking his obvious loss of concentration. "She does not own a car. She has rarely traveled outside of Chicago since she moved here. Further, all the deposits made to her various accounts were relatively small. Not at all what I would expect of a gem thief. In short, she appears to be an honest, unwitting accomplice."

"Still, she may be useful."

"Again, you are correct. We need to work on several leads at once. You find out what the team is learning about the pottery angle. I intend to spend more time with Miss Bradley and try to unravel these issues." He waved at the documents on his desk. "Once I've reached the bottom of it, I'll solicit her help in finding the elusive Mr. Dimas."

"And if she fails to cooperate?"

"Then I'll simply have to use my powers of persuasion." Constantine smiled, imagining the form that persuasion would likely take. "Now, Edmund, I need you to do a little research and engage some undercover operatives for a little soiree I'm planning for the benefit of Miss Bradley this Friday."

Chapter 6

The Friday night crowd pressed around Jill, swaying to the pulsing music that spilled from the Excalibur dance club. The throb of the bass speakers quivered through her body, turning sound into sensation and heightening her awareness.

She scanned the crowd waiting in line, straining for a glimpse of Phillip. *This is lunacy.* After almost a week of interruptions and delays, she'd agreed to meet him at the club, but now, waiting in line, second thoughts assailed her. The mantle of responsibility she'd donned at eighteen didn't slip off as easily as she thought it would.

She smoothed her hands down the silk of her burgundy slip dress, grateful that her stepmother had taught her to sew. The Dior pattern flattered her figure and fooled everyone who looked at the dress. She knew, as always, she looked like she belonged. Too bad it wasn't true.

"Jill." She looked up at the sound of her name and saw Phillip waiting for her at the front of the line. A flutter of butterflies instantly assaulted her stomach, and she felt his eyes trail from the glittering Marcasite clips in her hair to the faux rhinestones of her spiked heels. By the time his gaze returned to her face, she was as warm as if she'd run a mile.

"Hello, Phillip." She took his extended hand. Instead of helping her up the steps, he lifted her hand to his lips. The courtly gesture was from another century, or another world, or at least, from a dream.

But the sparks that shot through her at the touch of his lips were straight from an X-rated film. Especially when they settled warm and low and filled her with a pulsing urgency. Her nipples tightened against the sheer fabric of her dress.

In for a penny, in for a pound, she reminded herself. She'd wanted an irresponsible fling. She deserved it. Intimacy and loss had been linked in her mind for too long. Jill shuddered at the memory of how she'd lost her virginity only hours before the accident that had taken her father. The memory—stronger than any attraction she'd felt to the men in her life—kept sexual intimacy at bay. But not tonight. Not with Phillip.

Before she could think, she closed the distance between them, threaded her fingers through his hair and kissed him. In a moment of surprise, as Phillip yielded to her, she felt a rush of feminine power. She deepened the kiss, moving beyond the press of lips to explore the warm recesses of his mouth.

His hands closed over her back, and he molded his body to hers. No longer simply yielding to her, Phillip returned her kisses, claiming and relinquishing control until she was aware of nothing but the ebb and flow of desire between them.

"That's the kind of greeting that makes the wait worthwhile," he said, pulling away from her lips and resting his forehead on hers. "Shall we go inside?"

Jill stood for a moment, trying to calm her racing heart and steady her ragged breathing, but his nearness made it an impossible task. In the end, she simply nodded and followed his lead.

Phillip placed his hand on the small of her back and guided her up the stairs. At the top, the staff waved them inside. Before she could take in the throng of partygoers on the main floor, a waiter directed them to a secluded table in one of the private party rooms on the upper floor.

Here, the music was quieter, the crowd more sophisticated, and the service more solicitous. And here, the diamonds were real. Jill wondered how much he'd had to slip the doorman and the rest of the staff to assure this royal treatment.

The private lounge was appropriate for the old Jill, the one who thought a wealthy husband was the key to solving her family's dilemma. In the last few months she'd begun to hope that, maybe, her years of hard work and frugality would be enough. Maybe she could help her family without having to settle for a loveless money match. And then, maybe, she could find the love she had been living without.

Jill reached almost involuntarily for the good luck charm at her throat. The touch of the warm filigree beneath her fingers calmed her. Phillip watched her every move, at ease despite the upper-class atmosphere of the private room. A server stopped and put icy, bubbling flutes of champagne on their table.

"I hope you don't mind," Phillip said, picking up his glass, "but I took the liberty of ordering some refreshments for us."

Jill picked up her glass and turned to face him. "In that case, here's to tonight."

"And here's to you, a rare, and unexpected gem." He touched the rim of his glass to hers.

The champagne was cold, dry, and expensive. She'd come a long way from the girl who'd once drunk Everclear-spiked punch and five-dollar jugs of wine. Now she could evaluate quality at a sip, separate excellent wine from the merely expensive. Her senses told her this champagne was both excellent and expensive.

"Phillip, this is wonderful." She laid her hand on his arm. The fine fabric of his jacket lay smooth and elegant beneath her fingertips. "But you didn't need to go to all this trouble and expense to impress me. I would have been just as happy dancing with you on the main floor and drinking beer."

Something flashed in his eyes—a look of surprise, quickly hidden. He waved a careless hand. "This is nothing. Merely a more pleasant way to enjoy the evening. I have a generous travel stipend. Shall we dance?"

He rose and offered his hand to her. Compared to her own, his hand was large, square, and strong, yet gentle. On the dance floor, he pressed her close and swayed to the music. The exotic scent of Melesian cologne lingered on his shirt, enticing, but not overpowering. Just like the man himself. She relaxed against him, savoring the warm, crisp cotton beneath her cheek and the occasional brush of his lips against her hair.

For the first time since she'd met him, nothing seemed out of place. His casual elegance belonged here. He belonged here—in a way he didn't belong at the office or in the dim pizzerias of Chicago's more desolate streets.

"Isn't this better than beer and crowds?" he murmured in her ear. "You're the kind of woman who appreciates the finer things in life."

"I didn't agree to go out with you to experience the finer things in life. I went out with you because I wanted to be with *you*." Jill stopped dancing and looked up at him, her hands resting on his shirt front.

When she had his full attention, she continued. "I've been on dates in some of the finest restaurants and clubs in Chicago, and I've been on dates in out-of-the-way taverns. What makes an evening special isn't how much it costs. It's who you're with."

His eyes darkened, and he tightened his hold around her waist. "And is tonight special?"

"Yes." She lifted one hand to brush it along his temple. "For the first time in a long time, I'm enjoying myself. So please, stop trying to impress me and simply be with me."

He pressed her close and as they moved to the music, her doubts and his pretensions lost in the magic of the dance.

Jill stood at the mirror freshening her makeup in the relative privacy of the bathroom. Beside her, another young woman from the private party room applied a coat of lip gloss.

"That man you're dancing with sure is a looker," the woman drawled. "And he must be connected to get admission to the private room. Young, good looking, and rich. How'd you get so lucky?"

Phillip was a lucky catch, but not for the reasons the woman seemed to think. "To be honest, I think he's just trying to impress me. I'd rather he'd saved the admission fee and danced with me on the main floor."

"Don't be too sure, honey. Sometimes the stars align just right and drop a wonderful package at your feet." She sighed and leaned against the wall, regarding Jill. "The only wealthy ones I seem to find are old and fat. I'd snatch your man up in a minute if I were you."

"I've been through my share of old, fat money myself," Jill said. Something about the stranger reminded Jill of her past mistakes. She warmed to the woman. "It took me a while, but I finally figured out that money with strings attached isn't worth it. Believe it or not, I don't want to snag a rich husband. I'm holding out for love, not money."

"Sounds like you've been burned before."

"Let's just say I've learned the folly of trying to sell myself to the highest bidder." Impulsively, Jill grabbed the woman's hands. "Don't mistake a rich, connected man's attention for love. More often than not, they just want arm candy. You deserve more. Every woman does."

"Honey, you have a point, but I'm a little too addicted to my toys." She waggled her fingers under Jill's nose, showing off her rings. "After all, diamonds are a girl's best friend."

"They're beautiful," Jill said. "But most people wouldn't know a cubic zirconia from the real thing. Relationships shouldn't be measured in karats. You'd be surprised what you can learn to do without. Good luck with finding whatever it is you're looking for."

Jill left the ladies room feeling lighter than a penitent leaving a confessional. She was on the right path at last. Phillip was the kind of man she could love—someone decent, honest and simple. He was perfect for her.

Too bad the ocean between them decreed that they'd never be able to share a life together.

Chapter 7

A week later, Constantine scanned the "art fair" where Jill had brought him, amazed at the booths filled with stuff. He stopped short of calling it junk, more out of consideration for Jill's feelings than out of any sense of certainty.

The exhibit occupied a full story of a spacious warehouse and contained everything from delicate blown-glass ornaments, fragile as a baby's touch to hand-painted "bathroom art." Constantine couldn't fathom why any civilized person needed a neon green sign to remind him to flush.

"Is this art fair a common event in Chicago?" he asked Jill as they passed a booth of stitched rag dolls.

"Crafters and artists come from all over the states. They usually attend several art fairs and festivals in a season." She rounded a corner and headed down another crowded aisle. "One of my best customers is located at the end of this aisle. I promised I'd stop by and get his order."

She darted through the crowds with an ease that defied Constantine. He struggled to keep up with her, his progress suddenly hampered by a bearded, flannel-clad bulk of a man.

"Hey, buddy." The man turned to Constantine and gestured toward a booth. "What do you think?"

The entire display wall was covered in mounted, lacquered fish, each on a glossy walnut plaque. "Which one should I get for my den? That one looks like a big ol' Muskie I caught a few years back."

Constantine stared in the direction of the man's pointed finger. In Melesia, rare exotic fish were bred for study in museums and universities. Several new species had been discovered in the protected area known as Neptune's Crown Reef, the domain of his younger brother, Stephan, the royal champion for conservation. But here, the only fish in sight were these mud-brown specimens that resembled old boot leather.

The specific fish in question was about six inches wide and stretched eighteen to twenty inches across the plaque. Burned underneath into the walnut mounting were the words "you shouldda seen the one that got away."

"I, uh…I've never seen anything like it," Constantine managed. "It will make a fine addition to your…den." Without another look at the man, he escaped and headed in the direction Jill had taken.

On impulse, he returned to the booth and found the second ugliest plaque he could—his flannel-clothed friend had the ugliest—and had it engraved for his younger brother. Stephan may be the man he was counting on to be his chief science and technology advisor, but he was also adept at playing the obnoxious little brother. The fish was a small payback.

He resumed his search for Jill and found her in a roomy, tastefully decorated vendor booth filled with pottery. Some he recognized as Melesian island art, and some he did not. Jill motioned to him.

"Phillip, I'm glad you caught up. I saw you had a little trouble."

"A thoughtful woman would have come back to rescue me."

"Too bad. You're stuck with me." Her face glowed as she returned his teasing banter. "Besides, it looks like you succumbed to temptation."

"This? Just something for my younger brother. A specimen of North American aquatic wildlife to enhance his collection."

"Is your brother a fisherman?"

"Actually he's a naturalist and a talented scholar and scientist. Just don't tell him I said so if you ever meet him. It would upset the family dynamics."

"Don't worry, I have a little brother too. I understand a bit about family dynamics." She motioned him into the booth. "Here's the reason I brought you to the art fair. I want you to meet Mr. Latimer. He's my best customer for the small to medium sized pots."

Mr. Latimer stuck out his hand. "Pleased to meet you, Phillip. Jill here tells me you're from Melesia where they make these ingenious little best sellers."

Constantine nodded. He picked up a nearby pot, about four inches in diameter, and examined it.

"What you're holding there," continued Mr. Latimer, "is what we call a self-watering pot. It's really just a good planter with a built-in drainage system. See, here." He pointed to the interior of the pot. "There's a lip halfway down where they glue in a false bottom with drainage holes. Underneath, it's packed with pebbles and shells.

"They rattle a bit when you shake 'em. I like to tell folks that it's good luck to rattle the pot before you put your plant in it. Makes 'em grow better. Really, it's the drainage, but folks like a bit of a story to go with their purchases."

Constantine examined the pot, then wandered around the booth as Jill and Mr. Latimer began discussing orders and payments. Several other bits of Melesian pottery were on display, but nothing was more exotic than the pieces sold in the tourist shops back home. Considering the prices Mr. Latimer charged,

Jill could easily save a tidy sum from the sale of small, unexceptional pots. Especially given the generous nature of her supplier, the elusive Mr. Dimas.

Despite nagging questions about Dimas, a weight lifted off his shoulders. The deeper he looked into Jill's financial and business dealings, the more it appeared that she was neither a thief nor or a willing accomplice. Moreover, his spies from last night's party confirmed what his gut told him.

Despite her contradictions and quirks, Jill appeared to be the honest, hard-working, somewhat shy woman he'd hoped to find under her sexy exterior. His words from the first day they met came back to him. *I see someone who sparkles with as many facets as a diamond, who cannot see her own worth.*

Mentally, he reviewed her moods. Her sexy persona was designed to keep people at a distance, a shield for the sharp mind that created a thriving market from simple clay pots. The tender woman who pampered that lucky palm tree, and the shy girl who fidgeted under his gaze and sidestepped compliments were, he suspected, the most honest sides of her.

Then there was the street-smart advocate for the less fortunate. It was clear she was more at home with simplicity than wealth. It wasn't the profile of a high-end smuggler or a knowing accomplice.

With his conscience clean on the smuggling issue, he could relax and concentrate on Jill. She was, indeed, a fascinating woman. Someone he wanted to know much, much better before this day was through.

She laced her fingers through his and led him away from the booth. The warm softness of her touch awakened emotions he hadn't felt for a long time.

Protectiveness for the soft-hearted woman who could so easily have been used as a front for smugglers and needed someone to look after her.

And possession. He'd been the one to find the real woman under the façade. This side of Jill belonged to him.

He squeezed her hand and watched a smile light her face in response. He noted the slight hitch in her breath as he caressed her fingers. She was more affected by him than she pretended to be. But he'd known that since the first day they met. And his spies at the dance club last week confirmed his hunch. She didn't know about, and wasn't interested in, his money or status.

Constantine cursed himself for ever thinking otherwise. He looked down at her animated features, loving the sound of her voice as she chattered about nothing and everything, unaware of the need she'd roused in him.

The last of his worries slipped away. From now on, his sole mission, at least where Jill was concerned, was to make her happy. To give her what little luxuries he could during the limited time they had together.

Her eyes sparkled when she stopped at a jewelry booth displaying cut glass earrings. He selected a pair with a clear crystal dangling in a silver setting and held them up to her ear. "These would look lovely on you. They match your necklace."

Damn. His gut clenched. Even when he wasn't thinking about his assignment for Melesia, that necklace bothered him. Someone—likely the mysterious Mr. Dimas—was tweaking the nose of the Melesian royal family by passing the symbol to a commoner.

Constantine shifted uncomfortably, remembering that his own mother was once a commoner. A commoner with American roots whose status had sent shock waves through the country that still reverberated today.

Tradition decreed the insignia was worn only by members of the royal court. *And the intended bride of the monarch.* That blasted legend. He tried to ignore the voice of tradition. These were modern, enlightened times. But the voice taunted him.

The legend was the source of his discomfort. It had to be. Seeing the necklace reminded him that he must one day marry and produce an heir. And his future bride could not be the vivacious, open-hearted, American girl by his side.

So much for modern, enlightened times. I'm as bound by tradition as the ancient rulers of my land. When his mission for his brother was accomplished, his freedom would come to an end. Duty caged the monarch as tightly as steel bars.

He shook off his dismal thoughts and instead watched Jill study the earrings in the mirror, turning them slightly to catch the light. Her smile flashed as brightly as the crystals until she flipped the price tag over. The hesitation in her movements when she put it back tugged at him.

How many women had he showered with gems? Yet he'd given nothing to Jill but suspicion and dishonesty. When the Crown Jewels were found and he took his place as leader of his country, he could give her much more. But for now, he could at least give her the crystal earrings.

"I thought they looked lovely on you, Jill. Is something wrong?"

"No, of course not. I just changed my mind."

"Let me buy them for you."

"Phillip, no. It's not necessary."

"I want to." He took the earrings to the counter, overruling her protest. Despite her cash from Mr. Latimer, she refused to indulge in a small luxury. It was another puzzle.

Maybe instead of comparing her to a diamond, he should compare her to the fabled Gordian Knot, where nothing was as simple as it seemed.

According to legend, the gods decreed that whatever mortal unraveled the knot would rule the world. Impatient, Alexander the Great simply slashed it with his sword and went on to rule the ancient world. Like Alexander the Great, Constantine wanted to cut through Jill's pretense and get to the heart of the matter. Her heart. Now.

Liar. Who was he kidding? Her heart would be nice, but what place did it have in his life? He, who had nothing to give in return? What he really wanted to strip away was the tight, little barely-there jacket and prissy white blouse she wore. He wanted to slide her jeans down those long, lean legs and uncover her secrets. He wanted to close the distance and burn away the pretense that lay between them.

But this wasn't the place. He tossed a couple of bills onto the counter and swept the earrings into his shopping bag, anxious to be away from this bazaar. "Jill, let's go somewhere where we can be alone."

He made no effort to disguise the desire in his voice. He ran his hand down her arm, gently, and she sucked in a startled breath. Unconsciously her fingertips grazed the necklace, a fleeting touch as if in search of courage, then she laced her hand in his and led them from the building.

Tension curled in Jill's stomach, and a flutter of awareness prickled her skin every time she looked at Phillip. Her hand was tucked in his, not loosely, but securely, with his warmth surrounding and invading her.

Whenever they stopped at a crosswalk, he looked at her, the aqua blue of his eyes deepening, his pupils flaring behind the lenses of his glasses as he slid his gaze over her body. From breasts to belly, she tightened and quivered in response. And when he looked in her eyes as if nothing else in the world mattered, her knees went weak.

No one had ever looked at her quite that way before. Lots of men had admired her body. Some had openly flirted, others had ogled, a few had ignored her. But no one had ever looked at her like she mattered. Like she was both desirable and important. The effect was as intoxicating as his deep blue gaze.

They walked to the train stop, hand in hand, as the clouds gathered in the afternoon sky. The temperature, warm this morning, dropped. Damp wind gusted through her thin jacket, yet she felt on fire.

Beside her, Phillip seemed impervious to the weather. His hair was wind tousled. His denim jacket hung open revealing the familiar blue crew neck sweater.

When they reached the platform, he smiled down at her, heat in his gaze. The approaching train rumbled on the tracks. The rickety wooden platform shook and creaked, but the sensations dimmed in comparison to the thundering of her heart and the pulsing urgency to see him, touch him, feel his naked skin beneath her palms.

The easy banter of the morning was gone, swept away by a restless, urgent need as sharp as the rising winds. Passion twisted and curled in her gut, stoked by his smoldering looks and burning touches. And her heart—that lonely, icy fortress where all of her failures and fears lurked—melted under the heat of his gaze.

She'd started to thaw the minute he'd peered beneath her disguise that first day, offering praise instead of criticism. *I see…intelligence…beauty…someone who sparkles…a diamond, who cannot see her own worth.*

His simple words had warmed her then, just as the heat from his body warmed her now. His actions had forced her to live again, to feel something.

And with him, feeling didn't bring pain. Not the wrenching, knife stab of loss. Not the dull ache of guilt. Not even the needle-sharp pain of something numb waking up after a long time. With Phillip, she felt only the warmth of returning life and the surge of energy and purpose.

"Where to, now?" he asked as soon as they'd boarded the train. He stood by the door, one hand holding his shopping bag, the other resting on the upright pole beside her. He swayed easily with the movement of the train, unconcerned with the bumps and jolts of the track. Focused only on her.

His intense regard made her stomach tighten and quiver, turning somersaults in a drunken, giddy rush. All from a single, searching look.

When his gaze left her eyes and slid along her skin, she shivered. His look was as enticing—and arousing—as a touch. He studied her neck, and a shiver whispered across her skin. He lingered on her breasts, and they tightened. He swept lower, and spasms of longing pulsed through her body.

A sensual, tantalizing light sparked in the aqua-blue depths, hot as a gas flame. Jill licked her lips, feeling naked when his eyes retraced their path. Her heart raced, her skin burned, and her body quivered in every secret place she'd ever known or imagined. By the time he looked in her eyes again, she knew what he saw. Desire.

Weak-kneed and breathless, she gripped the pole harder, the cool, hard metal giving her temporary relief from his sensual bombardment. Then he leaned close enough for her to catch a whiff of his scent, earthy and lush as his homeland, and her desire exploded into white-hot shivers that danced down her spine.

Jill swallowed and focused on the slow, steady pulse at the base of his throat. Her own heartbeat answered in erratic thumps. *Now or never. Now or never.*

"My place," she whispered, tearing down her last barrier. "I'm taking you to my place." Phillip's breath fanned her cheek. Barely an inch separated their jostling, swaying bodies.

Passion shimmered between them. The clack of the train echoed her heartbeat.

She'd never allowed a man into her apartment. Never courted anything more than the illusion of intimacy. Until now. Until Phillip. But this time, it seemed right.

The realization that he would soon disappear injected a hollow, half-frightened emptiness into the passion building in her gut. She wrapped her arm around his waist and closed the inch-wide space between them, letting his heat push the emptiness aside.

At their stop, she pulled him out of the train and set a brisk pace for home. The sky was darker and the wind colder, piercing her desire with unwanted memories. Even Phillip's warmth couldn't fully protect her.

The last man she'd trusted with her heart–her father—had died without warning, leaving her empty and alone.

And now she was giving her heart to another man. One she knew would leave. One who promised nothing but today.

She slammed the door on thoughts of the past and the future and looked in Phillip's eyes instead. If today was all they had, she was going to grasp every second, memorize every detail and live a lifetime in an hour.

Beside him, Jill was silent. Constantine wondered if she was having second thoughts until she snuggled close and wrapped her arm around his waist.

"Is your home far from here?" He knew the address but didn't have any idea how to get to it. The neighborhood seemed deserted, and slightly sinister, with cramped houses and apartments lining the narrow streets.

"Only a couple of blocks more," she murmured.

Thunder rumbled and the wind blew colder, piercing through the loose knit of his sweater. Yet the thought of being alone with Jill was enough to warm him, at least temporarily.

She paused at a corner where several streets intersected. A jumble of neighborhood businesses clustered there, flower shops, pharmacies, bistros, and boutiques happily coexisting within a few crowded blocks. Quiet residential streets radiated out from the business hub like spokes from a wheel.

She pointed to a flower shop. "That's where I sell most of the large pottery. They make high-end arrangements for hotels and corporations. One of their clients is an art collector who buys some of the more rare pieces."

Constantine looked at the store. Buckets of cut stems surrounded the front stoop and the sidewalk outside. A few elaborate arrangements sat on display in the bay window. Nothing was remarkable, and yet curiosity, and a feeling of unease, nagged at him. He turned to investigate.

Thunder rumbled again in the dark, nearly black sky. Jill tugged him toward one of the residential streets. "I'll take you there another time. He's been pressuring me about a new shipment lately, and I'd rather not confront him again. Besides, we'd better hurry." She scanned the sky, worry causing her eyes to darken as black as the clouds.

Half a block later, the storm came. Great sheets of icy rain drenched him from head to toe. The wind seemed to be in a frenzy, blowing from every direction at once, driving cold water into every crevice. Constantine sloshed through puddles, soaking his leather shoes.

He glanced at Jill. Rain streaked her dark hair as it clung to her face highlighting her delicate features. It plastered her white shirt to her body, outlining her curves in near transparent perfection. Her soaked, useless jacket only framed the view, highlighting her beauty. Unaware that he'd stopped, she skipped ahead of him. Even her jeans molded to her butt, which wiggled with an enticing, natural, come-hither invitation.

He could stare at her glistening, wet body for hours. Soon enough, he'd entice her to his islands where he could drench her in his private, sun-kissed bathing pool. He would lick the moisture from her body until she melted for him. His groin tightened at the thought of her hot, wet, and naked.

His chattering teeth reminded him how far they were from home. He was chilled to the marrow. She must be freezing. For now, they needed to get warm and dry.

Jill unlocked a rusty, blackened security gate and led him down a narrow path to a tiny building squeezed between two much more modern structures. The bricks looked as black as the security gate, wrapped in a century-old layer of grime.

She fumbled with another key and let him into a dim entryway, lined with gunmetal gray mailboxes. They moved to a stairway at the back of the building. A dozen smells assaulted his nose. Heavy grease and frying fish. Exotic spices and roasted meats. Garlic. Onions. Sauerkraut. Each floor of the high rise seemed to have a different ethnic scent permeating the air.

She sprinted up the stairs, just enough ahead of him to lead the way. Three flights. Four. The walls seemed to narrow with each story. Finally, six flights up she led him down a short hallway to her door. A freight elevator stood across from it, the entrance crisscrossed with yellow warning tape. A tattered sign, which looked about a decade old, declared maintenance was in progress. Somehow he doubted it.

No wonder every inch of her looked like she worked with a personal trainer, even though she didn't belong to a gym. Her stairs alone were a grueling workout.

She grabbed his hand and hauled him into the dim apartment. Once inside, she turned to him and said the words he'd longed to hear.

Or rather, the one word.

"Strip."

Chapter 8

A wicked smile played across his lips at her command. To her delight, Phillip obeyed without a protest. The gift bag fell from his fingers with a clunk.

He dropped his jacket unceremoniously on the scarred wood floor and slowly peeled the sweater from his body. Inch by inch, his progress revealed dark golden-brown skin stretched across taut muscles. A sprinkling of dark hair dusted the expanse of his chest. His nipples puckered with the cold, but his smile and his gaze simmered with heat.

The sweater plopped in a wet pile beside the jacket. He kicked off his shoes, then dropped his hands to the fly of his jeans. Slowly, he complied with her wish, bending to ease his jeans and briefs off while skewering her with that hot gaze. When he straightened, he took one step toward her, leaving every stitch of clothing behind.

Dear heavens! A sizzle shot through her, hot enough to make her wet clothes steam. He was perfect. Broad shoulders, narrow hips, long, elegant feet and toes, just the right amount of coarse dark hair, and desire. Desire, displayed without modesty. Thick, hard, pulsing need unveiled before her eyes.

"Better?" he asked, his voice rolling over her like hot molasses.

She nodded, her sense of bravado not quite extending to her voice.

He took another step forward, a thrilling, yet slightly predatory approach that caused her heart to thump and her breath to come in quick, harsh gulps. Thunder accompanied his step and a jagged flash of lightning brightened the room. Another crack of sound, then they were plunged into darkness. Outside, the entire block went black.

As if heightened by the darkness, her other senses raged. She could feel his heat. Almost taste his nearness. He framed her face with his hands and touched his lips to hers, holding her firm, preventing any contact between their bodies, yet devouring her with his lips and tongue. Tasting and taking from her as much passion as he gave.

She'd started the encounter intending to tease him into a carefree night of passion, but she was in over her head. This wasn't a game where she could control the outcome. This was real. In her home. Leading to an inevitable conclusion that she both desired and feared. After tonight, there was no turning back.

Already, despite the fact that he was naked and she fully clothed, he'd taken control of the situation, giving and withholding passion at his own pace. Commanding the fire that whipped through her at the touch of his lips.

When he pulled her across the small room to the window, she didn't resist. The storm raged; lightning created fireworks in the sky, filling the room in a ghostly half-light. "Now it's your turn," he said softly in a voice that brooked no refusal. "Strip."

Jill's fingers trembled as she shrugged out of her sodden bolero jacket, dropping it to the floor in haste. She reached for the top button on her blouse.

"Slower," he ordered, his words snaking out of the darkness and wrapping around her. "I want to watch."

Suddenly her lips were dry and her throat thick. His eyes followed her every move, and even in the darkness, she knew he could see her. His gaze was like a tangible thing, sizzling along her nerve endings.

How different from the hurried, clumsy intimacy of her youth when her boyfriend pushed her skirt up over her hips and raced to satisfy himself while another couple pounded on the door of his bedroom and an out-of-control party raged in the background. It had been dark then, too, a shameful, secret darkness. The memory had held her hostage for years.

She unbuttoned her blouse, slipping each button free with an agonizing slowness as he watched. Tonight the darkness was heady, rich, and full of promise.

She finished with the blouse and dropped it to the floor. Beneath his gaze, her nipples hardened, throbbing. The lace of her bra scraped them with each breath. With his eyes watching every move, she unclasped the front closure and dropped it, too, to the floor. Her hands slid to the button on her jeans.

"Stop."

She didn't even consider questioning him, but stood frozen in place, waiting for his next move. Yes, she'd relinquished control of this game, but for once, she felt no need to sway the outcome. No desire for control. No desire for anything but the man in front of her.

Jill's eyes drifted closed. The electric crackle in the air could have been from the storm or Phillip. She didn't know. She didn't care. She just gave herself to the feelings crashing through her.

A tickle alerted her to his hands on her breasts. His fingertips slid slowly down the slopes, teasing, but stopping short of touching her aching nipple. He traced full circles from the top down the sensitive sides, across the heavy bottoms.

Sparking, fiery jolts raced through her with each stroke, tingling along her skin before pooling, warm and low, at the juncture of the thighs. Wave upon wave of hot and cold shivers followed the same path, leaving her longing for more. All with just the touch of a fingertip.

She moaned, only one word coherent enough to understand. "Please."

"No." It was a command, gently given, but irrefutable, despite his quiet tone. Cool air rushed in where his hand had been moments ago. "This time, I give the orders and you obey. Agreed?"

She pulsed and ached for his touch, quivering in anticipation, longing for him to cup her breasts, her thighs. Could she trust him? Give herself to him completely? The demands of her body gave her no choice—and her heart urged her to put her doubts aside. To trust him—even if only for tonight.

"Agreed," she whispered.

"Good." He stroked her breasts again, the sensation all the more intense for the brief separation. When she thought she could stand it no more, he tweaked her nipples gently. She cried out, without words this time.

"Very good." His voice was warm and full of satisfaction. "Now, turn around."

She pivoted.

"Take off the jeans. But leave the panties. And Jill?"

She nodded to indicate she'd heard him.

"Do it slowly."

The rasp of her zipper was loud in her ears, and her hands shook from excitement. She eased the jeans down her hips, wiggling to keep her panties from being entangled in the wet, clinging denim. Behind her, Phillip chuckled at the move, his laugh sending shivers of anticipation down her spine.

Jill could feel his gaze raking her, even though she couldn't see him. She bent to push the jeans farther down her legs. They caught on her shoes, and she fumbled, all the while aware of her butt in its sheer white, wet panties exposed to his view. And the wet wasn't only from the rain.

She tugged off her jeans, shoes, and socks. But when she started to rise, his hand on her back held her in place.

"I like the view from here." His palm cupped her bottom, burning through the wet fabric, searing her. He squeezed, then moved to nestle her bottom against his groin. "I like this very much. I could take you this minute."

The blatant dominance of his act was countered by the gentle touch of his hand on her spine and the soothing stroke of his thumb against her sensitized skin. A forbidden thrill shot through her. Trust transformed would-be danger into anticipation. If only her chaotic emotions could be tamed as easily as her body.

His penis nudged the crotch of her panties, sliding in and out of the tight vee of her thighs while he held her hips steady. Each stroke increased the throbbing in her center. Each stroke milked more wetness from her.

She begged for more, her earlier promise forgotten.

He scored his fingernails along her spine while one hand still cupped her butt. But he pulled away from her, slowly, completely, leaving her empty and wanting.

"Who's in charge, Jill?" The gentle chastisement was edged with laughter, but it still sent shivers of playful warning racing across her skin.

Every exposed inch of her skin begged for his touch, and the spot between her thighs ached and pulsed, protesting the emptiness.

"You are," she replied in a breathless moan.

"Don't make me remind you again." Again, the hint of danger lurked in his smoky, velvety voice, adding dark excitement to the moment.

He peeled the panties off her body, lingering, exposing her more slowly then she'd believed possible. She shivered in the cool air, her damp skin breaking into goose bumps now that he wasn't close enough to warm her.

Still, she held her tongue, trembling at the intimacy of the act, feeling desire build even as he denied her relief. When her wet panties pooled at her feet, he gave her a brief, searing pat on the behind. She moaned.

"Stay here," he said, commanding in the darkness. "Don't move a muscle." He padded away, leaving her awash in need, shivering more from desire than from the cool evening air.

A moment later, he returned. Jill heard the crinkle of plastic and his own sharp exhalation, then he nudged her again, the thick bulk of his erection sliding along her wet cleft, separated by nothing but the thinnest of latex barriers.

"Thank you," she murmured, squeezing her thighs to draw him deeper.

"My pleasure." More laughter colored his voice this time, but it still didn't break the sensual spell he wove around her. He eased along her wetness again, his rhythm fast, then slow.

With one hand, he held her hips while the other stroked her belly and caressed her breasts. Yielding to his gentle direction, she rose and snuggled against him. His chest hairs tickled her back, and his breath was warm as he dipped his head to kiss the sensitive place where neck met shoulder.

"Oh. Phillip."

"You are so beautiful, so perfect. Soft and hard in all the right places." He flexed his hips to her bottom causing his length to throb against her cleft. "And wet and hot in all the right places too."

She moaned. Her body was already languid and limp in his arms. Yielding to her desires brought joy instead of the pain and loss she'd feared. "I never knew. I never imagined…" Her voice trailed off while he kissed his way up from her shoulder to her jaw.

"Don't imagine, Jill. Don't think. Just feel. For once in your life, let go. Trust me, Jill." His voice wrapped around her in the darkness, as tender as the touch of his hands on her body. The danger-filled foreplay melted into something mesmerizing and sweet.

"I do." She turned in his embrace and threaded her arms around his neck. "I do," she repeated as she raised on tiptoe to kiss him.

"Then lead me to your bedroom, and let me have my wicked way with you," he murmured against her lips.

Stumbling, unwilling to let his lips go for long enough to cross the small living space to her even smaller bedroom, Jill urged him to the bed. They tumbled in together, and he rolled on top of her, pinning her to the soft mattress.

With a slow, firm caress from her shoulders to her wrists, he forced her arms above her head and pressed her knuckles into the wall at the head of the bed.

"Stay there for me, *Er'hona-mei*. Be still, and let me look at you."

"But it's dark. You can't see."

"Then let me feel my way." He caressed her with his palms, sliding them down her arms to cup her breasts. His lips fastened on her nipple, and he sucked gently, drawing her into his mouth and teasing her with his teeth.

She sucked in a breath, startled by the dizzying sensations assaulting her. Without thinking, she reached for him.

"Please, Jill." His voice was thick and rough with passion. "Not yet."

Slowly, she returned her hands to the wall. His words imprisoned her more effectively than any physical bonds. Stretched out beneath his gaze, as helpless as a harem slave in the sultan's bed, she quivered in anticipation. "When do I get my turn?" she asked, her voice coming in breathy gasps.

He laved her other breast, suckling it thoroughly before lifting his head. His eyes shone in the darkness, and his voice was tender. "I've waited too long for this moment to ruin it by rushing. We have all night, *Er'hona-mei*. We have all night."

Er'hona-mei. My desirable one. Every time she heard the words, her heart melted a little more. She'd never been *Er'hona-mei* to anyone before. Warmth spread through the frozen corners of her heart and mind.

Phillip kissed her stomach then moved to her thighs, kissing and caressing with his one-finger-to-drive-her-crazy technique. She squirmed when he grasped her ankles and eased them apart, spreading her wide with gentle insistence. The intimacy of the physical act mirrored the open and vulnerable state of her exposed heart. She had nothing left to hide from him.

When he slid his hands to her thighs and buried his face between them, all she could do was lie still and breathe deeply, pulling in the pleasure he offered and riding waves of tightening, spiraling, heart-pounding sensation.

He found her sensitive spots and teased them. A long, slow lick across her wet entrance, then a teasing flick of his tongue at her sensitive core.

Lick, flick.

Lick, flick.

She writhed, screaming out with frustration until the lick, flick gave way to a hard, insistent sucking. The tight ratcheting of her senses peaked and erupted in an explosion of light, color, and a shuddering release.

In the aftermath of orgasm, she collapsed, limp and so sensitized that even the wisp of Phillip's breath across her stomach was an agonizing pleasure. He nibbled his way back to her breasts, his gentle ministrations igniting that coiling tension again.

This time his teeth and tongue teased her nipple. The head of his shaft pressed against the exquisitely tender flesh he'd just kissed so thoroughly.

She ached for him. He slid along the slick cleft without entering, teasing her with his nearness. She throbbed and clenched, her body ready to draw him in.

"I want you," she whimpered. Her hands, still pressed to the wall, fisted. "I want you inside me. Don't make me beg."

"Never, *Er'hona-mei*. I live to fulfill your wishes." He kissed her, deeply, thrusting his tongue into the soft recesses of her mouth. One hand cupped her breast, alternately squeezing the rounded flesh, then rolling her nipple between thumb and forefinger. His other hand cupped the curve of her bottom, angling her as he slid along her cleft one more time before entering.

Jill's body accepted him eagerly, tightening around him in a rhythm she couldn't control. Maybe it was the aftershocks of her last orgasm. Or the beginning of her next one. Each pulsing, burning stroke over her already sensitive flesh demanded more of her coiled response. Each slide of skin on skin brought her one step higher.

"Jill, look in my eyes."

Through her own haze of passion, she saw his eyes gleam in the darkness. "I want you," he said. "I want you. Come with me."

She clasped her arms around his neck and wrapped her legs around his hips, opening herself deeper and more fully to his touch. With his next thrust, lightning flashed, thunder roared, and her body splintered into a convulsing, writhing heap. Her constrictions squeezing him until he, too, collapsed in a shudder of completion.

They rolled onto their sides, and in the quiet of the aftermath, her body pulsed and his body answered, each time more gently, until their breathing slowed. Outside, the storm calmed until nothing was left but the soothing patter of rain on her windows. Lying beside Phillip, the thrill of orgasm faded into the contentment of being in the arms of the man she loved.

She hadn't bargained on love. Too late she realized that she wasn't capable of feeling desire without love. All of her sophisticated veneer peeled away revealing the girl she thought she'd left behind. The one who believed in love and happily ever after.

Phillip would return to his island home soon, leaving nothing more than a memory. She'd known it, thought she could accept it. But her foolish heart had gone and fallen in love.

Now in every spring storm for the rest of her life, Jill would see him in the flashes of lightning, feel him in the rumble of the thunder and hide her tears in the falling rain.

Chapter 9

Constantine woke to the dim light of a small bedside lamp. Through the doorway, he could hear Jill moving about.

"Hi, sleepyhead," she said as she appeared in the doorway holding a plate and a couple of mugs.

"Hey, beautiful," he replied. "Why'd you leave me?"

She came into the room and put the mugs and plate on the bedside table before perching beside him and leaning down to give him a kiss. She was as sweet and warm as she'd been hours before. Only better.

Her mussed hair and worn terry cloth robe giving her a softer, more approachable look. Or maybe it was the lovemaking that softened her protective shell. Either way, she was beautiful.

"Mmm, that's the way a man likes to wake up in the morning."

She laughed. "Maybe I'll get a chance to wake you that way in the morning. Right now, it's only nine o'clock in the evening. The power came on about an hour ago. I took our clothes down to the dryer and fixed you a sandwich and some coffee."

"Thanks, but you didn't have to go to any trouble. We could have gone out."

"Not in our wet clothes, we couldn't. And besides, I want you to gather your strength. If I remember correctly, it's my turn to give the orders and have my wicked way with you." Her smile went straight to his gut, warming it and starting a fire he'd thought thoroughly quenched.

She passed him the mug and plate. He sat up, balanced the plate on his knees, and took a slug of the coffee. "Thank you."

In all his adult years, he'd never had a lover care enough to make him a simple meal. They'd ordered elaborate room service. Or called for the palace catering staff. Or made reservations. But no one ever did something as simple as bring him a sandwich in bed. The warmth spread from his gut to a place dangerously near his heart.

Jill stayed for a while, sipping her coffee while he ate. Then she excused herself to retrieve their clothes. Constantine watched her leave, frowning when he realized she'd just left the apartment in nothing but a bathrobe. But what did he know of her habits? Maybe she always did laundry in her bathrobe.

If she wasn't back in five minutes, he'd go after her. He'd…He'd sit and wait because he had no clothes and no idea where she'd gone off to.

He tossed back the rest of his coffee and took the plate into her kitchenette, all the while straining to hear her footsteps. He helped himself to more coffee, then, almost as an afterthought, washed and dried the plate. When he opened a cupboard to put it away, a small packet tumbled out.

Ramen noodles, according to the package. Specially priced at ten for one dollar, according to the bright orange sticker on the front. He frowned as he replaced the packet alongside dozens of others, in all flavors.

Curious now, he checked the other cupboards. More noodles. Some rice. And a selection of dented cans of various vegetables, all bargain priced. A quick look in the refrigerator revealed almost nothing. When he finally put the plate away, he was in a state of humbled awe. In offering him that simple sandwich, she'd offered him the best she had.

He wandered out of the kitchen and almost jumped when he saw the figure standing in a shadowed corner. A headless, life-sized mannequin, swathed in an expensive gown, peered out from the shadows. Or would have peered if it had eyes.

An ironing board propped nearby held homemade pattern pieces, cut from tissue paper. One fragile piece was pinned carefully to the gown.

Constantine smiled to himself. Another mystery solved. The expensive gowns, returned a few days after purchase, were inspiration for a home sewn creation. Another way to pinch a penny. Just like her empty kitchen and this cramped apartment under the eaves of a crumbling building.

Behind him an ancient cordless phone in the kitchen rang. He stopped himself just as he reached for it, remembering at the last minute that this wasn't his home. He ambled back to the bedroom. Over the click and whir of her answering machine, a concerned voice spoke too loudly for him to ignore.

"Jill, honey, it's Mom. I'm looking forward to seeing you next weekend for your high school reunion. I know you're busy, probably working late on the weekend again, but I needed to talk to you about Gracie.

"She's never home—always either working or studying. But she's restless. The community college isn't challenging enough for her, even with advanced classes. Maybe if we pooled her college savings with Amber's, we could get her into a better school, sooner. Amber and Char can always wait another year or so. We'll talk soon. Love you, sweetie. Bye."

In the silence another piece of Jill's puzzle fell into place. He didn't know how many siblings she had, but based on the information his spies had uncovered about her finances, he'd guess there were four of them. One for each large bank account. Leaving the small one for Jill.

Why she felt compelled to skimp on herself to support her family, he didn't know. But he knew he could help. She held the key to finding the thief who stole the Melesian Crown Jewels.

He was convinced that if she traveled to Melesia with him, she would see or hear something that would help him uncover the thief's identity. He was asking her to take a risk for his country.

The least his country could do to thank her was to see that her siblings got the finest education possible. The minute he got home, he'd arrange it.

After all, he was soon-to-be crowned king, and what good was it to become king if you couldn't help your friends? He was giving up his freedom for his country. It was the least he could ask for in return.

And if the Bradley children attended the Royal Academy of Melesia on scholarship, maybe, just maybe, Jill would come to visit them. And him.

Jill propped her head on her hand and watched Phillip with sleepy eyes. Her limp body throbbed with pleasure and her mind filled with wonder. Phillip lay curled beside her, hair tousled, a shadow of a beard covering his jaw and a faint smile etched onto his face.

She ran her hand down his side, and he scooted closer to her, instinctively seeking her and looping his arm across her waist. A sigh escaped his lips, and he settled into a deeper sleep.

How easily she'd dropped her guard around him as if she'd been waiting her entire life for him. Like a key fitting into a lock, he'd opened the door to emotions she'd almost forgotten she had. She combed her fingers through his hair, raking her nails gently against his scalp in the way that he loved. His smile deepened.

She knew little about his family and nothing about his background, but she knew him, intimately. From his sensitive scalp to the tiny star-shaped birthmark at the top of his left thigh, nothing was hidden from her.

Like Sleeping Beauty, she'd been awakened from a long, dreamless slumber. Now, she was ravenous for the kiss and the man who'd brought her back to life. The warmth of his body, the sound of his breath, even the smell of his sweater when it came out of the dryer, only made the hunger more intense. She'd gorged herself on pleasure with him twice tonight, yet she craved more.

It wasn't only about the pleasure—although she could grow used to giant-sized helpings of that too. No, it was more. She wanted to crawl inside him, become part of him, bond to him in a way she'd never wanted before.

The desire to know him, open up to him, share with him, was meat and vegetable, bread and milk to her affection-starved soul. The lovemaking was dessert—delectable, but not quite enough to satisfy her for long.

With one last look, she slid from beneath the covers. Her restless hunger would surely wake him if she stayed put, and she didn't have the heart to disturb his slumber.

Jill padded out to the kitchen and turned on the radio, adjusting the volume to a mere whisper while she brewed herself a cup of herbal tea. Her favorite guilty pleasure—celebrity talk news—greeted her with its usual irreverent, humorous spin on the antics of the rich and famous. Her friend Claire had gotten her addicted to the entertainment tabloid *The Weekly World Stir* and its sister radio station. Jill smiled at the memory of how many hours they'd spent sharing celebrity gossip before Claire married her billionaire chocolatier. Maybe the talk show could distract her from thoughts of Phillip.

" …and now WSTR has an international tidbit. The island country of Melesia, a popular vacation destination renowned for its rare perfumes and exotic marine life, may be in the midst of turmoil. Speculations abound, hinting that King Alexander Augustus Tyronne D'Malia had a falling out with his brother, international playboy, Prince Constantine Phillippe Ramon D'Malia. The palace spokesperson denied any rumors of family unrest, but unofficial sources disagree.

"The Stir super sleuth team confirmed that the popular prince was nowhere on the island. So, late-night listeners, here's tonight's topic: did the prince leave the island to calm a family feud? Or is he in hot pursuit of an amorous adventure? After the break we'll take your calls."

Jill switched the radio off, disturbed by the host's flippancy. Phillip had once accused her of being an American royal watcher. She'd denied it, but the remark stung because it was close to home.

She occasionally still splurged on the radio station's sister publication, the *Weekly World Stir*. Not that she believed the fantastic stories. But the tabloid entertainment journal's prime reporter, Mack the Pen, had an often humorous insight into the lives of celebrities and royals worldwide. He'd specialized in Melesian gossip, always finding juicy tidbits to entrance his readers.

Yet after seeing Phillip's devotion and the affection he held for the Melesian royal family, she cringed at her small and voyeuristic indulgence in such drivel. In contrast to his patriotic respect, even her youthful fantasies about the charming Prince Constantine, which were inspired by the royal wedding all those years ago, seemed like an invasion of privacy in a family who deserved better from her.

She closed her eyes and focused on the real man asleep in her bed, not the adolescent fantasy. Her body tingled at the thought. Who needed Prince Constantine Phillippe Ramon D'Malia when she had Phillip Raym… Phillip Ra… Phillippe. Ramon. The bottom dropped out of her stomach leaving an aching vacuum in place of the tingle.

This wasn't real. It wasn't happening. It couldn't be. But even as she searched for the thick text on Melesian culture and history she kept on her bookshelf, her mind already knew what she would find.

She opened the book to the photo section. Her fingers trembled as she flipped the pages past the historical kings to the current royal family. There in regal splendor was the portrait of that scheming, lying, betraying dog-of-a-prince.

Constantine Phillippe Ramon D'Malia.

The man in her bed.

Chapter 10

"*L*iar!" Constantine jerked awake. A book whizzed past his head and slammed into the wall. He rolled aside just before it thumped harmlessly on his pillow.

"Wretched. Underhanded. Slimy." The shrieks and the missiles kept coming. Shoes. A tiny pot that shattered against the wall beside the bed. Then another. And another.

"Get out, you…you…bastard."

"Jill, wait. There's no need—"

"No need? No need for what? The theatrics? The disguises? The little intrigues? No need for the truth?"

She stormed to the bed and snatched the sheet away. "I want you out of my apartment and out of my life. Now."

Her eyes flashed with rage as she threw whatever was in reach. A pillow. A magazine. The alarm clock. "Get out. Get out. Get out." The mantra seemed to feed her frenzy until, with nothing more to throw, she launched herself at him.

He grabbed her wrists.

"Jill. Stop." He rolled her onto her back, tangling them both in the sheets, pinning her wrists to the bed and covering her flailing body with his. "Stop this instant."

His anger accomplished what attempts at calmness hadn't. She went limp under him, deflating suddenly as the passionate violence passed. Her eyes scrunched tightly, but a trickle of tears still escaped, accusing him more effectively than her rage.

"Calm down and talk to me," he said, trying to keep his voice soothing and gentle.

"I don't have to listen to you." Her voice was a choked whisper. "I'm not one of your subjects."

"Ah. So you've uncovered my secret, have you? Is that what this is all about?"

"You lied to me. You lied and took, took…" She gulped for air. The movement beneath him was nearly as distracting as her distress. "Were you laughing at me from the very beginning?"

"Jill, *Er'hona-mei*, I may have kept my identity secret, but I never lied to you about anything important." He loosened his grip on her wrists and smoothed her hair from her face with one hand. Her red rimmed eyes and blotchy cheeks tore at his heart. "And I never laughed at you."

"Don't call me that. I don't want to be your *Er'hona-mei*." Her voice caught, belying her words. "Why are you here?" She opened her watery eyes and stared at him, demanding an answer.

"I'm here, because I met a wonderful woman who offered me a priceless treasure."

"I'm not a treasure. I'm just another addition to your international playboy legacy." Beneath him she stiffened, anger threatening to take the upper hand.

"Jill, that's a myth. A media fabrication. I've had women before, but they all knew the score. And, believe me, they all wanted something from me too."

"I didn't want anything from you." Bitterness edged the words.

"No, you didn't ask for or expect anything. You gave me tenderness and laughter and caring. You gave me your trust."

"You trampled it."

"I'm sorry, Jill. I didn't mean to hurt you."

"Why are you really here? I mean, why are you in Chicago? Surely you didn't come looking for me. Or for a meaningless fling with a nobody from Anytown, U.S.A."

Her accusation wounded him more than all the missiles she'd hurled earlier. Because she believed it. She believed the worst of him. "You are not just anybody," he said fiercely, willing her to believe him. "And what we have is not a meaningless fling."

She flinched at his harsh tone, causing his gut to tighten in agony. "It's a long story," he added gently. "It's a story I need to tell you, and one I want to share with you. But first, I want you to promise me something."

"What?"

"Promise me you'll listen and not start throwing things if I let you up."

She nodded. "I promise." The words came out in a broken whisper that tore at him.

"Good, because even with you angry at me, lying here with you is damn distracting. In about five more minutes, I won't be able to think about anything but how good you feel beneath me. And how much I'd like to bury myself in you again."

"We can't have that, now, can we?" A wry touch of humor fought with the bitter edge of her voice, but the quiver of her lips gave her away.

"No, we can't. Not until you hear the truth—all of it—and decide for yourself if you still want me."

He rolled aside, taking her with him, gathering her in his arms. When she didn't resist, he stroked her back until the stiffness seeped out of it and she relaxed in his arms.

Jill lay motionless beside Phillip—no, not Phillip anymore, Constantine. She lay motionless beside *Constantine* and tried to gather her scattered feelings. She'd always known he'd go back to Melesia. She'd told herself she just wanted a fling with no strings attached.

So why did it hurt so badly to discover he was a prince instead of a businessman? The end result was the same. A week, maybe two, of romance with no commitments.

But he used you. The tiny irrational voice nagged at her. He hadn't used her, not really, she argued. Not anymore than she'd used him. Or had she?

She'd used her other dates, the rich ones who promised security. The ones she'd kept at arm's length while waiting in vain for a marriage proposal. But had she used Phillip—correction, Constantine? Or had there been something more from the beginning?

The truth hit her, along with a fresh batch of tears she struggled to keep inside. His deception hurt because, from the beginning, she'd longed for more. Why else would she bring him to her home? Or her bed where no man had ever been? Why else would she make love to him if she didn't already love him?

His secret identity had shattered hopes she didn't even know she had. Commitment, love, a family of her own, things she'd longed for in secret, all disappeared before her eyes. Some dreams were never meant to become reality.

She swallowed her tears and forced her mind and heart back into that cold, tight spot where she'd spent so many dry-eyed years. But the warmth of Phillip's—no, damn it—Constantine's body, the thumping of his heart, and the slow, tender caresses of his hands wouldn't let her go back to the cold.

"What I told you about Alex and Helena's marriage was true," he said. His voice, deep and warm rumbled through his chest, beneath the spot where her palm was pressed. "It was a political alliance. At least that's how it started. Somewhere along the line, they grew fond of one another."

Fondness didn't sound like a much better basis for marriage than the political alliance. And even though she'd considered a loveless marriage for herself, her heart had never let her go through with it.

Phil— Constantine's hand covered hers, and he idly stroked her fingers as he spoke. "I think things started to change after their son, Ty, was born. Alex spent every free minute with the baby and his wife.

"When Ty was a toddler, he was seriously ill. During those weeks, his mother or father was by his side constantly. Alex canceled public appearances; Helena put her schedule of charity work on hold. The whole country was on edge to see what would happen to the newest heir to the throne.

"In the end, he recovered. And Alex and Helena fell in love with each other. So, in a way, they have a romantic ending, despite their beginning."

Jill twined her fingers in his and rubbed her thumb along the side of his hand, taking in the story, and the quiet emotion she'd heard in his voice. "Why don't you believe in love?"

"Me?" His astonishment surprised her. "I used to have the luxury of believing in love. I even thought I'd break all my commitments if I found the right woman. But that was a long time ago."

His hand tightened on hers. "Alex is ill. In a few weeks, he plans to abdicate and retire with Helena and Ty to try to regain his health. He deserves a chance to enjoy the happiness he's found."

"Abdicate?" Jill couldn't get her mind around the concept. "Surely, his son isn't old enough to…"

"Not his son, Jill. Me. Special Melesian law allows him to transfer power on behalf of his son as well, if it's done before the heir reaches the age of ten. So he's passing the kingship to me. With all the duties and responsibilities."

"Duty and power," she said, remembering his words. It seemed a lifetime ago that he'd said them to her, not merely a few days.

"Yes, duty. To my family, my country, and the world. And power. To help everyone but myself."

"With such important events going on in your country, why are you here?"

He rolled onto his side and propped up on one elbow, watching her. His aqua-blue eyes darkened to azure. The hand he stroked her with was gentle, warm, and hypnotic. "A king needs his crown, and a coronation needs its regalia. And the Crown Jewels have been stolen."

"What?" Jill jerked to a sitting position and pulled her robe around her. "It hasn't been in the news. When did it happen? Who took them?"

He pulled the sheet around him and sat up next to her, gingerly moving the history book out of the way. "You're one of only a handful of people who know. The thefts may have been going on for some time. Palace investigations pointed to Chicago as the most likely place for fencing the jewels."

Jill's throat went dry and the blood drained from her face at the unspoken implication. "And in Chicago, McKinley and Company was the most likely suspect."

He took her hand and placed it between both of his, hesitating before answering. "Yes. I came undercover with a small team to investigate further."

How much worse could things get for one woman? Yesterday the world was full of promise. Today it demanded retribution for every sin she'd ever committed. A chilling numbness gripped her. Within his grasp, her fingers trembled.

"Are we," she licked her lips and started again. "Am I a suspect?"

He shook his head, a tiny motion full of regret. But it wasn't an answer to her question. For a second, she wondered if she would see the island kingdom at last—from the window of a prison cell.

"In the beginning, everyone was a suspect. But you have to believe me, Jill. I wouldn't be here today, in your bed, or even in your home, if I thought you were guilty. I would never have slept with you if I still thought you were stealing from me."

"Still? So you did suspect me."

"Jill, your hands are like ice. Let's get dressed and I'll tell you over breakfast."

"Tell me now. Why did you think I was involved? And what changed your mind?"

"I don't *think* you're involved. I *know* you're involved." He lifted his hand and stroked her throat. Though his movement was gentle, a cold shot of terror rushed through her veins. He paused, lifting her necklace. "I know you're involved because of this. You don't even know what you're wearing, do you?"

"It's my good luck charm. The one from Mr. Dimas. The one he wanted to give to the daughter he never had."

"It's the royal insignia, Jill. Very few outside the royal court have seen it. No one is allowed to wear it but the royal family."

Her hands flew to the clasp. The necklace, once a good luck charm and symbol of her changed fortunes now choked her. She fumbled, unable to find the catch. Constantine laid his hand on top of hers, stilling the frantic motion. She couldn't look at him, didn't want to see disappointment in his eyes.

"Jill, please. I want you to wear it."

"But I can't. It's your tradition. It's—"

"It is a part of who you are. You've worn it for a long time. And I've never seen you without it. I want you to wear it." She let him pull her hands away, but the insignia weighed heavy against her skin.

"You didn't receive that necklace by chance," he continued. "Only a few people outside of the royal family know the exact design of the necklace. And I'll bet my crown—if we ever find it—that your Mr. Dimas is one of them. I don't know exactly how this man is using you, but I know he is. You're the only clue I have to the disappearance of the Crown Jewels. I need your help, Jill. I need you to help me find them and the thief. I need you to come to Melesia with me. Will you cooperate?"

"Do I have a choice?"

"Yes, Jill. You have a choice. I'm asking, not ordering. Please. Will you help me?"

When she looked in his eyes, she saw not only the question, but also his hopes. She didn't really have a choice at all.

Chapter 11

onstantine pulled on his clothes with short, jerky motions, cursing himself for mishandling the situation. Calling himself the biggest fool on earth. He glanced to the bathroom door. Jill had disappeared behind it, and he doubted he'd see her anytime soon. It was the only place in this tiny shoe box of an apartment where she could get away from him.

He should leave now, and have his security guards, or Edmund, take over. She didn't need to be reminded of his selfishness every time she looked at him. He could have told her about his identity and the mission before he started thinking with his groin instead of his head. He should have told her then. No wonder she felt used.

Part of him—probably the same part that was in control last night—didn't want to give her up. Anyway, she was his responsibility. It was his Crown Jewels that landed her in this intrigue. Besides, his suspicions may have raised the stakes for the thief. Jill could be in danger because of him. There was a justification if he'd ever created one. Still, he wasn't going to leave her alone.

And he sure as hell wasn't going to let her go to Melesia alone. If, as he suspected, her presence on the island shook things up, she could be in for an unpleasant visit. Once people recognized her necklace as the royal insignia, rumors would fly. He couldn't let her face that alone, or even with a contingent of bodyguards. No, only his presence at her side could temper the gossip.

He heard the shower turn on. Listening to the sound he imagined Jill slipping out of her robe and standing under the steamy spray. He could almost smell the scented soap as the lather glided over her wet body. His hands itched to follow the path of its slick smoothness.

This was nonsense. He didn't belong in that shower with her, even if he longed to be there. Frustrated, he searched for his shoes. He'd kicked them off in this very spot yesterday. He peered under the couch and behind the TV. Then he remembered where he'd seen them last—hurling through the air, aimed at his head. At least he thought they were his shoes.

He found them, half hidden under the bed, covered in the broken shards of pottery. Jill could get hurt if she walked in here in her bare feet. He frowned, trying to remember if she'd worn slippers earlier. Either way, it was just a matter of time before she stepped on something and cut her feet.

He searched until he found a broom, dustpan and dust cloth in a tiny kitchen cupboard. He hadn't grown up so privileged that he couldn't make himself useful. Starting on his side of the bed, he picked up the discarded missiles, wiped them free of dirt and broken pottery and tossed them onto the bed. Then he swept under and around the bed, corralling the sharp bits into a neat pile.

"What are you doing?"

He turned at the sound of her voice. Jill stood, wrapped in the familiar worn terry cloth robe, her hair still damp from her shower.

"Stay where you are." He held up a hand to ward her off, regretting how she stiffened at his tone. He glanced down at her slippered feet then lowered his hand. "Unless you have something on your feet, that is. There's broken pottery every-where in here."

Jill turned red and rushed to take the broom from him. "I'm sorry about that. You shouldn't be cleaning up my mess. You, you're…"

"I'm the one who made you angry enough to throw things in the first place." He turned her to face him and gently cupped her jaw. "While I sincerely hope that isn't your normal way of handling disagreements, no one was hurt."

"There's probably some sort of a law with horrible conse-quences for people who hurl pottery at the future king."

She clutched her broom with a charmingly distraught ex-pression that somehow poked holes in all the musty traditions of a centuries-old monarchy. He burst out laughing, instinc-tively gathering her close. "I'm sure there is, *Er'hona-mei*. For your sake, we'd better keep this quiet lest the royal guards take you away in the middle of the night and strand you on one of our remote islands."

Her arms snaked around his waist, and he thought he heard her muffled attempt at laughter, although with her face buried in his sweater, it was hard to tell. He pushed his luck a little more. "Of course, you'll have to find a way to insure my silence. I'm open to bribes of all sorts. Although I am getting bored with the usual things, you know, money, priceless gems, rare antiquities. But I'm sure you could think of something."

This time, he knew he heard laughter, and when she lifted her face, he bent down and stole a kiss from her. It was as sweet, unhesitant, and full of affection as it had been yesterday. As if she not only forgave his deception, but also as if she didn't care who or what he was.

Outside of the kiss, her awkwardness over his status lin-gered, but here, they were equals in every sense. The softness of her lips, the press of her body, still warm from the shower, the tightening of her grip around his waist, all spoke of desire, affection, and—

His stomach rumbled. Loudly.

"Perhaps breakfast would make a good bribe, Your Highness." The teasing in her tone didn't quite off set the awkwardness of the situation.

"I was hoping for something more along the lines of another kiss." His stomach interrupted again. "But it looks like I'll have to settle for breakfast. As a starting point." He arched an eyebrow and tried to arrange his face into an expression of mock sternness.

When she giggled and led him from the bedroom, he relaxed, certain that with a little effort he could restore the easy, uncomplicated companionship they'd shared before.

It was wrong to want her when he couldn't offer the kind of future she deserved, but for once, he wasn't thinking about right and wrong. For one selfish moment, he gave free rein to his heart—logic and tradition be damned.

Jill poured them both a second cup of coffee and leaned back to watch Phillip. Constantine. She growled silently at her mental slip. Dressed in his standard weekend attire of jeans and sweater, he looked exactly like a normal, available male. Except he wasn't.

He was the crown prince of a wealthy archipelago. All the clues she'd seen but not understood came together. Expensive cologne contrasting with everyday work suits. The slight aloofness he showed to everyone but her. Edmund's poorly disguised deference. And even his current behavior.

"What exactly did you smear on this toast again?" he asked, inspecting the toast with a slightly nervous tilt of his head.

She bit the inside of her cheek to keep from laughing. "It's peanut butter. Almost everyone in America eats it, either because they're kids and they love it or because they're on a tight budget. It's safe."

As he took a cautious bite, a sudden horrible thought occurred to her. "You're not allergic to nuts, are you? I mean a lot of people are, and I guess it could be a problem if you were sensitive. If you've never had it before, you wouldn't know."

His eyes bugged out of his face, and he grabbed his throat, suddenly gasping. Jill raced halfway to the phone in a panic, turning back only when she heard his laughter. "Jill, no, I was just teasing you. I'm not allergic to any food that I'm aware of."

"You rat." She launched a couch pillow at him before she could stop herself. "Oh no. I've done it again."

He picked up the pillow off the floor and tossed it back at her. "I'd much rather have you throwing pillows at me and laughing than sitting across the table biting your lip and looking at your fingernails. I'm the same person I was last week, and last night for that matter. Come back to the table and finish breakfast with me."

She joined him again, but could only fidget with her coffee cup, restless under his gaze. He watched her with such intensity, a troubled frown puckering his forehead. She cleared her throat and tried to break the silence.

"It's just a lot to take in at once," she began. "It was amazing enough last night when I realized I was with someone who made me want to…well, someone who made me care. It's been a roller coaster since early this morning."

She looked up at him and attempted a smile. "I can't even get your name right in my head. I keep thinking of you as Phillip. Constantine sounds like such a mouthful."

"You should hear the whole thing. It's not so bad for formal ceremonies or when the reporters say it, but my mother had a way of making me tremble in my shoes with nothing more than my name." He took a breath and mimicked the high-pitched tone of his mother. "Constantine Phillippe Ramon D'Malia, how many times do I have to tell you…"

Jill burst out laughing. "I thought Jillian Louise Bradley was bad. I guess mothers everywhere are the same, aren't they?"

"Well, yes, and no." He leaned back and took a leisurely sip of coffee. "Most of the current political turmoil at home, what little there is, stems from my mother. She wasn't the typical, aloof royal parent. Being a student of history, you probably know that Alex's mother died when he was a toddler and that my father remarried soon afterward."

She nodded. "Some of the people thought your mother was a poor choice."

"Most of the royal court thought she was a poor choice," he corrected. "The citizens, however, loved her. In a way, it was the classic Cinderella story. She worked in the palace as part of the late queen's staff. After the queen's passing, my father decided he'd done his duty. He'd made the expected marriage, produced an heir, and that was that. Something about my mother intrigued him, and I truly believe they married for love.

"Mother raised both Alex and myself, as well as our younger siblings, giving us as much of a childhood as one could have while living in a glass house. I was lucky. I didn't have the pressure of being the heir, plus I got to travel with my maternal grandmother to visit her parents in the United States. They had a farm up in Wisconsin. They died when I was still quite young, but I remember those days well."

"Your mother was an American?"

"My grandmother was American. My maternal grandfather was a Melesian businessman who swept her off her feet."

"There's a lot of romance in your family for a man who doesn't believe in it for himself."

He shrugged, then picked up the discarded toast again. "You know, I probably did eat this as a kid, when I visited in Wisconsin. I just forgot about it. Anyway, since I was born a good two years after their hasty wedding, my mother thwarted most of the nasty rumors. But whenever there's a disagreement about the country's future, someone is bound to bring up my 'tainted' blood line."

"Could your mother's heritage and prejudice over your ancestry be behind the thefts? That would explain why the jewels were being routed through the United States."

He polished off the toast while considering it. "It fits. There are factions who would be against my coronation. Giving you the necklace could be a symbolic reminder that my mother—who wore the royal insignia after her marriage—had common roots. It's subtle, but possible.

"I tend to think, however, that it's a sign to someone in the smuggling ring. They may be shipping the jewels in with other imports bound for McKinley and Company. You could have been followed when you inspected the crates."

Jill left the table, unsettled by the talk of smugglers, schemes, and political turmoil. She'd changed into her loose jeans and her father's frayed varsity sweatshirt, but even their familiar comfort couldn't help her shake her unease. Memories of her father were no match for the emotional tangle Constantine had brought into her life.

She wandered to the bedroom, concentrating instead on cleaning up the bits of broken pottery that still littered the floor by the bed. Constantine's shoes were covered in dust, shards marring the expensive leather. She swept up the piles of pottery then knelt to clean his shoes, upending them to shake the clay from inside. Something shiny was buried in the smashed clay. "Oh, my God! Phillip! I mean Const-"

He was on his knees beside her before she could finish. "I'm here, Jill. What's wrong?"

Mutely she held out her hand, a tiny pair of earrings flashing amidst the smashed pottery. He picked up one of the gems, the color draining from his face.

"These belonged to Helena. I helped Ty pick them out for her birthday two years ago. She thought she'd lost them."

The truth hit Jill with the force of a speeding car. She was smuggling the stolen gems in her pots.

She, unwittingly or not, was an accomplice to theft and treason.

Chapter 12

The plush luxury of Jill's suite at the Melesian embassy, with its continuous flow of fine foods and wine, contrasted sharply with every dank, colorless holding cell she'd ever seen on television. But despite the physical comforts, an interrogation was still an interrogation.

Her head pounded, and she fought a wave of nausea. Outside the window, the sun dipped low, painting the horizon in red.

"Tell me again exactly how this Mr. Dimas approached you," the security officer asked, his voice dry and without expression. "I need to make sure we didn't miss any details."

She looked up from the book on her lap. Every wanted criminal in the northern hemisphere seemed to be profiled in it, but none of the profiles fit the man she'd so innocently trusted. In an exhausted monotone, she repeated the story of their first meeting, bracing for the inevitable interruptions and diversions.

What were they looking for? She longed for blessed silence and something familiar to ground her in the midst of this nightmare. Even though Constantine sat beside her, holding her hand, she'd never felt more alone.

Here, surrounded by his bodyguards and loyal subjects, she saw him as he was, every inch the crown prince and soon-to-be-King. Staff members worked to anticipate his slightest demand. Everyone kept a respectful distance and treated him with deference. No one laughed, or teased, or—heaven forbid—threw things at him. She cringed at the memory of the morning.

She didn't belong here. Not in the embassy. Not with him.

She wanted to pull her hand away and shrink from the spotlight, like the common nobody she was. But she didn't have a choice. She owed it to herself, and to the royal family of Melesia, to help catch this thief she'd unwittingly aided. With her free hand she rubbed her throbbing temples.

"Miss Bradley, how long have you been working for McKinley and Company?" He'd asked that only an hour ago. Did the security team have a short memory? *Listen to your recordings*, she wanted to scream. *Check your beat-up little note pad. Search your memory.* She took a breath, but it came out shaky, not calming.

"Gentlemen, Miss Bradley is tired. She's answered enough of your questions for one night." Constantine stood, took the book from her, and escorted the security team from the room.

Jill sank back against the brocade covered couch, thankful for the silence now that the army of interrogators was finally gone. Grateful that she was alone at last.

She hugged a pillow to her middle, kicked off her shoes and drew her knees to her chest. She didn't need to be strong now. The tears brought on by exhaustion and frustration fell freely.

"I'm sorry, Jill. I should have stopped them an hour ago." The couch dipped as he sat beside her again.

She wasn't alone in her misery. Why had she assumed he'd go? She wouldn't have given in to the urge to cry if she'd known he was still there. But now, she couldn't stop. And she couldn't resist him when he cupped his hand around her neck, gently urging her to curl up against his shoulder rather than the hard arm of the couch.

She shouldn't do this. He was a prince, for crying out loud. He was a world leader. He was… He was warm. Solid. Comforting. And the only thing familiar in this strange, luxurious, foreign world she'd been thrust into. No matter what, or who, he might be tomorrow, tonight he was here, offering her the solace she needed.

When he pulled her on top of him and sank into the couch, she didn't resist. When he kissed her temple and wrapped his arms around her, she didn't struggle. She just snuggled close and took what he offered. Until morning. When her troubles returned.

Constantine shifted on the hard couch, a mere fraction of an inch, careful not to wake Jill. She sighed and cuddled against him, still asleep. Even though hours had passed, he could still feel a damp patch where her tears seeped through the loose weave of his sweater to wet his skin. Right over the place where his heart should have been. Now the spot was filled with the cold ache of seeing Jill broken and defenseless.

As soon as they'd walked through the embassy doors, the security team descended, holding back their questions only long enough for him to order a comfortable suite and some food. They'd questioned, taken notes, and questioned again, trying to glean every scrap of information from Jill. With each tactic, he could feel her slipping farther away, withdrawing into herself.

When he came back into the room after dismissing the investigators, he'd found her in tears. She'd startled at the sound of his voice, shrinking back against the couch pillows. Jill wasn't the kind to show weakness or fear, and he'd seen both in that minute.

More than that, he'd caused both. Because of who he was. Because of his damned duty to king and country. He wouldn't blame her if she felt like a suspect again. He'd understand if she hated him in the morning.

But for now, at least, she rested in his arms, trusting him. He held her close, soothing her as she murmured in her sleep. Caring for her, despite all the reasons he shouldn't.

Outside the window, lights from the skyscrapers twinkled against the inky blackness of the chilly Chicago night. He longed to be home, lounging in the sand of a private beach, feeling its warmth seep into his skin. Stars, not artificial light, would twinkle in the sky. The only restlessness would come from the waves surging onto the beach. And Jill would be in his arms, sharing the wonder of it with him.

But he was a prince, soon-to-be king, and such wishes were for ordinary men. The discovery of the stolen earrings strained the fragile trust they'd forged, destroying the illusion that they were just two people sharing a peaceful Sunday morning.

The memory and the accompanying dread that gripped him burned in his gut like cheap whiskey. His investigation had exposed the smuggler's mode of operation, but had it also put Jill in danger? Instead of an asset, she was now a liability to the culprits. How far would they go to protect themselves? Until that moment, he hadn't thought Jill in danger, not really. But now, he was obligated to protect and shield her.

During the long, grueling day, she'd given the palace in-vestigators plenty of information to work with. Mr. Dimas was still a mystery, but teams had been dispatched to check on her contact at the craft show, Mr. Latimer, and the flower shop owner to see if they were co-conspirators, or mere pawns in a larger scheme.

Others, posing as collectors, were poised to make offers on the flower shop merchandise in the hope of finding the art collector who, according to Jill, purchased "rare" pieces.

Rare pieces with smuggled gems. He'd stake his life on it. But not Jill's life. That's why he had to keep her close and guarded at all times.

Unfortunately, the undercover officers had little to go on. Jill's involvement consisted of sorting the pieces according to size and selling them to her various clients. The security team's tactics to jog her memory were unsuccessful. She simply didn't know how the pots were marked.

She shifted in her sleep and a hint of floral shampoo drifted up, reminding him of a more pleasant part of the day. She moaned slightly, mumbling.

"What is it?" He whispered the words and stroked his hands lightly across her back.

"I told you everything." The agitated, sleep-slurred words were laced with contempt, likely aimed at his security team. Then, as quickly as the restlessness came, it was gone. She snuggled against him, deep asleep once more.

He closed his eyes, impossible thoughts of his private beach, and Jill, tempting him as he drifted into a peaceful sleep.

"I know where it is."

Constantine jerked awake at the sound of her voice and stared at Jill. His eyes were groggy, and her animated figure seemed to weave drunkenly above him.

"Wake up, Constantine. Wake up. I know where the stolen jewels are. I had an incredible dream, and I suddenly knew where they were." She rolled off the couch, and an unwelcome wave of cool air washed over him, replacing the luscious warmth of her body.

"Dream with me." He tried to pull her back to the couch, wanting to recapture a pleasant dream of his own. The beach seemed so real. The ocean and moonlight were within reach if only she'd snuggle against him and sleep once more.

"Come on." She tugged at his hand. "I know where the jewels are."

Her words finally penetrated his sleep-numbed brain. The jewels. She'd remembered something to help them find the jewels. He pushed the fragments of his own impossible dream away and sat up. Reality, and Jill, demanded his attention.

"All right, Jill. Where are they?"

"They've been under our noses the whole time."

The offices of McKinley and Company were deserted at this time on a Sunday night. Or was it Monday morning already? She'd lost track.

Jill shivered despite the warmth of the building, and Constantine pulled her close. Edmund hovered in the background. Constantine spoke briefly to Edmund before turning back to her.

"I must be crazy to let you talk me into coming here without a full security team."

She pulled him into the office, leaving Edmund in the hallway. "Mr. Aims at the florist shop has been bugging me recently, asking when I'm due for another shipment. I've avoided him as much as possible, but he's been insistent. He said his collector was breathing down his neck. I sold him all the large pots I had, but he didn't believe me. I must have been dreaming about it, because when I woke up, I remembered."

Constantine nodded, understanding what he'd missed before. Not *I told you everything* but *I sold you everything*. "You were talking in your sleep. I thought you were having nightmares about the security team."

"They don't inspire good dreams," she muttered. "But that's not what was on my mind. I've been trying all day to remember anything that could help. My mind must have put it together while I was sleeping. It's been here all along." She gestured to the window where the struggling palm tree sat nestled in its pot.

"Oh my God." Constantine stared at the pot, his eyes first widening in amazement, then narrowing as if he could peer inside it by the force of will alone.

"This pot was chipped when I got it. Normally I send the defective ones back to the address Mr. Dimas gave me, but I brought this one here instead, because it was painted in the national colors, green and gold."

She moved to the pot and knelt. "I also liked the designs. I didn't realize until tonight what made it so appealing to me." She pointed to the design, almost hidden where the pot faced the wall.

"The royal insignia," Constantine said as he knelt beside her and looked where she directed. His voice was rough with emotion.

"Until you told me about my necklace, I didn't realize the importance of the mark. I just thought it was lucky, like my necklace."

"What about Mr. Aims and his collector? Were all the pieces he bought marked with the insignia?" Constantine grabbed the pot and shifted it to look at the design more closely.

Jill shook her head. "I don't remember. I think some of the pots had the mark on them, but I'm not sure."

"But you think the gems were all smuggled in pots marked with the royal insignia."

"It makes sense, doesn't it? Why wouldn't Mr. Dimas use it to mark the smuggled gems? The royal insignia marks the royal Crown Jewels."

"Too bad we didn't get a look at the pot in your apartment," he mused.

"Well, there's only one way to find out if I'm right." She lifted the hammer she'd asked Edmund to bring with them.

"Wait." Constantine's voice stopped her as she was poised to strike. He rose and grabbed a coffee mug then dragged an empty waste basket over to the window. "Let's see if we can't make your tree comfortable in his new home first." He scooped dirt from the pot to the waste basket with the empty mug.

Jill's heart did a little flip, and she sat back on her heels feeling the sting of fresh tears in her eyes. Prince Constantine Phillippe Ramon D'Malia, rich, handsome, and on the brink of his own coronation, was concerned about saving her palm tree when most men would have tossed it aside for the sake of the gems.

His country would be well cared for in those hands, mud-encrusted though they were now. And despite the strange circumstances that drew them together, she was glad she'd met him, glad she'd opened her heart and home to him. She scooted closer to the pot and joined him, scooping dirt from it, and gently loosening the roots of the tree.

Their fingers brushed and a thrill of anticipation shot through her. Would her body always react this way to him? She wondered if she could ever see his face on the news or hear his name without this sense of heightened awareness. Without this tingling urge to touch him, to kiss him.

Impulsively, she stilled his hand with hers and leaned over to kiss him. He responded, his initial surprise melting into a languid play of lip on lip. A sweet tenderness, more powerful than passion, tugged at her heart.

"What was that for?" he asked when she pulled away.

"It was to thank you for..." her throat swelled as she thought of all the new emotions he'd brought into her life. She nodded to the tree. "For being kind."

They finished the job in silence, bound together by memories. When the tree was transplanted, he moved it carefully away from the pot and dusted off his hands.

"Edmund, I need you here for a witness."

"Yes, Your Highness." Edmund appeared at his side almost as quickly as if he'd materialized out of nowhere. The quirk of his eyebrow and a tightening of his jaw made it clear that he was uncomfortable standing while Constantine knelt in the dirt. Constantine paid no attention. Instead he pointed to the insignia and explained Jill's theory.

"Go ahead, Jill." He nodded to her. "See if you can break the drainage platform inside and remove it. We can keep the pot intact for evidence."

She carefully tapped on the platform until it cracked down the middle. Then she removed the fragments.

Constantine reached into the pot. "Let's see what we have here." He pulled out a bulky package. Brown paper wrapped in plastic concealed the contents. Layer by layer, he removed the wrapping until only a thin bolt of richly woven green-and-gold cloth covered the piece. He held it out to her.

"Jill, would you do the final honors?"

Her fingers were as cold as ice, and stained from working in the dirt, but she pulled the cloth back as he indicated. There, before her, rested the royal Melesian crown. She glanced up at the portrait of King Alexander. It was no mistake. Forged of heavy gold and encrusted with gems, the crown twinkled in the dim light of the office, identical to the one in the official portrait.

"Look inside." Constantine's voice was quiet. "Every ruler of Melesia has inscribed his mark on the gold of this crown. Without it, the coronation would be invalid."

Faint scratches, worn by hundreds of years lined the scalloped top of the crown, looping around where the jewels were embedded. Deeper, more lasting inscriptions lay below them, signed by more recent royal hands. She gently rubbed an empty spot near the last name. A rich tide of history seemed to flow through her fingers as if she were touching a living relic. "This is where you will be."

"Yes." That single word bore the weight of generations. Duty, responsibility, sometimes privilege, and always loneliness. Although he didn't say the words, the expressions that flickered across his face told her this and more.

Behind them, Edmund cleared his throat. "If I may suggest, Your Highness, I'll contact the palace security and see that the crown is safely packed away for our return journey."

Constantine nodded. "Thank you, Edmund. Meanwhile, Jill and I have matters to discuss."

Constantine watched as Jill paced across her small bedroom, transferring clothes between the bed and the closet for the third time in fifteen minutes. He was glad, for her sake, that he'd ordered the small team of agents to wait downstairs.

"This plan is crazy," she said, hanging her red suit back in the closet and pulling out the champagne-colored one. "You've recovered the stolen jewels. You don't need me to come to Melesia with you."

Constantine pushed away from the door jamb and moved to her side. "Now that we've found the jewels, Alex wants me to wrap things up here and come home as quickly as possible."

"I guess even you're not immune to the wishes of the king."

"I want to go home, Jill. It's time. And I want you with me. Alex and Helena agree. Having you in Melesia is the best way to ferret out the thief. You've seen him. You'll be able to recognize him again." That wasn't the only reason he wanted her with him, but it was the only one he should have.

Jill tossed the suit on the bed beside the slip dress she'd worn at the dance club with him. She'd been so innocent and fresh that night. Before he'd smashed her romantic illusions with his political reality.

She returned to the closet, reaching into the back to pull out an emerald green gown. The gown was exquisite, but he knew that he wouldn't find a designer label or a private tailor's mark inside if he looked.

He knew she'd fashioned the intricate details with her own hands during sleepless nights. Jill gave freely to everyone but denied herself any hint of luxury. He intended to change that. If he did nothing else, he would see that her trip to Melesia was filled with every luxury money and power could buy.

"What do you think?" Her voice quivered, and she bit her lip as she held the dress up for his inspection.

He tossed it on a chair and wrapped his arms around her. "I think you're worried about nothing. You'll be perfectly safe on the islands. You'll have around the clock security."

"From a team of trained professionals who think I'm a thief."

He stroked her hair and wondered how to quell the edge of panic he heard in her voice. "No one thinks you're a thief. And no one will question your motives when you come back to the islands with me."

"That's exactly why they will question me. Rumors will fly. They'll think that we—" she broke off in mid-sentence and waved toward the bed. "That we—"

"We did." He pulled back and gave her a quick peck. "And I don't regret a minute of it. But what we did, or did not do, is nobody else's business. Remember that and hold your head up. Unless you're ashamed of what we've shared."

"No. I'm not. I don't regret a minute. I'd do it all over again. Except maybe for the part about throwing things." A hint of mischief crept into her voice, a sure sign her spirits were stronger.

"You will need to reel in your temper," he said watching her face. "I won't be able to stop the palace guards if they think I'm in danger. And by the way, I think you still have some serious bribing to do if you want me to keep silent about that little incident."

"Oh, yeah?" The saucy grin on her face replaced the trepidation he'd seen since she agreed to accompany him home.

"Oh, yeah," he murmured, bending down for a kiss. The minute their lips met, everything fled from his mind except the sight, sound, feel and taste of Jill.

It was another hour before they stuffed her rumpled clothes in a bag and left the building, the picture of propriety.

Chapter 13

*J*ill watched Constantine's hands on the steering wheel of the rented Jaguar as the miles between Chicago and Ohio disappeared. It was like sleepwalking through a twisted dream—a crown prince accompanying her to a high school class reunion couldn't be anything else. A week of living at the Melesian consulate under constant scrutiny and cross examination must have destroyed her sanity as easily as it had ground her optimism into despair.

"You don't have to do this."

"So you keep saying." He flashed her a grin. "And I keep telling you I want to visit your family."

"You were supposed to go home. Your brother needs you."

He placed a hand on her knee, stilling her protests with a warm caress. "There are some loose ends to tie up first. I'm planning a very public return to Melesia. Shortly after, Alex will announce his intent to abdicate in my favor. I don't know if the publicity will make the thief more careless or less so, but it will make my security team's investigations more difficult."

"What investigations?"

"They are searching for leads among the independent potters and artisans hoping to discover the identity of Hector Dimas. Given the size of our archipelago, you can imagine that some of the islands and inhabitants are quite remote. It takes time to follow all of the leads."

Jill nodded distractedly then turned to the window and watched miles of nearly empty fields slip by, still looking winter-desolate despite the promise of spring around the corner. The sight reflected her own bleak turmoil.

Even now, days after they'd discovered the stolen crown, the enormity of the situation weighted on her. How many women let their actions jeopardize the stability of an entire country? How many initiated a casual fling only to discover the object of her desire was an undercover prince and a world leader? Or fell in love with a man whose closest allies had reason to hate and distrust her?

After ten years of being mature and responsible, everything had fallen around her ears in a matter of days. Her means of helping her family was a scam, her attempt at finding love was a titillating bit of international gossip ready to break at any moment, and her future was out of her control. She was just…screwed. Royally screwed, as it were.

"This is all my fault," she muttered.

Beside her, Constantine cleared his throat. "I'm tired of hearing those words from you. If you say it one more time, I'll pull this car over and do whatever it takes to convince you otherwise. You'll have no one but yourself to blame if you're late for your mother's dinner."

"It's kind of you to spare my feelings, but we both know I brought this on by trying to make a fast profit with Mr. Dimas."

"That's it." He edged the car toward the exit lane. "We're going somewhere private to get to the bottom of the matter."

Jill slumped in her seat. His calm, almost congenial manner was a sharp contrast to her inner turmoil. "My father used to say that whenever one of us was about to get a swat on the behind. Usually me."

He slid an assessing gaze over her. "I take it you were the headstrong one."

She nodded. "I remember dreading the moment we'd reach the next rest stop or gas station. The anticipation was worse than the punishment, because I knew I deserved what was coming."

Painful childhood memories crowded in beside adult guilt. "When it was over, he'd hug me and say he loved me, no matter how badly I'd behaved. Believe it or not, everything seemed to fall into place after that."

Constantine gave her fingers a gentle squeeze. "If I thought something as simple as a swat on the behind would snap you out your mood, I'd consider it. But adult matters are rarely so easily solved." He headed to the parking lot of a small chain hotel and killed the engine.

Ten minutes later, they sat facing each other in a tiny, dingy room. She flicked a glance at the bed. "I don't think anything we do in here will solve our problems, either."

He sandwiched her hands in his, chasing away some of the chill that gripped her. When he spoke, his tone was patient, but with an underlying steel that forced her to pay attention.

"You've changed since we found the jewels. There's no more confidence, no sparkle, no life in you. You're slipping into the shadows. I had hoped this trip would restore your spirits. So far, it hasn't. *Er'hona-mei*, I can't help you unless I know what's going on inside your head."

He raised one hand and smoothed the hair from her face. "I miss the spunky girl who threw the history of my country at my head for misleading her. What happened to her?"

"It's…" She shrugged. The slight movement required more effort than it should. But his unyielding gaze dominated her silence, its unspoken demand weakening the apathy that held her prisoner.

Jill sucked in a breath and spilled out her jumbled thoughts. "It's everything. Living at the consulate instead of my apartment. Watching your staff hover around you, reminding me we're from different worlds. Edmund, glued to my side while I try to do my job at McKinley and Company." She hesitated.

"And?"

"The security guards. They follow me everywhere and watch everything I do. They think I'm a thief. A thief who's getting off scot-free because I...we...because..." Her gaze flicked to the bed again before returning to his face.

Emotions raced across it and disappeared in an instant. Concern. Compassion. A flash of pain. Anger. And finally, nothing. An emotionless mask settled over his features. Only the stormy blue of his eyes hinted at the anger he held tightly in check.

"I feel guilty all the time about what I did, even if I didn't do it on purpose." She rushed on, compelled to explain. "I'm used to taking responsibility for my actions. I don't expect leniency or forgiveness because we—"

"Stop." Constantine rose and paced a few steps away. His already erect posture stiffened. The man who turned back to her was a stranger. "Let me be sure I understand," he said with more steel than patience now. "You don't want the sexual favors we've traded to cloud my judgment when it comes to Melesian national security. Is that it?"

His sudden change of demeanor made her head swim. And his cold summation of her worries sounded both right and wrong, turning the warmth they'd shared into a tawdry attempt at diversion from important matters. Yet wasn't that what she feared the world would see?

"Yes or no, Jill. Answer me."

Even in his faded jeans and sweater he exuded an aura of absolute power that left her mouth dry. Yes? No? She didn't know anymore. She wobbled, her head in a confused gesture that was neither yes nor no, silently pleading for his understanding.

Instead, he pinned her with a look, gauging her like a judge sizing up the accused. "Never again question my integrity. I don't tolerate it from my staff, and I won't tolerate it from you. When it comes to my country, I will sacrifice everything—even my life—for her.

"No matter how desirable you are, if I believed you were a willing accessory to treason, you would be in a holding cell in Melesia awaiting trial at this very moment. Do you understand?" His quiet words were all the more forceful for their utter lack of emotion.

Cold realization washed over Jill. She opened her mouth then closed it again, swallowing a knot of fear. "I understand," she whispered, forcing the words out despite the raw, burning tightness of her throat.

He held her eyes for a moment longer, then, satisfied, returned to his seat. Power still crackled through the room, bouncing off the bare walls, but the emotion slowly returned to his face.

Jill trembled when he reached for her hands again, not sure how to react to the autocratic stranger he'd become. But his touch was gentle, almost a caress. "Since you're here with me, sharing this," he glanced at the threadbare carpet and the shabby bedspread with a hint of a smile, "luxurious accommodation, can you assume I don't believe you're guilty of any crimes?"

"I want to believe you. I—"

She stopped at the imperious look on his face accented by a single raised eyebrow. The commanding, emotionless stranger hovered just beneath the surface. "Yes," she corrected herself. "I believe you."

"Thank you." Gratitude laced his words and warmed the cold space between them. His jaw relaxed and the hard, stormy glint to his eyes faded. He pulled her into his lap and settled his arms around her, quietly soothing her while she struggled to reconcile the image of the monarch he was to become with the man she loved.

Her quivering subsided under the familiar heat of his hands. His touch was the only real thing in a bizarre, tilted world. She closed her eyes and counted her breaths until her heartbeat slowed and she relaxed slightly in his embrace.

He tucked her head more snugly against his shoulder and ran a languid, unhurried hand down her back. "I'm sorry I had to be rough with you, *Er'hona-mei*."

"I've never seen anyone look so detached as if you had no soul. It was terrifying." She shuddered. "On the whole, I would have preferred a swat on the backside."

He chuckled and let his hand drift down to fondle her bottom. "I'll keep that in mind for future reference. But I'm afraid this," he gave her a playful tap, "could make you squirm—" it did "—which might land us in that lumpy looking bed. Given the nature of your concerns, it would have been a bad option."

She nodded, feeling a twinge of optimism as his teasing soothed the imbalance between them. Things almost returned to normal. Or as normal as they could ever be.

"Let's put the unpleasantness behind us." He nuzzled her temple and smoothed a hand down her hair, taking his time as if nothing else mattered. "Feeling better?"

"Please believe me. I never doubted your devotion to your country."

"I know. But sooner or later your over-active conscience could have caused problems for me. Perceptions—real or otherwise—have a way of turning into reality. Which brings us to the next order of business." He snagged the other chair and propped his feet on it while he shifted them to a more comfortable position. "Clear your mind, *Er'hona-mei*, because you're about to get a crash course on international politics and diplomacy."

"I should warn you, I'm not a good student."

"But I am a good teacher." He drew her into a kiss that put the last of her fears to rest and reminded her of how much she'd missed by keeping him at arm's length all week. "There's your first bit of incentive."

"I could get used to studying."

"I thought so." Laughter warmed his voice as he stroked her from knee to hip, trapping her between the warmth of his palm and the heat of his body. The gesture brought back images of simpler times when they'd been together. Times when she'd trusted him to safeguard her vulnerabilities. Now she trusted him to lead her through a maze of unknown complexity.

"Lesson one," she prompted, slipping her hand beneath his sweater to touch warm, bare skin. The connection gave her confidence.

"First, a short lecture. Followed by plenty of practice, with unlimited encouragement and rewards—yours for the asking. Fair enough?"

"Fire away, professor."

"A minute ago, you accused me of being detached and emotionless." His voice was quiet, almost introspective. He paused to let the words sink in. "I'm neither. Royal families are judged by their image as much as by their policies. We can't always control our emotions, but we're trained from birth to control our responses. It can mean showing any of a dozen public faces, or it can mean shutting down completely to hide strong emotions."

"Like anger?"

"A public display of temper could wreak havoc on our ability to govern well. So could the appearance of weakness, or indecision. For example, Alex never looks worried or exhausted at press conferences, even though he's often both. I always appear confident and positive in public, no matter what the media throws at me."

"What about love? Can you display love?" Jill held her breath waiting for the answer.

"Love for country, loyalty to family, confidence in the future, all of these are positive emotions. I won't have to hide my affection for you, either. But passion is best kept behind closed doors."

Affection. Passion. Jill tucked the words away in her heart and tried to ignore her pain at the one emotion he'd never feel for her. Love.

"You must learn to control your responses to the world, just as we do. No doubts about yourself or your involvement with me or the jewels, no matter what anyone says. You already have poise, polish, and grace. Simply project the image of a confident woman, who's an asset to the crown."

"I wish I could be that person. I'm not. But I can be a convincing imposter." After all, she'd climbed the corporate ladder at McKinley and Company by faking it.

"You're more of an asset than you know. Consider this. If Dimas hadn't found you, he would have used someone else. Someone who wouldn't love my country enough to put herself at risk for it."

"I won't let you down."

Constantine kissed her again, letting his lips and tongue speak for him, reminding her that he was neither passionless nor cold, despite the mask he sometimes wore. His taste filled her mouth. His scent wrapped around them. And his steady heartbeat gave her courage.

Jill responded in kind, nibbling his lip and clinging to him, pouring her love into the kiss. She'd be the woman he needed, no matter what it took.

Chapter 14

"Jill, honey, you're so late. I was getting worried about you." Jill's mother swept her into an embrace before carefully scrutinizing her daughter's face. "You look tired."

Constantine thanked his instincts for making them stop when they did. Jill's enthusiasm had returned—more slowly than he'd hoped—but he saw glimmers of the woman he knew and lo— The woman she should be.

"It was a long drive, Mom, nothing else." She held her hand out to him. When he took it, her smile brightened slightly. "Mom, I'd like you to meet my friend, Mr. Phillip Raymond."

"It's a pleasure, Mrs. Bradley." Constantine kissed her hand, letting courtly, rather than American, manners rule his actions.

"Oh, dear. How romantic. Well, it's a pleasure to meet you Mr. Raymond." She swept him into a hug like the one she'd given Jill. "Any friend of my daughter's is welcome in our home."

Constantine held her for a moment longer than necessary, savoring the feel of a mother's arms. Fifteen years melted away and the lush surrounds of his childhood replaced the chilly Ohio cornfields as the memory of his own mother surfaced. He reluctantly let Mrs. Bradley go and followed her into the rambling two-story frame house.

The family crowded around and a flurry of introductions followed. Gracie, the smart one. Amber, the talented one. Charlene, the shy, dreamy one. Geoff, the only son. Mrs. Bradley tagged each of her children with labels as lasting as the ones he and Alex wore as children.

"May I introduce to you Prince Alexander, Heir to the Throne. And my son Prince Constantine." The Spare. No one said it out loud, no one needed to.

No wonder Jill doubted her intelligence. She'd always been just *the pretty one*. But things changed, as he well knew.

"Mom, I've got to go before the library closes. I wanted to check out a couple of non-circulating journals for the weekend." Jill's next oldest sister, dressed in an oversized school sweatshirt that cast a pallor over her skin, crept toward the door obviously hoping to avoid notice. Blonde hair, which might have been lustrous, was scraped back into a purely functional style. The smart one.

"Not tonight, Gracie. Stay for dinner." Mrs. Bradley motioned the group toward the dining room.

"I'm not hungry, Mom. Besides, the library closes in half an hour." She gave Jill a look that was an odd mixture of apology and something else. "I could have picked the journals up earlier if I'd known you were running late."

"Grace Susan Bradley, your sister's had a long drive. It won't hurt you to stay in for tonight. I'd like to have a family dinner while I have the chance."

Gracie's shoulders slumped a bit more, but she complied. "I'll go early tomorrow. That way I can also try to pick up a breakfast shift at the diner. Tips at breakfast are usually good."

Mrs. Bradley flashed Constantine an apologetic smile. "We almost never see her anymore. If she isn't studying, she's working every odd job and extra shift she can find. Just like Jill."

Before he could reply, Charlene—the youngest—grabbed his hand. "I want to sit by you."

"Jill said I could sit with them." Amber tugged on his other arm. "You go sit by Geoff."

"But I want to tell him about school. My teacher got us a class hamster, and it runs around in its cage on a little wheel and…"

"I'm in the school play this year." Amber interrupted, drawing his eyes to her. "The lead went to a senior girl, but I get a speaking part and a solo and…"

They led him to the dining room amid chatter, sighs and occasional pleading looks. He caught Jill's eye as they neared the table and shot her a wink.

"I must admit," he said turning to the girls, "I have rarely had the pleasure of sitting with two such beautiful and accomplished ladies. I find I cannot choose between you. May I sit with you both?" Letting courtly manners rule again, he pulled out chairs for both of the girls, then moved to Mrs. Bradley's side.

Geoff rolled his eyes and started to plop down, but Jill stopped him with a hand and a whisper. "Gentlemen let the ladies sit first. Why don't you help Gracie and me?"

"I'm fine." Gracie handled her own chair while Geoff seated Jill. Constantine could swear Gracie rolled her eyes just like her brother.

When they were all seated the uncontrolled conversations began again. Amber's play. Char's classroom and the antics of the hamster. Jill and her mother, catching up and making sure everyone's plates were filled. Only Gracie and Geoff were silent. Geoff, because he was fully occupied with emptying his plate and refilling it, and Gracie because she was studying him with quiet, intense looks.

"I hope you don't mind meatloaf, Mr. Raymond. It's our standard Friday night dinner." Mrs. Bradley perched on the edge of her chair, following his movements with a sharp gaze. One wrong move on his part, and he suspected she'd fly to the kitchen to whip up a rack of lamb, pheasant under glass, or any other delicacy he might request. He gave her a warm smile, meant to reassure.

"Please, call me Phillip. And I'm certain anything you cooked would be delightful." He eyed the unusual meat on his plate and the accompanying mashed potatoes, gravy, and green beans. At least he recognized the vegetables. Besides, he'd eaten stranger things on his world tours. He took a bite, projecting the image of casual confidence he'd tutored Jill on scant hours ago.

"It's like deep-dish pizza and peanut butter toast," Jill murmured from across the table. "It'll grow on you." She favored him with a smile and a look that sent his heart rate soaring. He breathed a prayer of thanks that his gamble in the hotel room had worked out. His autocratic manner could have sent her scrambling into her shell beyond reach. Thank God she'd chosen to fight instead. All was right between them again.

"And like Ramen noodles?" he asked, teasing in return.

"Jill, tell me you're eating something more nutritious than that," her mother chided. "You need to take care of yourself."

"Actually, Jill's introduced me to a variety of American foods since I've been here," he said, steering the conversation away from Jill's sacrifices. She shot him a grateful look. "She's a wonderful host."

"How long have you two known one another?"

"Mom—"

"We met about three weeks ago. But I feel I haven't known her nearly long enough. I've invited Jill to visit my country for a vacation. She knows so much about it already, I think she would enjoy seeing it firsthand."

Mrs. Bradley hid a look of surprise, and the girls demanded to know about his country. As he spoke of home, all eyes turned to him. Except Geoff, who was occupied with a third slab of meat loaf and a plate full of potatoes.

"You mean there's a real prince?" Char whispered her eyes wide.

"Of course, there is," Amber said. "If there's a king, there's got to be a prince, silly."

"Is he handsome?"

"Some people think so," Constantine replied.

"Passably attractive is more like it," Jill added from across the table.

Geoff snorted and turned back to his food.

"How would you know, Jill? You've never seen anything but pictures." Amber sent her a questioning look.

"Yes, Jill, how would you know?" Constantine enjoyed the pink tinge on her cheeks and the way she shifted in her chair. If they were staying in a private hotel rather than a bustling household, he was sure he could tease her into sharing his bed tonight. Instead, he cut off her response with a benign twist. "Prince Stephan is said to be both handsome and charming."

"All princes are handsome and charming. It's a rule." Char spoke with authority. "It's in every movie. Would you like to see? I can show you."

Constantine was ready to promise her anything.

"I'd like to meet a real prince." Amber clamored for attention on his other side. "Do you think I could come to Melesia too?"

"Amber, you may be an actress, but you're too old to believe in fairy tales like Char." Gracie spoke for the first time. "Even Char is too old to believe in fairy tales. I stopped filling my mind with that sort of nonsense when I was younger than she is now."

"That's because princesses are pretty like Jill, not smarty pants like you." Char crossed her arms across her thin chest and glared at Gracie.

"That's the problem with fairy tales. It teaches girls to focus on things that don't matter. Like being pretty."

"Girls, stop." Mrs. Bradley hastily passed the food dishes around the table again. "Here. Someone eat the last of these potatoes. And finish the meatloaf."

Geoff grabbed the bowl and scraped the potatoes onto his plate, plopping the meat in the middle of the mass.

Gracie, Char, and Amber shot each other pointed looks.

Jill shrank into her chair, trying to hide the flash of pain Gracie's comment had elicited. Constantine caught her eye. "You matter, *Er'hona-mei*," he said in Melesian. "Don't ever let anyone tell you otherwise."

"My what a lovely language, Mr. Raymond." Mrs. Bradley smiled at him, and he sensed she was trying to steer the conversation away from the awkward moment. "What was it you were saying?"

"My apologies for slipping into my own language. I was merely sharing one of our proverbs with Jill." He looked at the bickering girls surrounding him. "*When Beauty and Brains struggle for the Crown, Kindness is King.*"

"Huh?" Char looked at him with wide eyes.

"It means we should be nice to one another," Amber said quietly. "Doesn't it?"

"It does indeed," Constantine answered. "Disagreements are a part of life, but respect for your opponent is a great virtue. It would be a shame to hurt someone's feelings for the sake of winning an argument."

Char nodded. "I'm sorry I called you names, Gracie."

"I'm sorry too."

The room fell silent, the only sound the scrape of Geoff's fork against his plate. After a moment, Constantine spoke, softening his first words with a wink and a smile for Gracie. "Although most people tend to think of fairy tales when they imagine a royal family, there is much more to it than that."

Gracie speared him with a look. "Is it true, Mr. Raymond, that Melesia is an absolute monarchy? Does the king really have the final say in all matters of government?"

"Even the king is subject to the laws of our country."

"With all due respect, that argument is a moot point. The king can change the laws or add new ones as he wishes. Right?"

"Technically true, but—"

"So if you disagreed with him on matters of policy, you could find yourself a political prisoner, or worse."

"I assure you, I've disagreed with the king many times in the past. Although, I admit, I'm unlikely to continue to do so in the future."

Jill kicked him under the table, and he felt a rush of pleasure, despite the pain to his shin. His spitfire was back. He sent her a warning frown. Payback for that kick was going to be sweet.

"What happened?" Amber's hushed voice made him turn to her. "Did you get in trouble?"

"Of course not. The king's first concern is for the health and safety of the country. He is always willing to listen to the people."

"Maybe this king does," Gracie interjected, "but what about the next one? And the next? What happens when someone irresponsible and spoiled by privilege is at the helm? Sooner or later, even the best of intentions can be corrupted.

"And your country has no checks and balances to prevent disaster when that happens." She paused and sent him a triumphant look. "Face it, Mr. Raymond, your ruling class is an anachronistic government that should have been abolished a century ago."

"Gracie! Don't insult our guest." Mrs. Bradley flushed. "I apologize, Mr.— I mean, Phillip. I'm sure you don't want to argue politics over dinner."

"Actually, I'm a fan of spirited political discussions. While I think government by experts, such as our king and his advisors, is an excellent way to run a country, Gracie brings up some interesting points. I've given considerable thought to the matter.

"It is the responsibility of the current government to make sure the next doesn't rule by whim, but by fair and evenly applied law."

While Mrs. Bradley served apple pie, Constantine and Gracie discussed the state of affairs in his country. She shot out facts and statistics as quickly as some of his best advisors, supplying detailed analyses to accompany her often insightful opinions.

"So you admit we have the highest per capita income of any Caribbean nation? On par with that of your country?" He pinned her with one of her own facts.

"Of course, but the disparity between the nobility and the common man—"

"—is due to wise investment and money management by the monarchy. Not by milking the country with excessive taxes, as you imply." He asked for a pen and paper. "Here are several government websites that describe our tax laws and other policies. You might find them interesting."

The conversation shifted and the younger children drifted away while the rest of them moved to a cozy sitting room. Constantine relaxed over coffee with Gracie, Jill, and Mrs. Bradley.

"Politics aside, I'm impressed with your knowledge of Melesia, Gracie. It is refreshing."

"Jill's the expert. My teacher, Miss Foster, still talks about how quickly Jill learned your language and came to appreciate your culture. I only know about the country because I'm interested in your marine life preserves."

"Gracie's studying to be a marine biologist." Jill's voice held a tinge of pride, and a hint of something else. "I've told her as much as I know about the conservation and marine study programs on the islands."

Constantine took her hand, wondering if anyone else in the room saw her insecurity and self-doubts. It would take more than a fit of royal temper to banish those thoughts, but he swore he'd do it. Whatever else he did, he'd gift her with a clear vision of herself before their lives went in separate directions.

He kept Jill's hand tucked in his own but addressed his words to Gracie. "You should consider applying to our Royal Academy. It has an excellent undergraduate curriculum and a world class graduate program in marine biology."

"It also has a world class price tag."

"Gracie's a little young to be so far from home." Mrs. Bradley gazed at her younger daughter with pride as she rose to refill the coffee cups. "She skipped two grades of school. She's the youngest undergraduate at the Clarkson Community College. I'd prefer she continued her education at a university closer to home or at least one close to Jill."

"I may not be able to study in Melesia full time, but I'd love to do a research semester at your academy someday." For the first time since he'd met her, Gracie had a wistful tone to her voice. The longing in her eyes was almost as poignant as Amber's desire to meet a real prince.

Once his country was safe, he could make all of their dreams come true. He concentrated on the warmth of Jill's hand in his. She anchored him to the moment, filling him with impossible longings of his own. He wished, once again, he were merely a man.

Because to make his country safe, to make the dreams of the little girls possible, he'd have to risk the safety of the woman beside him.

And then, he'd have to give her up.

The next evening, Jill sat in her old room, preparing for the night ahead. She touched up the last of her makeup and ran a brush through her hair, fighting memories. The dressing table was the same one she'd used as a girl.

The same mirror she'd primped in front of before the fateful night her father died.

The same stool she'd sat on to paint her baby sister's nails neon pink to match the ribbons in her hair a day earlier.

Everything was the same, from the bedspread to the wallpaper. Everything but the two women whose eyes met in occasional, fleeting glances in the mirror.

"It was polite of you to accept Phillip's gift today, Gracie. I know how hard that was for you."

"Yeah, well, he didn't really give me much choice." Gracie curled up on the bed and toyed with the deceptively simple pearl bracelet that was part of a set he'd given her earlier that day. "After he talked Mom into accepting the abalone bracelet, I would have looked petty to refuse. But it was underhanded to tell her he would have given it to his own mother if he could. He made it seem like we were doing him a favor by accepting."

Jill smiled at the way Constantine had manipulated her family into accepting his lavish gifts. Even Gracie, who'd refused to accept gifts—including Christmas and birthday presents—after their father died had had no choice.

And despite her sister's aloof manner, Jill had seen a glimmer of excitement at Constantine's simple compliments. Gracie's brief smile was a ghostly reminder of the vibrant child she'd once been.

"What about you? Did he give you that?" She pointed to Jill's necklace. "It doesn't look expensive."

Jill touched the filigree—the royal insignia—that branded her as a temporary part of his life. The intricate knot, which should have marked its wearer as a royal bride, coiled and twisted in knots, like her own situation. It rested against her throat, as cold on her skin as the knowledge in her heart: they had no future. She was an imposter. "No. He didn't give me this. I've had it for a while."

"I know about the other jewelry," Gracie said half to herself.

"What?" Jill swiveled on her stool to face her sister.

"The jewelry you sold. I never told anyone, but when we visited you years ago, I heard a pawnbroker leave a message about the jewelry you sold to him. It came from men you dated, didn't it?"

Jill closed her eyes against the accusation in Gracie's voice. Painful scenes from her early days in Chicago surfaced. She'd dated the richest men she could find, letting them think they had a chance in her bed while she waited in vain for a wedding ring and a prenuptial agreement that would provide security for her family. Selling their trinkets after they left had been the easy part.

"They were meaningless pieces from men who wanted something I couldn't give."

"It's okay, Jill. I didn't mean anything by it. I just…wanted you to know that you don't have to do this. Especially not for me. I've got a couple of scholarships from the state schools, so I'm set. That way there'll be enough for the others to go to college when the time comes."

Gracie looked at her with the vulnerable eyes of a child. The years washed away and for a moment they were just sisters, sharing secrets instead of burdens. If only it were true. Jill turned back to the mirror.

"Community college was good enough for me, but you shouldn't settle for it. Mom says you're already bored with the classes they offer."

Gracie shrugged. "I found some online courses in advanced physics and calculus. It's not so bad. I just wish I could get advanced diving and marine biology classes online. But I'll catch up when I get to a bigger school. There's no rush."

"I want to help. You deserve the best school money can buy."

"Not if you have to sell yourself to get them for me." Gracie slipped the pearl bracelet off and regarded it with haunted eyes. Jill knew even taking money for her education grated against Gracie's self-imposed rule of not accepting gifts.

"It's not like that. And the school money isn't a gift. It's a loan. You'll repay it later by helping Amber, Geoff, and Char."

Only the click of the pearls sliding through Gracie's fingers broke the silence in the room. Jill resisted the urge to go to her and wrap her arms around her slumped shoulders, fearing that Gracie would as soon flee as accept comfort from her.

"What about this new man? Do you like him?"

Like him? Jill closed her eyes and tried to control her surging emotions. When she was with him, nothing else mattered. His tenderness seemed real, her dreams possible.

But when she walked away, she remembered who and what he was. A man forever beyond her reach. "It doesn't matter how I feel."

A rustle of bedclothes and soft foot falls told her Gracie was leaving. The warm, unexpected press of her sister's hand on her shoulder startled her. "Jill, don't do anything you'll regret. Please."

"I won't. I promise." She squeezed Gracie's hand before they both turned away—Gracie to her own room and her books and Jill to her reflection and the impossible dreams in her heart.

Chapter 15

ill shivered in the damp evening air. Her footsteps dragged on the concrete path to the community college assembly hall where her high school reunion was being held. She glanced at Constantine when they passed under the lamplight.

"I'm beginning to recognize that look," she said.

"What look?"

"Your public face. The one with the smile that doesn't quite reach your eyes. The one you wore when you first tasted my mother's meatloaf."

He stopped and turned to her, his smile broadening into something real. "Thank the gods. I was afraid it was my soulless monster look."

"I don't understand."

He tipped her face to his. "You're wearing your 'prisoner on the way to her execution' face. It's not exactly flattering to my ego."

"It's not about you. It's the memories. My father died in a car accident my senior year of high school." She closed her eyes and leaned into the warmth of his hand as it rested on her jaw. "I'll tell you the whole story on the drive back to Chicago."

"If it bothers you, we don't have to go to the party. We can go back to your home if you want."

"No." She let him gather her into his arms. His body heat soothed away the chill of the night and of her memories. His scent teased her with more pleasant thoughts—of the nights she hoped they still had together. "I want to enjoy tonight. With you."

"Then we will." He pushed her arm's length away and studied her face, his smile darkened by a hint of concern. "Are you sure you don't have any worries about me? About us? I haven't done anything to terrorize you lately, have I?"

Jill laughed and instantly his features relaxed into a goofy smile of his own. "Not since you challenged my brother to a "Monster Burger" eating contest at the diner and let him race your rented Jag up and down the driveway this afternoon." She tucked her hand in his and started toward the entryway. "He's now firmly a member of your fan club."

"He's a good kid. It can't be easy growing up in a single parent household. Especially when you're the only boy. All I did was give him a little male bonding time."

"Between bonding with Geoff and charming Mom and the girls, I'd say you were a hit with the whole family. Even Gracie. It meant a lot to her that you took her political opinions seriously."

"I see. I'd wondered how to interpret the venomous looks she shot me when we were leaving tonight." He pretended to frown at her, but his eyes glinted with approval. "She is protective of you. Or jealous."

"Either way, getting her head out of the books long enough to generate a reaction was a small miracle."

"Well then, since I have the family's endorsement, it's time to see if I can get the approval of your friends. I'm in your hands. Guide me through this foreign ritual of the high school reunion."

"And I thought you were the expert on international diplomacy." Jill checked them in and led him to the balloon and streamer festooned assembly hall, playfully briefing him on the school colors, the school mascot, the class motto, and the hierarchy of students.

"So," he said ticking off points on his fingers, "the official colors of the Valley Hills Fighting Farmers are orange and cream. The school mascot is a giant, pitchfork-wielding pumpkin, and your class motto is 'together forever.' How am I doing so far?"

"Your royal training is rising to the occasion. You haven't missed a thing."

"Good. Now on to the class politics. The most important people in your class were the athletes—"

"The jocks," she corrected.

"Followed by the music and drama students. Don't tell me. The performers."

"Right." She smiled at his use of their school jargon.

"And last came the scholars, or brains."

"That about sums it up."

"And which group did you belong to? I can make a convincing case for all three. You have the toned body of an athlete, the poise of a performer, and the intelligence of a scholar."

"I may have learned poise, but I definitely wasn't smart. I was—"

"Jill Bradley." Someone shouted her name and pushed between them, scooping her up in a full body hug and twirling her around in a breathless blur before setting her back on her feet. "We heard you might be in town for the reunion."

Tommy Jacobs, her high school boyfriend and the school's former star quarterback gave her a grin before turning to the crowd in the hall. "Hey, everyone," he shouted, commanding the attention of the hundred or so people filling the room. "Graduates of Valley Hills High, the rumors are true. All the way from Chicago, please welcome back our very own head cheerleader and class homecoming queen, Miss Jill Bradley."

A ripple of applause started in the room and Jill felt Constantine move behind her, resting his hands lightly on her shoulders. "So, a jock," he whispered. "And a popular one at that."

As the crowd broke up and her classmates moved toward them, Tommy turned his grin on Constantine. He stuck out his hand. "Sorry for the uproar, but we're all glad to see Jill. Most of us never left town, so it's a special event when a classmate returns. I'm Tommy Jacobs, by the way. An old friend of Jill's."

"Phillip Raymond. Her new friend."

The men shook hands. "Welcome, Phillip. I hope you don't mind if I steal Jill away for a few minutes. As her former homecoming king, I think she owes me a dance."

"As a mere date for the evening, I can only hope that you return her to me quickly." The teasing lilt to his voice made Jill flush.

"I'd rather not—" Jill evaded Tommy's grasp.

Constantine twirled her to face him. "I insist." He raised her free hand to his lips. "Protocol must take precedence even here," he murmured in Melesian. "I yield to the local dignitaries. But if he doesn't bring you back after one dance, I'm pulling rank on him."

"Behave," she whispered in return.

"Don't look so worried," Tommy joked as he led her to the dance floor. "The hunk with the accent isn't going anywhere. Although I gotta admit, I'm glad this is a fast dance. I don't think he'd stand by and let me relive old times without a word. Something about him makes me think people don't cross him very often."

Jill laughed and moved to the music, aware of Constantine's eyes following her every action. When Tommy led her back to him after their dance, he was surrounded by a knot of preening former students.

Some she recognized as old friends; others were only acquaintances. Girls who'd been popular in high school and those who'd been painfully shy all vied for his attention. Wives and mothers shot flirtatious, sizzling looks at him. Single women brushed against him.

Jill gritted her teeth as a knife-sharp stab of jealousy sliced through her. He might be a man who was beyond her reach, one who could never build a future with her, but he was hers for the night. She wasn't in the mood to share.

Dredging up a smile as false as the ones he sometimes wore, she joined the group, making introductions even as she edged between him and the women. She kept her tone light but wove in questions about husbands and children, families and roots, driving a gentle wedge between her friends and her man.

When the crowd dispersed, he slipped his arm around her waist and pulled her to one side of the room. "That was an impressive bit of diplomacy, *Er'hona-mei*. Tactful and polite, but firmly focused on your goals. I especially enjoyed watching you hide your jealous streak under that beautiful, serene smile."

"And did you enjoy the adoration of the masses?"

"Watch out. Your public face is slipping." Constantine chuckled. The soft sound sent shivers dancing across her skin. "For the record, I enjoyed meeting your friends, but I much prefer being alone with you. What about you? Did you like dancing with the homecoming king?"

"I'd rather dance with you."

"Later. First show me the photographs your friends were talking about. They told me I shouldn't miss the pictures from your graduating class."

Sure enough, posters filled with enlarged versions of ten-year-old high school photos lined the walls. A lone photo of her with the staff of the school newspaper, where she'd briefly worked, nestled among shots of the science and math clubs, where she was notably absent. Dozens of shots of her, midriff bare and pom-poms shaking, peppered the poster boards amid official cheerleading team portraits.

Constantine's gaze lingered over each shot, appraising her with an appreciative gleam. When he traced the image in her official cheerleading portrait, lingering over her bare midriff, a hot wave swept over her. Her stomach muscles clenched and her breasts felt sensitive, all from the stoke of his finger on a lifeless photograph. And the memory of how those same hands had once stroked her bare skin.

She pulled him from the poster board, blindly heading for the next in the series.

Bad move.

A display of photos from the homecoming dance filled the perimeter of the board, surrounding a large shot of her standing next to Tommy. Her arms were filled with roses and a cheap metal crown decorated with glitter and glass perched on her head.

"These are embarrassing," she murmured.

"Not at all. I find them charming. Like you." He tipped her chin up and kissed her tenderly, a mere grazing of lips that left her longing for more.

He walked to another poster, this one showing her with a group of friends at one of the bonfires leading up to the homecoming game.

The photo brought back a rush of memories. She'd been so young and carefree during that week. One wild party and one car accident later, she'd locked away her smile. Until Constantine. She turned her back on the photo and watched him instead.

"Dance with me?"

"Of course, *Er'hona-mei*. I live for your pleasure."

For tonight, she thought. *At least for tonight*. Two fast dances later, she'd forgotten everything but him.

When the music slowed Constantine pulled her close, mimicking the actions of other couples on the crowded dance floor. The press of her warm, inviting body against his had him hard and aching in an instant. How many days had it been since she'd been in his bed? Four? Five? More?

When they'd left her apartment for the consulate the last time, it was as if they'd left something important behind. Her smile. Her vibrancy. Her essence.

She'd withdrawn, barely summoning her professional persona for her brief trips to McKinley and Company. He'd asked Edmund, rather than a member of the security team she didn't know, to accompany her in case she needed assistance. And in case any of their subsequent investigations put her in danger. Edmund had reported that she was as dispirited at work as everywhere else.

Worse, she'd avoided him, making every excuse to be alone that a woman could invent. If not for their passionate last moments in her apartment, he'd have thought she disliked him. But the memory of those moments and the occasional flash of longing in her eyes convinced him otherwise.

But here, in her home, the vibrancy returned. After the tense start of the trip, everything had settled into a warm, almost familiar pattern.

He glanced over her head at the posters that lined the walls of the room. Jill had been on nearly all of them, lighting each with a bright smile and laugher so genuine he could almost hear it echoing through the photographs.

She was a luminary. The star of her class. A leader who unconsciously drew people to her and bound them with ties of loyalty that outlasted time and distance. The enthusiastic greeting of her classmates after nearly ten years of absence wasn't feigned. And the stories her flirtatious friends shared with him were filled with admiration rather than jealousy.

A woman like Jill could go far in life. Too bad she couldn't do it with him. The image of her homecoming dance popped into his mind. Homecoming queen. A novel concept for him. She'd glowed in those photos, clearly enjoying her role as class royalty.

Even if he could offer her a place in his life, it wouldn't be one filled with such frivolity and fun. Real life royal duties involved a succession of boring requirements and events punctuated by gut-wrenching decisions affecting the lives of millions of people. All done with a false smile and a look of absolute confidence. It would crush her more thoroughly than a few days at the Melesian consulate.

No, they only had tonight, and whatever days they could grab before his coronation. Then, for both their sakes, they would part. Friends. Allies. Lovers with a fistful of memories. But nothing more.

Constantine pushed the thoughts aside, sliding his hand to her hip to palm the lush softness, instead of thinking of harsh reality. He pressed her closer still. She exhaled a soft sigh that fluttered across his shirt where her cheek rested.

It was like the first sip of an aperitif at an official state function—a tempting glimpse of what was to come. A tidbit to whet the appetite rather than assuage it. The first of many temptations during a long night of delicacies before reaching the after-dinner cognac and eventual satisfaction.

His hunger for her sharpened in a way that years of training barely controlled. "I like this American style of dancing," he whispered. "Rubbing up against your body and swaying to the music is so much more pleasing than the intricacies of ball-room dance."

"Is that how you dance at home? Formal ballroom dance?"

"You'll find out soon enough. Dare I hope that you'll need some private lessons to follow the steps?"

"Lessons, no. Practice, yes. If you can spare me the time."

"What about right now?" He squeezed her hip. "Can we find a few quiet minutes alone?"

"To dance?"

"For much more than dancing." He planned to kiss her senseless the minute they were alone. It was only the next nibble in a long list of appetizers, but he couldn't wait any longer. If finger food was all he could get, he'd gorge on it. Privately.

He maneuvered her to the edge of the dance floor. Instead of staying for the next dance, they slipped out of the darkened room.

Jill pulled him through the silent corridors to a remote classroom. As soon as the door closed behind them, he leaned against it and pulled her into his arms, wedging his thigh between hers in a parody of the intimacy he craved but couldn't have.

She moaned, the sound turning more raw and needy as he devoured her lips. He lifted her closer, filling his hands with her bottom, anchoring her to his body. When she was firmly in place, he cupped one breast through the thin material of her dress.

She responded by deepening the kiss, thrusting her tongue into his mouth with an urgency that rivaled his own. Gods, but she felt good pressed against him in this hot, uninhibited embrace. He'd give half his kingdom for a cheap hotel room and an hour alone with her now. More for a luxury suite and a week alone.

He wrestled them into a more comfortable position, not breaking contact with her hot, wet, possessive little mouth for a moment while he moved away from the hard doorknob that gouged him in the back. Finally, he found a solid wall with no obstructions. He leaned back, taking her with him.

As his shoulders hit the wall, he felt the soft click of a switch and the room flooded with light. He blinked against the brightness and Jill scurried out of his arms, looking dazed. Until she discovered they were still alone.

But as she reached for him to continue the kiss, he moved out of the way with a resigned shake of his head. Mere seconds ago, he'd have given half his kingdom for an hour alone with her.

But it wasn't his to give.

At the head of the classroom, his brother's official coronation portrait glared down at him from the wall. A Melesian flag stood beside it, and the room was decorated with posters and photos of his homeland.

The kingdom didn't belong to him.

He belonged to it.

Body and soul.

He straightened, pulling his suit coat to order as he did so. Slowly, with reverence born out of deep respect and love, as much as ever-present duty, he executed the formal half bow to the portrait. *No matter my longings, I will not fail you, brother.*

Chapter 16

Jill watched the emotionless mask descend on Constantine's face, driving away the passion that had burned on it moments ago. This time, she understood. She looked past his detached features and unreadable face into his eyes. Cerulean blue gave way to a deeper hue, flecked with aqua. His eyes spoke of his inner turmoil in a secret language she understood.

She followed his gaze as he stared at his brother's portrait, the image of him bowing before it burned into her mind. He'd told her this look—the one he laughingly dubbed his soulless monster mask—always hid strong emotions. The almost imperceptible clench of his jaw confirmed it.

Jill could only guess at the emotions he struggled to keep in check. Passion, she was sure. Anger, perhaps, at the illness that chipped away at his brother's health and his own freedom. Guilt, possibly, because he'd lingered with her for several stolen days while his country's fate teetered on a thin balance.

She placed a hand on his arm. "You do him honor. Your country will be in good hands."

He turned his gaze to her. Gratitude and relief flooded his features for a second before they rearranged into a softer version of his public smile.

"Thank you for understanding." More softness crept into his features. "If…if things had been different…"

"If things had been different, we wouldn't have met. And I treasure each moment of our time together." She let the words sink in, then gently guided him around the room, chatting as if nothing of importance had just happened. As if she hadn't all but admitted she loved him. Her own bittersweet thoughts slipped behind a mask as effective as the ones he wore.

"This is one of the college's language rooms. I spent most of my time here while I was at school." She spoke in soft Melesian, soothing him with the sounds of his own language as they toured the room looking at a more than a decade's worth of photos.

"Miss Foster kept a scrapbook from her first visit to Melesia. She also brought home some cookbooks with native recipes. We had party days when we'd eat regional foods—or at least as close as we could get with ingredients from the local grocery store. This area isn't known for its interest in international cuisine." She flipped through the scrapbook, watching his eyes light up as they lingered over photos of his home.

Eventually she found one of their class, dressed in flowered shirts, eating pineapple and star fruit while they grilled shrimp on a barbecue set up outside the school. "This was a party we threw during my last year to celebrate King's Day. Miss Foster was big on celebrating national holidays to help us immerse ourselves in the culture."

"Here's some historical trivia for you," he said, his voice losing the strained edge it held moments ago. "Once upon a time, King's Day was celebrated on the monarch's actual birthday. After a while it became too difficult to track and it was moved to the same day every year so the national holidays wouldn't change with each successor to the throne."

"You don't even get your own birthday celebration?"

He looked at her and cocked an eyebrow. "There are a few people who know—and remember—the real date. Family. Friends." He leaned close and whispered the date in her ear. "Now you."

Warmth seeped through her at his whispered words. She committed the date to memory. It was a small secret, intimate yet insignificant, like knowing the location of his birthmark, but it bound them more effectively than all the big events they'd shared so far.

Jill turned back to the photo album. "Someone—whose name I won't mention—smuggled a couple of bottles of champagne into the celebration. I spent a few extra hours in the language lab that night waiting for the effects to wear off."

She looked up and gave him a grin. With every story, he relaxed a bit more and the pained look in his eyes receded. "That was the night I learned all four verses to your national anthem. Off-key, I'm sure."

Constantine snaked an arm around her waist and pulled her close, as if seeking her warmth. "I'll expect a private concert in the car on the way home. And if you play your cards right, I'll even teach you a fifth verse." His voice was lighter with a hint of laughter simmering beneath his words.

"They're aren't five verses and you know it."

"Actually there are several unofficial verses. My brothers and I made them up when we were children." He looked at her, his eyes warm and sparkling, his face as full of joy now as it had been devoid of all emotion moments before. His smile was filled with a mock arrogance. "There's a separate verse for Alex, one for me, and one for Stephan. And one for general purposes. I'll teach them all to you."

He skewered her with a look that sent hot shivers through her body. Beneath his teasing passion, laughter mixed with power and an unconscious dash of real arrogance.

A prince. A man. A lover. A friend. All stared out from those complex color-shifting blue eyes.

"It goes without saying that they are classified state secrets. Unauthorized use or dissemination carries stiff penalties. I'll forego asking you for the blood oath, however, out of deference to your gender."

"Shall I perform some other act of fealty to demonstrate my worthiness, Your Highness?"

"I can think of several possibilities." His voice washed over her in a silky, seductive slide. "I'll check my schedule to see when I can grant you an audience. Of course," he winked at her, "for someone as important as the homecoming queen of Valley Hills High, I'm sure that won't be a problem."

"I'm certain I rank right up there with all of the other dignitaries you entertain on a regular basis."

"You'd be surprised at how highly you rank with me, Jill."

The quiet admission slammed into her. No laughter. No teasing. Just a simple statement that sent her world off course and caused her heart to tighten.

She walked with him in silence until they reached a large bulletin board on a side wall. He lingered over it for a few minutes, his jaw tightening as he scanned the contents. "Tabloids? I'm surprised to find that drivel here."

"Miss Foster encourages students to bring in news articles about the various countries. She thinks it builds awareness of the culture and appreciation for the language and customs."

"I'd agree, except *The Weekly World Stir* and anything with Mack the Pen as a byline doesn't qualify as news." He examined the clippings, his lips curled in distaste. "Some of the other articles are worthwhile."

"We discussed everything students brought in. Even stories from entertainment magazines. Usually we talked about how they trivialized important international people and events. By the end of each semester, no one took gossip pieces seriously."

"That's wise. Look. This article has me purported to be 'hiding out' at either a Swiss chalet, an undisclosed honeymoon resort in Mexico, or in a remote cabin somewhere in North Dakota. My reputation gets around more than I do these days."

He read more articles while Jill watched him. Behind her, she heard the creak of the door.

"Jill? They told me you'd come home for the reunion. I suspected I might find you here when you weren't in the assembly hall."

Jill's attention flew to the door. "Miss Foster! It's so good to see you again." Jill crossed the room to hug her plump, petite former teacher, feeling a rush of affection. "You're the one person I didn't want to miss seeing while I was home."

"You're looking good. I hear you're doing a fine job at the import firm in Chicago. Your boss wrote a letter of commendation to our language department praising your skills. I understand you've picked up several new languages while working at the firm."

"I enjoy it. You know that."

"And I want to thank you again for all of the pieces of art and other imports you've sent me for our classrooms. Your generosity has made language come alive for so many students."

"North Dakota. Humph." Constantine's grumble caught her attention and she glanced back at him.

"Oh, dear, Jill. I'd forgotten that you were here with a date. How rude of me to chatter in Melesian with you while he's here. I sometimes forget that not everyone is as fluent with languages as we are."

"In this case, it's not a problem. Phillip is from Melesia." She pulled her teacher across the room toward the bulletin board. Constantine turned to them.

"Miss Foster, I'd like to introduce you to my friend, Mr. Phillip Raymond. Phillip, this is Miss Foster."

"My pleasure," he said, bowing over her hand to kiss it.

When he straightened, Miss Foster's cheeks turned pink. "What a lovely greeting, Mr. Raymond. If you were staying with Jill for a few days, I'd invite you to visit our class and speak with some of our senior students. I'm sure they would enjoy—"

Miss Foster's voice faltered as she looked at Constantine, her brow puckered in thought. Her cheeks went from pink to pale to flushed red as her gaze flew between his face and the framed portraits of the royal family which flanked the bulletin board. "You… You're… Oh my goodness." Recognition left her speechless.

"Yes," Constantine said, smoothing over her embarrassment with a smile as he tucked her arm into the crook of his elbow, "I am. And I am deeply impressed with your dedication to teaching both the language and the culture of my country.

"Jill's considerable skills are a tribute to your dedication and inspiration. As a matter of fact, Jill has done my country a great service. Something that would have been impossible without your excellent classes."

"Oh, dear. Jill's skills go far beyond my classes, I'm sure. Honestly, this is such an amazing turn of events." Miss Foster fanned herself with her free hand. She shot Jill a questioning glance. "How…that is if it's not too impertinent, how did you meet?"

Constantine smiled again. "That, Miss Foster, is a long story. Perhaps you would do me the honor of showing me your campus while we chat? Jill, would you like to join us?"

She started to join them, but stopped when her gaze fell on a small, glassed in cabinet by the door. "I'd like a few minutes alone. To freshen up. I'll close up the classroom for you, Miss Foster."

She stared at him, then at the cabinet where a trio of small pots rested—gifts she'd sent to Miss Foster for her language class. A memory of Mr. Dimas flashed through her mind.

"My dear, don't fall into the habit of keeping or giving away your wares," he chided, shaking his head when she told him she'd sent the pots to her language teacher. *"Many a new business has been bankrupted that way. Your best option is to stick to a few trusted venues."* He patted her hand. *"A couple of small pots are no great loss, but I advise you not to do that again."*

In the light of what she'd learned, his warning took on a more sinister meaning. *Don't sell pots where my associates can't retrieve them and the stolen gems inside.* She tipped her head toward the pots. Two were painted whimsically, with seascapes scalloping their rims in shades of turquoise and salmon. The third was painted a deep green with gold trim woven into a royal insignia on the front.

Constantine followed her look and understanding flashed in his eyes. He nodded to her. "As you wish, *mi'hona*. Perhaps we can meet back at the refreshment tables in twenty minutes or so."

Miss Foster perked up at the endearment, her sharp gaze flicking between Constantine and Jill. Jill breathed a sigh of relief, grateful he'd chosen to call her sweetheart—*mi'hona*—instead of the more intimate term he usually used. *Er'hona-mei.* My desirable one. Miss Foster would have picked up on it immediately and wondered.

She and Constantine might never have a future, but she didn't want their fleeting time together reduced to a tabloid tidbit. It was better that their words of desire stayed private.

Constantine turned back to her teacher. "Miss Foster, would you be terribly burdened to find yourself alone with me on our tour?"

"Not at all, Your Highness. The honor is all mine."

"Then let us go. If I could ask one favor of you, please, help me stay incognito for tonight. Call me Phillip. I'd like to keep this trip from becoming a bit of news on your bulletin board."

His deep voice and Miss Foster's breathless one faded away as they walked from the classroom. Alone again, Jill took a deep breath and turned to the cabinets.

Her necklace burned at her throat as she lifted the pots from their shelf. Did all pots with the insignia carry stolen gems? And if so, what other treasures had she innocently smuggled out of Melesia and into unsuspecting hands?

Constantine settled onto the couch and kicked off his shoes. He loosened his tie and popped the top buttons on his shirt before closing his eyes and leaning back against the cushions.

"You look exhausted," Jill said as she sank down beside him. "Can I get you something? Coffee? Cocoa? I might even be able to find a shot of something stronger if I look."

"No." He shook his head and blindly searched until he found her hand. "Nothing but a few quiet moments with you. I've been on my best behavior all night. Now I just want to relax."

Jill leaned against him, warm and trusting. He smiled at the way her body curled into his without hesitation. He didn't drop his guard around many people, but it felt natural to do so with Jill.

"Time to put the public face away?" Jill asked.

"I'm grateful to be able to be myself with you."

"Grateful enough to tell me why you were blank-faced and ultra-controlled when you returned from your walk with Miss Foster? Did she say something that disturbed you?"

Constantine hugged Jill closer, trying to offer comfort against the vague uncertainty he heard in her words. And trying to shield her from the shock he'd received earlier.

"Your Miss Foster was charming. I invited her to visit the islands again and to spend a semester or two at our Royal Academy. I also offered to update her supply of language materials or anything else she might need."

"Then what's wrong? You haven't said more than a dozen words to me in the last hour. Don't you even want to know what I discovered?"

There was no way to avoid what he had to say. "Jill, *Er'hona-mei,*" he hesitated "my security team called while I was with Miss Foster. A private, well respected firm on the islands—Ohanii Brothers' Security—found the artist they suspect made your pottery."

"Then we know who was smuggling the gems. Is he in custody?"

"He's dead. Murdered."

Jill stiffened. "How? Who?"

Constantine gathered her closer, wrapping both arms around her trembling body.

"He was shot. The Ohanii Brothers followed and apprehended his killer. Unfortunately, the killer also died within a few hours, before he was able to tell them anything. They suspect poisoning. A forensics team is investigating further."

"Did the potter leave any clues in his home or his workshop? If he was killed, it must be because he was working for someone else who didn't want to be discovered. Right?"

"Shortly after the killer left, the potter's home was destroyed in a fire. It appears his kiln blew up, engulfing both the workshop and the house in flames. Ohanii security believes the explosion was a result of tampering."

He ran a hand along her back, seeking the comfort of having her in his arms as much as he sought to comfort her. "It all happened on one of the small, remote islands. I don't think any more leads will come from there."

"Someone must really hate you. And me," Jill said in a small voice. She wound her slender arms around his waist, drawing herself a tiny bit closer to him. The gesture warmed him even as it fanned his need to protect her into full flame.

"Know this, *Er'hona-mei*. I will defend you with the same passion I defend my family and my country. You are mine to protect. My responsibility. I won't fail you."

"And I will guard you as fervently as any member of your court."

Her words, uttered with conviction and passion, lodged in his heart as no other woman's words ever had. It was dangerous to care for her this much. Dangerous to let her love him—he wasn't fool enough to believe her feelings were anything less—but he couldn't resist the temptation to do just that.

To care for her. To love—that is—let her love him. To forget the pain it would eventually cause both of them.

He pushed the thoughts away, lest he give in to the temptation.

"Now, your turn to update me. What did your detective work uncover? Were you able to look inside the pots?"

"Yes. The unmarked pots contained exactly what I'd expected under the drainage platform. Small gravel and crushed shells. The pot with the insignia had a ring hidden inside." She wiggled out of his arms and retrieved her evening bag. After rummaging in it for a minute, she held the ring out to him. "I don't know if this is significant or not."

Constantine took the gold ring from her. It was small, but heavy. He slipped it onto his pinky finger before turning to look at it closely under the light. The intricate engraving showed a lion's head at the top with two carved paws forming the junction between the face of the ring and the band. Between the paws a small beast cowered.

"Do you recognize it?" Jill's voice drew him from his study of the ring.

"It's the de Lyons family crest." He glanced up at her. "That's Helena's family. Her marriage to Alex solidified the union of our two most powerful political families—D'Malia and de Lyons."

"Just like ancient marriage contracts."

"Yes. But with a happy ending for them, at least until now. I don't know how—or if—this will change things. At the very least, it means more trouble and anxiety. Whoever wants to hurt the monarchy is going at it from both angles. First the Crown Jewels, now the queen's family crest."

"Could it be someone, or some group, who wants to abolish the monarchy? Maybe to establish a new type of government?"

"It's possible, but I think we would have known if a high level of discontent existed. There have been peaceful discussions about more participatory forms of government for decades. Theft, treason, and murder were never a part of the picture before."

"But they are now."

"So it seems." He hesitated, weighing the consequences of sharing his plans with her. One look at her eyes, and his hesitation fled. "I meant what I told your sister yesterday. A king's first responsibility is to listen to his people. One of the priorities in my government will be to add an elected body to represent the voices of the people. It will take time, and study, to accomplish it in the right way, but I believe it is what's best for the country."

Jill wrapped her hands around his, her grip both fragile and strong. "And I meant what I said once before. Your country is in good hands with you as its leader."

He gently pried one of her hands free and placed the ring in her palm, before focusing again on her face. "I am fortunate to have a supporter, and a friend, in you." He closed her fingers around the ring. "My family is fortunate as well. When you meet Helena, you should be the one to return this ring to her."

Before she could answer, he kissed her. Passion rocked his body again at the touch of her lips. Four—five?—long days had passed since he last buried himself in her warmth. At least one more would pass before he could do so again, devoting the leisure to her that she deserved. And then, who knew how many more days before they would be alone?

Somewhere, between this night spent in chastity as a guest in her mother's home and the nights spent in his home under the scrutiny of an entire royal entourage, he vowed to find a place where they could spend one last night as just Jill and Phillip.

Woman and man. Locked away in a place where passion was their only duty.

Alone.

Before their worlds tore them apart.

Forever.

Chapter 17

The plane banked to the right pressing Jill deeper into the plush leather seat of Royal Melesia One. She tried to ignore the queasy feeling in her stomach. A sip of her mimosa helped, but the platter of eggs Benedict on the tray table only intensified the nausea.

"I realize it's not peanut butter toast and coffee," Constantine said, squeezing her hand, "but you might feel better if you eat something."

She doubted anything would make the knot in her stomach go away, but she nibbled on a piece of buttered toast anyway.

At a slight movement and a quiet word from Constantine, the steward cleared away the platters and brought them coffee. It was strong, dark, and smoother than any coffee she'd ever had. Something about the simplicity of coffee and toast did take the edge off her nerves. Until she looked around.

She'd never traveled beyond occasional visits home, but even she knew the difference between flying coach class to Ohio and the opulent luxury of Royal Melesia One.

Elegant white linen topped the table and the chairs were upholstered in butter-soft, forest-green leather. Silk hangings covered the walls. It resembled a flying resort more than it resembled a plane.

"We'll be in Melesia within the hour," Constantine said softly as the plane settled back into a smooth, straight path. "I took the liberty of picking out a few additional items for your wardrobe. Lovely as you are in your business suit, I thought something more casual might be appropriate."

She followed his gesture to a small, richly appointed private bedroom with a private bath. Definitely a step above coach class to Ohio. Draped across the bed was a soft, flowing chiffon skirt in with a tropical flower print in shades of orange and yellow. Coupled with it was an orange, scooped neck top in a sumptuous summer weave. A pair of strappy leather sandals completed the outfit.

She unbuttoned her jacket and shimmied out of the tight, black skirt, tossing them carelessly on the bed where they lay like a discarded, too-tight second skin. The new pieces were light, airy. Sensual, without the revealing confinement of her shed wardrobe.

Jill sat on the bed to put on her shoes and came face-to-face with a stranger in the cabin mirror. The woman who looked back seemed years younger with a radiance and vibrancy that she'd lacked. This woman seemed alive.

Was it only a few weeks ago that she'd decided to have a fling with a handsome client? That she'd deviated from her plan of working, saving, and forgoing her own dreams to provide her siblings with an education? That she'd dared to give herself a chance at what she really wanted? To feel passion and life pulsing through her veins? To hope for a chance at love? Was it really only a few weeks?

Life pulsed through the woman in the mirror. Jill could see it in her reflected face, and feel it radiating through her body. Fear, anticipation, and desire raced along her nerves, sizzling and crackling, knotting in her gut, and weakening her knees.

She'd unwittingly fenced Melesian treasures. She'd located the lost crown. She held the key to uncovering the thief. And she'd made love to a prince. A real, headline-catching, drop-dead-gorgeous, wealthy soon-to-be-monarch of Melesia.

She shook her head clear of the fantasy and focused on what was real. It wasn't the prince who filled her mind and thoughts. It was the man. The man who'd kissed her so tenderly, yet believed royal unions were only about duty and power.

Despite his father's love for his mother, and his brother's love for his wife, Constantine refused to believe in love for himself. He was the reason she was here, she reminded herself.

He asked her to help him meet his obligations to family and country.

She came to help him be true to himself; to show him that love didn't need to be forever beyond his grasp.

Jill closed her eyes and counted to ten. Twice. She had to sweep away this most recent, dangerous fantasy. He wouldn't love her, and she shouldn't love him. She shouldn't. That is, she didn't. Not at all. It started as a fling. Now it was simply a ruse, designed to fool the public and to help a friend. Holding firmly to her thoughts and reining in her feelings, she turned to the main cabin.

Constantine rose, his eyes glowing with appreciation when he saw her.

"You look beautiful."

"Good enough to play the prince's love interest?"

"That depends," he said taking her hand and kissing the middle of her palm before twining his fingers in hers, "on whether the prince in question is me or some other random prince you've got waiting in the wings."

"There's no one else." All thoughts of friendship fled. Raw feelings rushed through her, colliding and bouncing off one another: desire, confusion, uncertainty, and the overwhelming need to kiss him. She stepped closer and twined her arms around his neck. He responded by wrapping his arms around her waist and pressing her to his body.

"I'm glad," he murmured before his lips touched hers. She closed her eyes, and in her memory, they were transported magically back to the night they first made love, when the storm and the darkness enveloped them as surely as passion. She'd trusted him then; she'd have to trust him now.

A soft chime interrupted the moment. The steward reappeared and discreetly cleared his throat. "Your Highness, Miss Bradley, we're preparing to land. If you'll please take your seats."

Constantine kept his arm around her waist, leading her to the plush recliners. "Thank you, Simmons," he said with a nod to the steward.

Once they were strapped in, she reached for his hand.

"Jill?"

"I'm scared. What if I can't pull this off?"

"All you have to do is be my guest until the coronation is safely completed. Even staying for the ceremony is just a precaution. Once we're seen together in public, that should be enough to lure the thief out. Your idea about bringing the potted palm with us was brilliant."

Something inside her warmed at his praise, even though she brushed it off. "It's just common sense. Only the thief knows the jewels were smuggled in that pot. If he thinks I've brought the stolen jewels back, he might give himself away."

"As I said, it was a brilliant idea. No, don't shake your head and turn away." He grasped her chin with his free hand and turned her face to his. "You undervalue yourself, Jill. You are an intelligent, compassionate, beautiful woman. The man you give your heart to will be lucky, indeed."

"Lucky," she echoed. The plane bumped down on the runway and the force of their taxi pressed her against the seat, stealing her breath and forcing her thoughts away from the man beside her. She was grateful for the distraction, because if she'd had more time to think, she'd have to admit she'd already given her heart to a man who didn't believe in love.

The landing, the limousine, the smiling, the waving, the popping of flash photos all passed in a blur. Jill kept her fears hidden behind a perfect public façade and navigated the unfamiliar territory with the grace of an accomplished actress.

But now, inside the cavernous foyer of the royal palace, her knees quivered, as weak as melted wax ready to pool onto the expansive marble floor. The room was cool compared to the tropical weather outside.

Ceiling fans circulated the air in tantalizing wisps around them. In front of her, the marble hall ended in six wide steps leading to a sumptuously carpeted, sunken sitting area. On either side, stretched passageways wide enough to accommodate a small army.

A movement across the room at the bottom of the steps caught her eye. The wall was living. Not living, exactly, but an expanse of glass and sea rock forming an indoor aquarium stretching nearly the length of the room and towering to the ceiling.

Glass windows framed it, looking out onto the ocean, providing the illusion of an undersea playground. As she watched, a swordfish swam by, dove, and disappeared beneath the floor.

"I brought you in the public route," Constantine said beside her. "The aquarium reaches another story below ground. There's a complete tour route that winds beneath the palace and shows this tank and many other tanks of marine life. We open this area for tours from time to time."

His voice seemed quiet, and all the more regal in the cool expanse of his home. The weight of tradition made her feel small as she gazed at the room. A touch on her elbow drew her from her reverie.

"I'll give you the rest of the tour later. The ballrooms and government chambers are located in the east wing." He motioned to his right. "The central rotunda also contains an arcade where merchants traditionally bring their wares for the queen to do her shopping. Our private apartments are off this way."

He led her to the west, opposite the direction he'd indicated earlier. "The upper floors are all enclosed, private and secure. Only members of the royal family and their guests are allowed to enter."

The first floor of the palace opened to the outside. He ushered her onto an outdoor path leading to the private wing. Wide porticos overlooked serene ponds, sparkling in the sunlight. Terraced walkways meandered through sculpted fountains, trickling waterfalls, lush gardens, and private pools. Beyond everything, on all sides was the ocean.

Constantine stopped beside her. "Royal Island is connected to the main island through the guarded bridge behind us. The island itself houses only the royal family and select staff and guests. It is half a mile wide and three miles long, with white sand beaches, and—"

"I know," she interrupted his monologue with a grin. "I read it in a guidebook. I want to see Melesia through your eyes, not the text of a guidebook."

"Private tours can be arranged. Perhaps tonight, after you've had a chance to settle in?" His voice was like a warm breeze, sliding over her skin and igniting her senses.

"Not now?" She flashed a teasing pout, but he only shook his head.

"I need to show you to your rooms, then meet with Alex and handle some business. I could pick you up in a couple hours for a tour of the island and dinner on the terrace."

"That sounds lovely."

He led her through a maze of courtyards and corridors, past the security guards and onto the upper floors of the palace, where only the royal family and their guests were housed. Finally, he stopped at a door.

"You can move about freely here without any security worries. This is our best guest suite. It overlooks the private lagoon. Someone will arrive with your things shortly, if they are not already here. If you need anything, just ask. I will be back as soon as possible."

His fingers tangled in her hair, and he gave her the briefest of kisses. With her lips still tingling from his touch, she took her first step alone into the unknown world of royal Melesia.

Constantine frowned as he listened to the reports from the royal physicians. He'd seen with his own eyes how Alex had declined in his absence; day-to-day duties and appearances tired him until he seemed like a much older man. Constantine turned his attention back to the specialists.

"…symptoms vary. In His Majesty's case, the primary symptom is fatigue, although he has also experienced some dizziness. The disease"—Constantine couldn't catch the complex medical name—"had been in remission for some time after his marriage, however, the flare ups are becoming more frequent. Although it is not medically proven, it is my professional opinion that the stress of the monarchy is exacerbating the symptoms."

The young doctor paused to consult his notes, but before he could speak again, a small, round, woman with graying dreadlocks stepped into view.

"Enough of this rambling," she said, taking control of the discussion. "This isn't a medical conference or a research case." She reached for Constantine's hand and patted it, something none of the other doctors dared to do.

He took the comfort she offered. The cool, dark hands that gripped his had soothed him through childhood fevers and scrapes and had safely delivered more than a generation of D'Malias. He trusted her to cut through the medical jumble for him. "Your diagnosis, Dr. 'Oodsoon?"

"Your brother is tired, young prince. He's poured himself out for the country from the day he was born. He'll do it till the day he dies, unless someone stops him. It's his nature. What he needs is rest, time with his family, and a chance to heal.

"I will personally oversee his care, but you're the only one who can give him the medicine he needs. The question is are you ready to do what has to be done?"

It was the same question she'd always asked him when he was a boy facing a painful procedure or a bitter medicine. Her eyes held the same faith in him now as they did then. He nodded.

"In light of Dr. 'Oodsoon's observations," his advisor said from across the room, "I believe we should move forward with plans for your coronation, Prince Constantine. Now that the— that is, now that you have returned."

Constantine nodded. "Make the necessary announcements," he said to the press secretary, "and continue with the preparations." The assembled team filed from the room, leaving him alone. He paced toward the windows.

Afternoon sun poured through the narrow mullioned glass panes lining his office wall between bleached stone buttresses.

The sparkle of light on the ocean danced before his eyes, tempting him like a mirage—beautiful but out of reach.

Duty tightened around his neck like a noose. First the coronation, then the increased official duties, followed by the pressure for marriage and a successor. Each responsibility was another tug on the knot that threatened to choke him.

Yet, he'd always known it was his duty to take over should his brother need him. And even in their childhood, it was clear that he was the stronger of the two. It had never really bothered him before. Before he went to Chicago. Before Jill came into his life and tempted him to want more. Now wealth, power, and the adoration of the crowds didn't stack up to the affection of one woman.

It was ridiculous. He'd been honest with her from the start—he wasn't interested in love. He wasn't capable of love. At least not romantic love.

He'd loved his parents. He loved his younger siblings—Stephan with his playful, scholarly disposition, Lydia with her contemplative, almost brooding nature, and the reckless Dimitri, locked in teenaged angst like Jill's younger brother. He loved Alex, both as a brother and a king. He loved his country. But there wasn't room in his heart for a woman.

Why, then, would the image of Jill not leave him alone? Maybe because he'd been in intimate contact with her for days. Proximity was making him edgy and hungry for her, like a man who smells chargrilled beef then craves a steak. That was all.

Cravings could be ignored. Now that he was home, it was time to return to the real world, his real world. A world that had no place for outsiders, no matter how beautiful or vibrant.

Reluctantly, he sat at his desk and penned a note of apology, excusing himself from dinner and their plans. Then, because he needed to focus on who he was, not the dream he wanted, he signed it with the official royal seal. He would see to it that Jill was amply rewarded for her services to the country.

He would see to it that she enjoyed her stay on the island. He'd assign her the best guards, the most experienced guides, and ensure she'd have her pick of any of the delights their island kingdom offered. All of the amenities he could buy or command would be at her disposal.

He'd give her everything. Everything but himself.

Because he couldn't afford to see her alone again. Not knowing she had the power to invade his thoughts and sway his decisions.

Jill sank onto the couch in her sitting room, the monogrammed letterhead and envelope dangling from her fingers. He wasn't coming. She hadn't expected the fairy tale to come crashing down around her ears this soon. Foolish romantic thoughts had left her unprepared to face reality.

Not that her room reflected reality. Instead, it surrounded her in opulence that she'd never even imagined. The spacious, airy sitting room was larger than her apartment. The polished wood and intricately laid flagstone of the floor kept the room cool, despite the warm, sea-scented breeze that ruffled the curtains.

Through an archway she could see the flutter of gauzy, golden bed hangings that surrounded the massive canopy bed of bleached white wood and gilt trim.

Even the selection of gourmet chocolates—the Fantasy Fudge brand created by her friend Claire's billionaire husband—felt foreign in their wrappers bearing a royal seal of approval. She nibbled one, but the sweet brought sadness rather than solace.

She wandered onto the balcony and let the breeze lift her hair, cooling her neck. Her only connection to Chicago—the beautifully potted palm tree with its hidden secrets—was displayed prominently in one corner of the balcony.

The rest of her suite, with its elegant furnishings, the closet full of luxurious island wear—another gift from Constantine—and the young woman assigned to act as her maid were all foreign and fit for a princess. The palace even had gleaming turrets and sparkling spires rising to the sky.

But despite the surroundings, the only thing she'd really longed for was the prince, or rather, the man he'd pretended to be. She lifted her gaze to the horizon. Beyond the beach, the lagoon glinted in the afternoon sun, its waters ranging in color from teal to aqua to deepest blue. The ever-changing sparkle of color, so like the eyes of the man she loved, brought a tightness to her chest.

She didn't want to love him, damn it. She hadn't planned on that. All she wanted was a night or two of passion with a wonderfully sexy man. And that's exactly what she'd gotten. With this trip to a tropical paradise of royal palaces and endless luxury thrown in. So why was she miserable?

Nothing was ever accomplished by wallowing, Jill. Her father's voice sounded in her head, reminding her of her obligations. With Constantine by her side, or without him, she'd promised to lure a thief from hiding. She had a duty to do, and she knew exactly where to start.

Behind her, Alia, the young woman assigned to help her, moved about the room tidying an invisible mess. Jill returned to the room.

"Alia, you don't have to clean up after me. I've been taking care of myself for a long time."

"Oh, no, Miss Bradley. It's part of my job."

"It's all right. I don't need someone to look after me."

"If you're unhappy with me—"

"No. Of course not. I'm just not used to being waited on. It's a little uncomfortable, if you want to know the truth."

Alia smiled and seemed to relax at Jill's admission. "Put your mind at rest, Miss Bradley. Think of it as a vacation where you don't have to lift a finger. Besides, all the students at the university are required to work as a part of their education. I was excited to be assigned to the main palace. If you send me back, they may put me in the kitchen washing pots."

"If you're sure I'm no trouble…"

"Please, Miss Bradley, I'd like to stay."

Jill looked at the young blonde, who was only a few years older than her sister, Gracie. A wave of homesickness struck her with unexpected force. "All right. You can stay. But please, call me Jill."

Half an hour later, after learning a bit about the university, Jill and Alia hurried off to the palace library. Alia led the way, relishing her role as guide while Jill followed, organizing her scattered thoughts. The sooner she fulfilled her obligations and found the thief, the sooner she could pack up her broken heart and head home.

Constantine wrestled himself from the tangle of sheets and paced his room, the evening air cooling the sweat from his naked torso. The sounds of the surf, the balmy ocean breezes, and the scents of home hadn't been enough to lull him to sleep. Every time he closed his eyes, images assaulted him.

Alex and Helena sitting together, holding hands. He could hear their affectionate laughter ringing in the silence of his room. His brother was sick, dealing with pain, illness, and the abdication of his duties. He shouldn't sound happy. Not at all.

But it was as if nothing, even an incurable disease, could take away his joy. He and Helena radiated happiness.

Constantine doubted he'd be so lucky. The public's idea of a suitable bride—someone with impeccable bloodlines and a far too sheltered upbringing—left him cold. Just as surely as the right woman left him cold, the wrong woman—Jill—left him hot. Hot and aching. Keeping his distance from her throughout the long afternoon and longer evening hadn't dulled his need for her. Instead, his hunger increased to the point of obsession.

He wondered idly if she would stay if he asked her. But he knew in his heart that she wasn't the kind of woman to take second place to a wife—not even a cold, political wife with appropriate blood lines and no interest in him. And though the press portrayed him as a playboy, he refused to be unfaithful in his marriage, even if it meant being unhappy.

No, the proper thing to do was to leave Jill alone. Yet, even as his rational mind argued against it, the undisciplined longings filled his imagination with decidedly improper images. His body hardened and throbbed, begging for the touch of Jill's fingers and the hot tightness of her wrapped around him.

Unable to resist, he grabbed a robe and raced to her rooms with as much dignity as he could muster. Fortunately there were few servants in the hallway to see exactly how undignified he was.

He hesitated for a second outside her door, rallying his tattered self-control. He would be honest. There was no future for them; there was only now. He would take whatever she offered. A day. A week. A month. An hour. Or even a minute, to say good-bye.

His knock, soft at first then increasingly urgent, didn't awaken her. After five long minutes, he admitted defeat. Perhaps it was for the best that she slept alone, rather than with him. He had his country and his duty. There wasn't time for pleasure, especially not pleasure that would leave Jill feeling used and alone.

He returned to his suites and began making plans, despite the late hour. In the morning, he would be on his way for a countrywide goodwill tour. There, he would make peace with his future as king of Melesia. A future without Jill.

Chapter 18

$\mathcal{J}$ ill stretched out on the lounge chair beside the pool and let the distant sound of the surf and the warmth of the morning sun lull her into a deep relaxation.

Visions of newspaper headlines flashed before her closed eyes. She'd scoured the library for the past two days, spending well into the night with stacks of dusty, decades-old documents and blurry images on microfilm.

What else was there to do? Constantine had left, the morning after their broken date, without a word to her. Ironically, she learned of his departure from the Melesian newspaper that covered his multi-island tour announcing his upcoming coronation.

The humiliation and the gut-wrenching anger of being used and abandoned carried her through the first hour before everything coalesced into blinding, stabbing pain.

The migraine that followed robbed her of every sensation but pain, inside and out. Pain like she'd experienced nearly every day in the weeks after her father died. Pain that eventually moved from her body and lodged in her heart.

That pain, too, started with a charming boy. One who gladly took the innocence she offered then left her for another conquest while she fought waves of nausea and the aftereffects of too much spiked punch.

Only now, she was a grown woman. She'd offered herself to Constantine without any strings attached. With no thoughts of tomorrow. He'd done nothing more than take her at her word. And though she wanted to heal her broken heart in the privacy of her Chicago apartment, she'd made a promise—one she refused to treat as casually as Constantine treated her.

She would do everything in her power to find the man who'd called himself Mr. Dimas. The one who'd started this whole charade. Then, after the coronation, she would fade away and leave her pretend lover to the adoring crowds.

His words haunted her every day, a litany that broke her heart as much as it imprisoned his. *Love and marriage are two separate things.* The frown that etched his brow at the words was as vivid in her memory as if he stood before her.

Modern monarchies are about duty and power. She hadn't known at the time that the words were directed at himself. Yet now they seemed prophetic. *People marry for all kinds of reasons. Love is the least of them.* She'd wanted to prove him wrong, but history was on his side, judging from the newspapers she'd read.

Political loyalties, seemingly at rest for centuries, had erupted during the early years of King Tyronne Phillippe I's reign. It was then that the house of Lyons, well established rivals to the ruling D'Malias, began making claims to the throne.

Ugly accusations reared their head as the house of Lyons claimed the D'Malias had diluted the blood of kings by marrying indigenous island elite, fueling the de Lyons' claims. Although the claim gained little traction among the people of the kingdom, the de Lyons side kept up to pressure.

Suggestions of a match between King Tyronne and Ophelia de Lyons, after the death of his first wife, were raised as a way to heal the rift. The plans were dashed when the king chose Constantine's mother, a commoner, instead. Thus, instead of ending, the feud accelerated.

Jill became as obsessed with unraveling the political history of the country and searching for clues to the current problems as she'd once been about learning their language.

She turned down an endless stream of opportunities for entertainment. The palace staff approached her daily with tempting offers, and daily, she sent them away. Not unkindly—because many of them were student workers or young employees of the palace—but firmly, because she refused to let Constantine assuage his conscience by buying her entertainment.

She'd promised to help lure out the murdering, thieving, treasonous threat to the throne. She'd keep her promise. Then she'd go home. But she wouldn't let him think that his current treatment of her was acceptable.

So she continued her grueling research despite the unending ache in her heart. Every night Jill left the library, eyes gritty and desperate for sleep; every afternoon she returned and worked until well past midnight. She needed a break, to assimilate all the facts she'd gathered. And she deserved to relax and soak up a little sun during her last days in this lonely paradise.

"Reach for the sky, stranger."

Jill cracked an eye open at the sound of the young voice beside her. A stranger, about four feet tall and clad only in a red felt cowboy hat and a pair of baggy swim trunks weighed down by a gun belt, stood over her. The gun he leveled at her wasn't one of the shiny metal toy guns. It was a far more lethal, large capacity, orange water pistol.

"State your name and your business here," the stranger drawled in oddly accented Melesian.

Jill bit the inside of her cheek to keep from smiling and slowly raised her hands. "My name is Jill Bradley, and I'm here at the invitation of—"

"You talk funny. Where are you from?" The water pistol wavered a bit.

"I'm from Chicago."

"The United States?" The pistol went limp in his hand, forgotten. "Do you know any real cowboys?"

"Well, I—"

"Master Tyronne!" A harried voice called from the paths beyond the pool.

"Oops. I don't want to get caught." The stranger turned big, aqua-blue, pleading eyes at her. "Pretend you haven't seen me, okay?" He darted off behind a cement planter twice his size and peeped out from the foliage.

"Master Tyronne! You know you're not supposed to run off." A slender woman of indeterminate age with graying hair and a weathered face raced down the path, ignoring Jill while searching for her charge.

Jill closed her eyes and feigned sleep, hoping that she wouldn't be asked to betray her young companion. She heard a soft rustle and felt the presence of someone beside her.

"Ty, Miss Celine has been calling for you," said a cultured, gentle voice. "You don't want her to worry, do you?"

"No, Mama."

Jill peeked out from half closed eyes as Ty emerged from his hiding place and raced over to them.

"I was just playing with my new friend. Hi, Miss Bradley." He waved at Jill. "Would you like me to introduce her, Mama?"

"I'd like that very much, Ty. Then I want you to find Miss Celine and apologize to her for running off." Ty's mother sank gracefully to a lounging chair opposite Jill. A swimsuit peeked out from her simple, elegant cover up, but she made no move to remove either the cover up or her wide brimmed straw hat.

Ty drew himself up to his full height. "Mother, may I present to you Miss Jill Bradley of the United States. Miss Bradley, my mother, Her Royal Highness Helena, Queen of Melesia."

Jill had been hiding a smile at Ty's serious voice and demeanor until his words sank in. The protocol lessons she'd drummed into her head fled. "Your Highness, I..." she scrambled trying to rise, but the lounge chair didn't allow her to be graceful.

"Please. I'm simply Helena to my friends." The young queen offered her hand and motioned Jill back into the lounge chair. "Since my son has already befriended you, it would hardly do for me to stand on formality. May I call you Jill?"

Jill nodded, liking the young woman immensely, but unsure how to react. Her work with business clients hadn't exactly prepared her to socialize with royalty.

Except for Constantine. And that had started with deception on his part. Her gut tightened as the warm memory of her carefree days with him fought the reality of their present situation.

"I feel as if I already know you," Helena continued, graciously ignoring Jill's preoccupation. "Constantine lights up when he talks about you. Of course, he's a typical man and tries to deny it, but I've learned a thing or two about love over the years."

She turned to her son, who was still standing there. "Ty, weren't you supposed to do something?"

"Oh, yeah. Bye, Miss Bradley. Bye, Mama." Ty turned and ran off, calling for Miss Celine as he skirted the pool and scampered out of sight on one of the paths.

"He's an adorable boy," Jill said, noticing how Helena's eyes softened at the compliment to her son.

"We almost lost him when he was little. Every time he leaves my sight, I fight a twinge of fear. But I can't keep him tied up. Besides, he's been a bundle of energy ever since his Uncle Con came home with a suitcase full of American toys. Especially that cowboy outfit."

"Uncle Con? Oh, you mean Constantine. So that's where Ty picked up his terrible cowboy accent."

"That's where he picked up a lot of habits that worry me."

"I don't think you'll have to worry about Ty's playboy image for quite some time. Although, he does practically ooze charm."

"Thank goodness it's only six-year-old charm and not the full grown D'Malia charisma." Helena chuckled and curled up more comfortably in her chair. "And thank goodness he has another uncle nearby to provide a more stabilizing influence.

"Stephan is the scholar in the family. He's been planning Ty's education since the day he was born. Of course, Ty thinks it's all fun and games, but he's learning and that's what is important."

"He seems to have a wonderful family around him. That's important too."

Helena smiled at her. "Since my brother-in-law is neglecting you in the name of his official duties, it would be my pleasure to introduce you to the rest of the family."

"I'm not neglected." Jill picked at the hem of her beach towel, avoiding Helena's eyes. "I've been treated like an honored guest. I'm under no illusions about why I'm here."

"You're here at the invitation of the royal family. And now that you've had some time to adjust, the rest of the family would like to meet you."

Jill's stomach sank at the thought of meeting more royals. Despite years of working with international clients in her job, she couldn't remember the intricate Melesian protocols governing interactions with the royal family. How did one behave as a guest? What was her status as a foreigner? And did anyone know she'd been Constantine's lover? A heavy, sick feeling settled in the pit of her stomach as the questions piled up.

But even she knew better than to turn down a royal invitation. "That would be lovely," she said.

Helena's gentle laughter shook her from her self-pity. "Don't look so worried, Jill. You've already successfully weathered meeting the extremes. Constantine is, in many ways, the most formidable of the brothers. And my son is easily the most charming member of the family."

Jill swallowed her nervousness and smiled instead. If she could only trade her bikini for a business suit, she'd be on safer ground. She'd met powerful people before. She could do this. "I'll look forward to whatever arrangements you think are best," she said with more conviction than before.

"Wonderful." Helena rose in a smooth motion. She placed a hand on Jill's shoulder to keep her from doing the same. "Don't bother getting up. Enjoy yourself for a while. Why don't the two of us meet poolside tomorrow morning to talk further? You can catch some more sun, and I can enjoy the breeze."

Helena's warmth seemed genuine, and Jill nodded, glad at the thought of being alone with her for another day before meeting anyone else. "Thank you for understanding."

"Not at all. Thank you for allowing me the chance to talk with another woman my own age. It is a refreshing opportunity."

Jill closed her eyes and listened to Helena's retreating footsteps. She forced herself to lie still but sunbathing no longer held fascination for her. As soon as she could leave—without appearing to run away—she would head to her room and beg Alia to give her an emergency course in protocol. She was going to need it. Soon.

Two days later, Jill lounged poolside again, desperately trying to relax. Helena's conversations over the past days had been fun, light, and almost like two friends getting to know one another. At times, Jill forgot the gulf in circumstances that separated them. But all of that was about to come to an end.

Tomorrow, like it or not, she was destined to meet the scholarly bother, Prince Stephan. Soon after, Helena had informed her, she'd meet King Alexander. And although Helena had called both of them less formidable than Constantine, Jill doubted it was true.

For the hundredth time in the last forty-eight hours, she wished she'd been born the smart sister instead of the pretty sister. The thought of meeting another prince was nerve-racking enough. But did he have to have a genius IQ to boot? She didn't know which aspect of Prince Stephan worried her more—his royalty or his intelligence.

She sighed and opened the protocol book Alia had loaned her in preparation for her upcoming introductions. Nothing in it mentioned appropriate behavior for guests of the royal family, but at least she could learn to behave as a citizen would. When in Rome, and all that.

She scanned the sections on the proper forms of address for all the members of the royal family, quizzing herself as she read. His Royal Majesty the King. His Royal Highness, the Crown Prince. His Highness the Prince. So far, so good.

She flipped to the chapter on presentation to the court—broken down by official function. Jill paged through the sections on presentations at formal balls, academic functions, and state sponsored award ceremonies, searching for something relevant. Like a section on "how to behave when meeting your lover's younger brother under duress." It wasn't there.

"Looks like some heavy reading you're doing."

Jill peered out from under the edge of her book to take in a pair of worn deck shoes. Khaki pants and a lightweight shirt, open at the throat completed the ensemble. She shaded her eyes and looked up. Way up.

The tall, lanky blond plopped down in a chair beside her and stretched out, kicking off his shoes to reveal bare feet. "I usually try to leave work and cumbersome textbooks behind when I get a minute to lounge by the pool." He smiled at her. "Unlike you."

Jill returned the smile. She rarely saw the young workers in anything but uniforms and never by the pool, but she was glad for the distraction.

"To tell the truth, I'm out of my league visiting here on Royal Island. I was reviewing protocol so I don't make any embarrassing mistakes."

He plucked the book from her and studied the title then shuddered. "The best thing you can do with this is to put it away and forget it. For that matter, take the time to escape Royal Island. It can be intimidating. Have you been out on the ocean yet? Been snorkeling? Or sailing? I'm sure you'd have a good time."

Jill held up a hand to stop him. "As tempting as your offers sound, I have work to do while I'm here. I'm only taking a short break by the pool. And you can assure His Royal Highness Crown Prince Constantine that I don't need any special, extravagant entertainment. I'm fine."

The man sat up and looked at her, humor sparkling in his eyes. Unlike the other students, he didn't appear at all disappointed by her refusal. He actually grinned at her.

"What's so funny?" she asked.

"You don't need that protocol book at all. From what I can tell. Not a single word you've said is less than polite. But the overall effect was as if you wanted me to tell his Royal-Pain-In-The-Ass just where to stick his offers." He broke out laughing. "I'd be happy to tell him for you."

Jill could feel her eyes widening, horrified at his comments. Everything she'd seen and heard in the country so far pointed to a people proud of their monarchy and steeped in tradition and politeness. Yet here was someone openly mocking. Was he capable of hating the monarchy? Of betraying it?

"I didn't mean it like it sounded," she began.

"Oh, I think a part of you meant exactly that. You're just reluctant to put it into words. But if you really want to put Constantine in his place, spend the day having fun with me. I take it you've turned down every entertainment he's tried to arrange for you?"

"Actually, yes, but I don't think enjoying the day with you will make him jealous—" Oh no. Had she actually said jealous? Her mouth and her brain were truly disconnected. "I mean, I don't think it would affect him in any way."

He sent her a wicked grin. "Trust me, it will. Spend a day with me and have some fun. I know how to needle him. I'm good at it. I just saw the pompous jerk on one of the other islands a few days ago, and I can't think of a better way to put his feet back on the ground."

Jill's mouth hung agape, perplexed by his flippant disregard for his crown prince. Surely the student workers and the palace staff were discouraged from such behavior.

"Don't worry," he said as if he'd read her thoughts. "I can call him whatever I want as long as I don't do it in public." He sat up and offered her his hand. "In case you haven't figured it out yet, I'm the annoying little brother, Stephan."

"Oh. My. You don't..." What was she supposed to say? You don't look like a prince? You don't act like a scholar? "You don't look like your pictures, that is."

"Ah. Imagine that. I don't look like a stiff and out-of-date official portrait. Thank the gods." He rolled his eyes, looking for an instant like her little brother, Geoff.

Jill stifled a laugh. Stephan had to be the least intimidating person she'd met yet. His ability to joke about himself chased away all the stuffy ideas she had about royalty in general and genius princes in particular. More than that, he'd made her laugh about Constantine. It took away some of the persistent ache in her heart.

"A woman who knows how to laugh is a rare treasure. My brother needs more laughter in his life. He's always been too serious." Stephan picked up the abandoned protocol book and handed it to Jill. "This book is crammed with information, but none of it applies to you. Royal families are guarded and extremely private, but among ourselves, I suspect we're a lot like any family. And you, Jill Bradley, are a valued friend of the family."

"Hey, Uncle Stephan! Miss Bradley!" Ty raced down the path, interrupting them. He plopped down on Jill's lounge chair and focused on her, bouncing with every word. "Uncle Stephan is taking me snork'ing tomorrow. He says there are lots of fish to see. And Mama says you're coming too. Are you? Please?" He looked at her quizzically then twisted toward Stephan. "Did she say yes?"

"There you have it, Jill. Ty's decided you're an honorary family member."

"Please say you'll come. I want to show you how I can swim." She couldn't refuse the look in Ty's eyes. The charming D'Malia clan was ganging up on her.

"I'd love to."

Before any further doubts about intruding on the royal family could enter her mind, Stephan grabbed Ty and bench pressed him over his head while the boy giggled. "Why wait till tomorrow, *ma'chido*? If you want to show Miss Bradley how you can swim, this is the perfect time." He walked to the pool and tossed the giggling, screaming boy into the deep end. Ty swam to the edge and scrambled out, only to have Stephan toss him in again.

As she watched, longing swept through Jill. This was what she wanted for herself. Family. Children. Laughter. She'd waited so long for these things. Put them on hold for so many years while she struggled to make up for her father's death.

The fractured bonds to her own family might heal, but she wondered if she'd ever have the children she longed for. Even if she someday did have kids, they wouldn't have the piercing aqua blue eyes or simmering, half arrogant smile that haunted her dreams.

They wouldn't have the mysterious, indefinable D'Malia charm.

Chapter 19

The gentle slap of waves on the side of the yacht lulled Jill into a dreamy state. All around, endless blue ocean stretched to the horizon. It had been a perfect day. Relaxed, fun, and energizing.

When Stephan scooped up a sleeping Ty and headed downstairs, she was alone on the deck with Helena.

"Jill?" Helena took a sip of her mineral water and looked into the ocean. "Do you ever think about marriage? Or love?"

All the time. "Not often," she said aloud, keeping her own eyes trained on the distance.

"You have a choice I never had." Helena's voice was soft, the voice of one confiding a secret to a sister or close friend. She sat and faced Jill. "I can barely guess how it must be for you. I'm sure Constantine told you that my marriage started out as a political necessity. I never expected it to be anything else. So you can imagine how surprised I was when I discovered I was in love with my husband."

"I can't imagine marrying someone without being in love first. You…" Jill hesitated, "you were such a radiant bride, and everyone believed it was a love match."

"I was terrified. Any radiance was an illusion created by a professional wedding staff, including some of the best makeup artists in the business."

"You were afraid of getting married?"

Helena shook her head. "I was afraid of not living up to everyone's expectations. The public wanted a romantic couple. The king wanted to right a perceived wrong. My father wanted a perfectly poised and groomed political champion. And, other than an heir, I had no idea what my husband-to-be wanted."

"What did you want?"

"I wanted to run out of the church, catch the first flight to America, and trade my duty and honor for a taste of freedom."

"Believe it or not, I understand exactly what you mean."

Helena nodded, seeming to accept Jill's claim at face value. "Somehow, I knew you would. Constantine told us you traveled to Melesia out of a sense of duty and a desire to help us. It's important for you to understand, Jill, that no one, absolutely no one," she repeated with emphasis, "in the royal family believes you are responsible for the loss of our Crown Jewels. You don't owe us anything. We are the ones in your debt."

"Thank you for your kind words, but I was involved in the plot. I should have known the pottery sales were too easy." She fingered the necklace, the cursed mark that implicated her in the treachery. It shamed her in front of the young queen.

"Jill." Helena gently moved Jill's hand from her throat and held it in her own, closing the gap between them that Jill tried so hard to establish. "Do you know why I went through with my wedding instead of running away?"

Jill shook her head, confused by the sudden change of subject.

"Alex and I were rarely alone before the wedding. Nearly every meeting was a carefully scripted photo opportunity. Even so, at times our eyes met, and I felt something, a reaction to him as a man. He was steady, kind, and believe it or not, shy. But what moved me most was how alone he seemed. When it came to the choice between walking down the aisle or fleeing for freedom, I knew I couldn't leave Alex alone to carry his burdens."

"Did you love him?"

"Maybe I did. Or maybe it was the D'Malia charm. What matters is that I love him now with all my heart. I wouldn't trade a minute of our lives together for anything, not even for the freedom I once craved."

Jill looked at the image of their clasped hands, through a blurry haze. She blinked away the film of tears.

Helena gave Jill's hand a squeeze. "Loving a D'Malia isn't easy, but it is worth the effort and occasional heartbreak. That's something I think you also understand."

Obviously her love for Constantine wasn't as hidden as she'd thought. Even though she'd dared to hope he loved her too, she couldn't expect a happy ending. His letter made it clear he was putting her aside to fulfill his responsibilities. She knew it would happen sooner or later.

And she understood, even though it broke her heart. Helena may have fallen in love with the man she married, but Jill could never hope to marry the man she'd fallen in love with.

"We have a great deal in common, you and I," Helena continued. "Whenever you need a friend, you can call on me. In fact, I'd like you to join me tomorrow afternoon for tea and light refreshments."

"I would be honored," Jill replied, more out of a desire for companionship than out of political correctness. The thought of having another woman her own age to talk to pushed aside the nagging loneliness that dominated her days. And nights.

Shortly after, Helena excused herself to go check on Ty. Staring at Helena's retreating figure, Jill wrestled with the question uppermost in her mind. Was love worth having, even if it was doomed to lose? She wrestled with it through the rest of the afternoon, returning to it again and again. By the time she returned to her suite at the palace she'd made a decision.

Love didn't come around more than once in a lifetime, and she wasn't going to give it up without a fight.

When Constantine returned to Royal Island, she would be waiting. And she would show him that love was worth whatever price they had to pay. She would seize the day and teach him to live in the moment, even if they were destined to part—he to a political match and she to a life of lonely memories.

Jill checked herself in the mirror one last time. The suits she'd brought from Chicago were too tight and revealing, too much like the old Jill, and they were totally inappropriate for an informal tea with the king and queen.

The new clothes didn't seem quite right either, but she'd finally decided on a bright yellow sleeveless dress with a matching jacket. She pulled her hair up in a tortoise shell and coral clip and waited. At exactly four o'clock, a page came to her door to escort her to the king and queen's private sitting rooms.

Jill forgot about her anxiety over the meeting as she followed the silent young man through the corridors. His pristine uniform and formal demeanor only accented his youth. Alia had told her that all students were required to work as part of the payment for their education at the Royal Academy.

Even citizens who didn't attend the university worked in public service jobs for several years of their career. The process, Alia explained, kept taxes lower and also gave the citizens a stake in their country and how it was run.

Observing the student workers on Royal Island, Jill wondered if there was a work-study program that would allow her sister to attend the Royal Academy. Although she hadn't admitted it when Constantine had accompanied Jill on her trip home, the Royal Academy had been one of Gracie's top picks because of its stellar reputation in marine biology. But even with Gracie's excellent grades, full scholarships were rare, and it looked like she'd have to settle for a state school.

Now Jill began to wonder. She wasn't asking for a free ride, but perhaps she could meet with the college administrators to discuss a work-study program. It may take Gracie a couple of extra years, but the experience would do her good. She'd always been a bookworm with little social life.

You're the popular, pretty one; Gracie's the smart one. Her stepmother hadn't meant the words to be unkind. That was simply how she looked at her children. *The smart one. The pretty one. The talented one. The dreamy one. The only son.* Simply statements of fact. What Jill lacked in intelligence, Gracie lacked in social skills. Work at the college might change that. Still, something made her hesitate.

"We're here, Miss Bradley." The page stepped aside and opened a door with a flourish. Jill hesitated, wondering if he would announce her, then took a step forward when he did not.

"Jill, welcome." Helena rose and came over to her. For a second, Jill had the impression Helena was going to embrace her, but instead, she simply put a hand on Jill's shoulder and motioned her toward a cluster of comfortable upholstered chairs and a settee arranged around a low table.

King Alexander Augustus Tyronne D'Malia rose from one of the chairs. Jill's breath caught. She would have recognized him from his portrait, but neither paint and canvas, nor photographic paper and light captured the man before her.

He was dressed simply in a pair of dark slacks and a tailored shirt, but he radiated a mixture of power, warmth, sex appeal, and — what had Helena called it? — the D'Malia charm.

Only one other man had ever affected her that way. And he was an obstinate, cold, arrogant…

"Alex, this is my friend Jill Bradley. Jill, may I present my husband, Alex?"

Jill finally caught her breath and moved forward, leaving thoughts of Constantine behind. "Your Majesty," she said, taking the hand he offered and wondering whether to curtsy.

"Welcome, Jill." He brushed her cheeks with brief kisses, European style, then grinned at her, easing her discomfort. "Please, call me Alex. I prefer to be informal when we're in private, especially among friends."

Jill glanced at the fine bone china, gleaming flatware, and sparkling Waterford crystal. "At home, when we're informal, we use paper plates and plastic cups," she blurted out. "Oh, my. I didn't mean to say that."

Alex cut her off with a hearty laugh. "I think I should like to visit your home and sample your version of informal. I envy my brother for spending time undercover these last weeks. He's told me how much he enjoyed meeting your family. Please, make yourself comfortable." He motioned toward the settee then settled back in his chair.

As they chatted and helped themselves to tea and sandwiches, Jill saw the weariness etched in his face. His charm had hidden it at first, but the effort must have cost him, for Helena carried much of the conversation, steering it toward innocent topics.

Finally, he spoke again. "You have done us a great service by helping to recover the Crown Jewels, Jill. Without the new king's signature on the gold of the crown, the ceremony would be unofficial."

"It's another of our legends and traditions that visitors find so appealing," Helena added.

"Yes. I am grateful that the delay in finding the jewels was not longer." Alex stared into his teacup for a moment, a frown marring his features. "I'm sure my brother has already told you my reasons for abdicating in his favor."

"He told me you were ill."

"Yes, and over the past years, I've learned that nothing is more important than my family." Alex looked at Helena, love lending a softness to his features. "I wish to spend my time and energy focusing on them."

"Family is important to me as well." Jill hesitated, thoughts of Gracie hovering close to the surface.

"I understand from Constantine that you have a rather large and interesting family. Tell me about them."

"I have three younger sisters and a younger brother." She gave him names and a brief description. "They're all brilliant. I think they must have gotten their intelligence from my stepmother, because, heaven knows, I don't have a fraction of their brain power."

"Constantine warned me you'd say that. Somehow, I don't think he agrees. But it doesn't matter. What is important is that you've done us all a great service by finding the missing jewels and agreeing to try to identify the thief. I should like to find a way to express our gratitude—mine and the entire country's—in a tangible fashion."

"I only did what anyone would do. After all, I was fencing stolen jewels. I'm pleased to be given a chance to repair the damage."

The king looked at her, studying her, gauging her intentions. Jill fisted her hands, resisting the urge to fidget under his gaze, fighting the temptation to touch the necklace that was once her good luck charm.

"There is a difference between fencing stolen jewels and being used as an unwitting courier," he said at last. "If I had any doubts as to which side of that line you fall on, your welcome on Melesia would have been very different. I assure you, I am not the fool some may take me for."

The blood drained from Jill's face in a sickening gush. She should have known. She'd seen the same transformation once before in Constantine. How easily Alex slipped from the role of friendly host to monarch. How insignificant Jill Bradley from Ohio must seem to him. "I never thought—"

"What Alex meant was that there have been people who sought to take advantage of him in the past. He has become quite good at discerning fact from fiction."

The king nodded. "Thank you, Helena. The one person whose judgment I have never doubted—besides my wife—is my brother Constantine. Having met you, Jill, I can say I agree completely with his assessment. Now, let us come back to the issue at hand. Is there anything I can do to properly thank you for what you've done on our behalf?"

Jill's mind and emotions started a dangerous tug-of-war. She hated to ask for anything, yet she was unwilling to let the opportunity pass.

"Surely there must be something I can offer you." Alex's calm voice interrupted her turmoil.

"I would like to ask you about the Royal Academy." She swallowed her pride and explained how she'd tried to provide for her siblings but was unable to give them the education they deserved. "If you would allow them to enter a work-study program to make up the difference between what I can pay and the cost of tuition, I'd be deeply grateful."

He was silent, again considering her with regal detachment and a gaze that seemed capable of reading minds. "I should very much like to offer your siblings full tuition without the need for any payment on your part."

"As generous as your offer is, I'm afraid I can't accept it. I'll pay for a portion of their tuition."

"You *cannot* accept my offer, or you *will not*, Jill?"

His quiet voice demanded attention, and Jill found herself at a loss to explain. Maybe it was her pride. Or maybe it was her need to redeem herself in her family's eyes. But even her guilt over her father's death didn't explain everything.

Over the years, she'd matured without even realizing it. Now, she truly wanted to contribute. She just didn't know how to explain it to the royal couple in front of her.

"Perhaps we can agree to discuss the specifics at a later date," he said, breaking the silence. "For now, be assured that your family, and you, are welcome to attend the Royal Academy under the conditions we will define. Is that acceptable, Jill?"

"Yes. Thank you." A rush of gratitude overwhelmed her, both for her siblings and for the way the king acknowledged and respected her pride.

"I'm glad that's settled." Helena rose and refilled their teacups. She added a splash of brandy to her husband's cup before turning to Jill. "Would you care for some brandy? Alex is partial to it, so my father sees we have a supply from his private collection. It gives me a headache, but you're welcome to try some."

Jill declined and accepted her fresh cup of tea.

"Now," Helena said, settling beside her husband, "let's talk about something more interesting. How did you and Constantine meet? He absolutely refused to give us details."

"Helena, don't pester Jill. She has a right to her privacy."

"Oh, hush, Alex. Even you said you were jealous because Constantine got to visit Chicago undercover. Admit it, you want to know details about his visit as much as I do." She turned to Jill. "In return, we'll tell you some childhood stories about the boys that didn't make the history books."

"My wife has turned into a romantic." Alex reached across the space between their chairs and clasped her hand. "Now she sees love everywhere. Even between you and my brother."

"I'm not, I mean, it's not like that," Jill stammered, not willing to examine or expose her feelings publicly.

"No?" For an instant Alex's gaze sharpened, searching again for the truth behind her words. Then he let it pass. "I'm sure you are correct. In any case, Helena won't be satisfied until she learns everything from day one, will you, *Ba'hona-mei*?"

My beloved one. My soul mate. My spouse. The endearment, similar to the one Constantine used for her, said so much more. And everything it spoke of was reflected in Alex's eyes as he looked at Helena.

"You needn't pretend I'm the only romantic in the room," Helena replied, the love in her eyes matching that in her husband's. "You've spent your share of years trying to convince Constantine there's more to life than duty."

The secret smile the two of them shared melted Jill's heart and sent a shaft of longing through her. Why did Constantine refuse to believe in love when he was surrounded by it? If only she could give her prince a happily ever after of his own. One that included her. One that made her his *Ba'hona-mei*.

A deep masculine chuckle and a female giggle drew her thoughts back to the couple across from her. Unbelievably, the warmth between them spread to encompass her as well, when they turned to include her in the teasing banter.

As easily as that, all remnants of formality disappeared and talk began to flow. Helena and Alex were as inquisitive as her own family would have been and as free with information. By the end of the afternoon, once again, she felt at home, and at ease, in Melesia.

"So, Your Highness, refresh my memory." Edmund settled into the couch across from Constantine in his private suite at the hotel. "Do I owe you a thousand U.S. dollars, or do you owe me?"

"What the devil are you talking about, Edmund?" Constantine took a gulp of his scotch and soda and willed himself to relax. A week of island-hopping, glad-handing, and generally paving the way for his new role had left him irritable.

Hearing his family gush over Jill while knowing she refused all the entertainment he'd arranged for her irritated him even more. At least with Edmund, he could forgo the politically correct façade and act as grumpy as he felt.

"Our bet. About the American woman. Or don't you remember? A thousand dollars that you couldn't tempt her into your bed without resorting to either title or money. I know she made it into your bed. What I don't know is what lured her there. Title? Money? Or your charming personality?"

"My relationship with Jill is off limits, Edmund."

"Ah. That leaves out the charming personality. Which, I might add, is more surly than charming, at the moment."

Constantine tossed back the rest of the drink and poured himself another. "You're like a dog with an old bone, my friend. Let it go."

"It's not like you to recant on a bet."

"She didn't know, damn it. Not until after. Are you satisfied now? You can keep your thousand dollars if you'll just drop this discussion." Constantine took a sip of his drink, kicked off his shoes and stretched out on the couch, grateful for the silence that followed his outburst.

It didn't last for long.

"I'd far rather pay you the thousand and continue to poke at this tender spot," Edmund observed in a deceptively lazy voice. "If you ask me, it sounds as if you have feelings for the girl."

"I didn't ask you."

"I'll tell you what I think. You're in over your head for the first time ever. You didn't need her to come to Melesia to ferret out a thief. You wanted her to come because you weren't ready to give her up."

"Ready or not, my people and responsibilities come first. I have to take a bride who will stop the feuding between the house of D'Malia and the house of Lyons."

Edmund snorted. "In case you've forgotten, the royal family already tried that tactic. It didn't work. The people of Melesia don't give a damn whether your bride comes from the house of Lyons, our most remote island, or the city of Chicago. Only a few mired-in-the-mud members of the court care one way or the other. That's an excuse. You're running from something. I want to know what."

So do I, Constantine thought. *So do I.* During the long week, he'd set a grueling pace, discussing politics with members of the Melesian nobility living outside of Royal Island, visiting local fairs, chatting with leaders of industry and private businesses. He'd traveled that route before, encouraging merchants to export perfumes, spices, sea salts, and island arts. His work had raised the standard of living in the country and added to the income they enjoyed from tourism.

Back then, the trip gave him satisfaction. Now, nothing seemed to satisfy him. Not the praise of the people, not the grudging acceptance of the nobles. Not the grand plans for the future. Nothing.

Worse, the pace didn't keep his mind off Jill. He'd assumed the need for her would disappear as soon as she was out of sight. But absence only intensified his cravings. He wanted to see delight in her eyes as she discovered his island home. He wanted to share her laughter. He wanted to taste her lips and feel her beneath him. And even more than that, he wanted to wake up next to her. Not just for a day, but every day.

Reality hit him with a force that ripped away his alcohol-induced relaxation. He dismissed Edmund with a curt good night then wandered into the bathroom and confronted his own weary image, knowing what he was running from and hating himself for it.

Of all the foolish things he'd ever done, this was the worst. He'd broken every promise he'd ever made to himself. He'd gone off and fallen in love. And there wasn't a damn thing he could do about it.

Chapter 20

Constantine signed the last of a stack of documents and passed it to his private secretary. The minute he and Jill had discovered the missing Crown Jewels, plans for his coronation had been set in motion and now, with his island tour out of the way, the pace was ramping up.

During the past week, the international press, with more discretion than he'd thought possible, covered the story, highlighting the country's long history and playing up its exotic image. Now, with the last of the papers signed, the details were official. In three days, the Coronation Eve Ball would kick off a week of events designed to bolster his country's pride and restore her confidence about the future.

Nothing was missing, no detail left to chance. Extra guards were assigned to cover the ball, the parade route, and all official functions. Security at the air and seaports was increased. No one would be able to enter or leave the country without royal permission during the ceremonies.

Discreet cameras for televising the events were already installed in the Grand Hall, the Royal Cathedral, and all along the parade routes. Arrangements had been made for the international dignitaries who would attend. Everything was perfect.

Everything except for the twisting in his gut when he thought of Jill. He no longer tried to deny that he loved her, but there was no point in letting her guess the truth. There was no future for them. For all her knowledge of history and languages, she didn't know how to be royal. That was something born and bred into a person, something…

Actually, it could be learned. His mother was a living example of how one could rise to royal status without being born to it. But could he ask Jill to give up her independence, her job, her close ties to family, all for him? Proposing was the equivalent of inviting her into his royal prison. Could he offer her enough to make up for all she'd sacrifice?

The attraction between them sizzled with ample fire to convince the public theirs was a love match. Hell, it was a love match, at least on his part. The more suitable bride candidates looked at him with an eye for pedigrees and price tags. Jill looked at him with longing, humor, and passion in her eyes.

And he was comfortable with her. Her laughter put him at ease. She was as American as, well, peanut butter and Coca-Cola. Which was another problem. His mother's mixed blood—half American, half Melesian—had been as much of an obstacle for her acceptance as her common birth, at least among the nobility. Some still viewed him as tainted by diluted bloodlines.

Now a quirk of genetics would turn him into a king. A smile touched his lips. Even those who questioned his legitimacy would come to heel, at least in appearance. After fighting for acceptance his whole life, it had been handed to him on a golden platter.

Edmund's words cut through the jumble in his mind. *The people don't give a damn whether your bride comes from the house of Lyons, our most remote island, or the city of Chicago.* Maybe he was right. Maybe Constantine had been craving acceptance from the wrong people all his life. He wished he could believe it.

A knock at the door pulled him back to the present. He frowned. His appointment book was empty for the rest of the day. "Come in," he called, leaning back in his chair.

Edmund sauntered into the room. "Your Highness, you have been working almost nonstop since your return to Melesia. I've checked your schedule and it is clear for the rest of the day. May I suggest you take a few hours to attend to other matters?"

"What matters?"

"Matters of hospitality, sir. You have an important visitor."

Diplomats were already arriving? Or was it a reporter? Either way, Edmund would not have interrupted if it wasn't important. "Fine, show him in."

Edmund nodded, then opened the door.

Constantine's jaw dropped. Jill walked in the room, dressed in a teal and royal blue sundress with a gauzy overskirt covering strips of material that swayed and shifted, alternately covering her and giving him tantalizing glimpses of bare thigh. She clutched her sunglasses in one hand.

"You promised me a tour of the island. I'm holding you to it."

Her voice was like fresh water on a hot day, cool and inviting, promising to quench the raging thirst inside him.

He tried to speak, but his parched throat wouldn't let the words come. His mouth didn't work. For that matter, neither did his brain. But his eyes were doing overtime, taking in the flip and sway of her skirt and the glimpse of long, lean legs with every step. Other parts of his body were working overtime too. He shifted uncomfortably in his chair.

"Jill, I would be happy to arrange a tour for you." The words came out in a dry, undignified croak.

"No. No arrangements." She leaned down and braced her palms on the desk. The neckline of her dress dipped low, revealing the golden, glowing, sun-kissed perfection of her skin.

She'd been winter pale when he'd left. He wondered exactly where her tan lines were, or if she'd lain naked on her balcony turning every inch of her skin to gold.

She moved slightly, and he glimpsed a swath of dark blue bandeau wrapped around her breasts. Dear heavens, he hoped it was a swimsuit and he hoped he got to see the other half of it. Soon. "I want *you*."

"What?" Another croak.

"I want *you*," she repeated. "I want to see your home through your eyes. You promised." She rose and perched on the edge of his desk, hiding the tantalizing view of her breasts, but exposing a delectable sliver of thigh once again. "Besides, you said yourself that we should be seen together. As a way to lure the thief out of hiding. I can't do that on my own."

"Miss Bradley is correct, Your Highness. You recall we did discuss the importance of luring the thief from hiding."

Damn Edmund. The man stood smirking behind Jill's back, reminding Constantine of the fragile house of cards he'd constructed when he lured Jill to the islands on the pretense of finding a thief. If the man wasn't his friend—and right-hand man—he'd fire him. Instead, he nodded abruptly.

"Thank you, Edmund. You and Miss Bradley are correct. She and I have business to attend to. If you will excuse us?"

Jill breathed a sigh of relief as Constantine took her hand and led her from the maze of offices buried deep within the private recesses of the palace. When she'd seen the dark circles under his eyes and the tightness around his mouth, a prickle of unease almost made her stumble. He looked like a man possessed, not like a man who could be swayed.

Nevertheless, she was determined to sway him. The haunted look hadn't been there when he was pretending to be Phillip Raymond. That man had smiled and teased. That man was someone who could hope for a happy future. Jill refused to believe Constantine had to choose between duty and happiness. One way or another she would show him he could have both. Even if she couldn't.

They stepped from the cool interior of the palace onto the flagstone lined portico leading to the public entrance. The enchanting vision of meandering garden paths, sunlit pools and cascading waterfalls took her breath away. No matter how many times she saw it, the beauty always touched her.

"So, what is it you'd like to see? Shall I take you to the beaches or would you prefer the gardens?"

"What is your favorite spot?"

"My favorite spot is right here with you." He squeezed her hand and sent her a bone melting smile. "I've been away from it for far too long."

"Is that true, or is it just the D'Malia charm talking?"

A warm breeze ruffled his hair and pressed the thin silk of his shirt against his body, showing her contours she longed to touch. His eyes, a deep, fathomless blue, fixed on her face. "It's true, Jill. I missed you. I was a fool to leave the way I did. More than that, I was a coward. I didn't want to deal with your reaction over my leaving."

"Exactly what reaction did you expect?" *Did you know I'd be heartbroken? Disappointed? Lonely?* Yet even as her mind challenged him, her heart recognized the naked, vulnerable honesty in his confession.

He hesitated. "I'm not sure." His eyes turned from serious blue to twinkling aqua. "Having experienced your throwing arm, I think I was a little afraid you might have a killer right hook."

The glint of humor belonged to the man she'd fallen in love with. Her heart squeezed tightly at the thought of how few days they had left together before he surrendered his life to duty and she went back to her cold, lonely home. Dwelling on it only wasted precious moments, she thought, shoving images of the future back into the recesses of her mind.

"So, if you were afraid of my right hook, what made you come with me today?"

"This." He pulled her to him and wrapped his arms around her waist then lowered his head to hers. Lip met with lip, his touch gentle and whisper-soft, but sparking an explosive rush of emotions.

The pleasure of his lips, the solid, comforting warmth of his body and the sizzle that shot through her veins blocked all rational thought. She poured her heart into the kiss, telling him without words that she would always love him, offering every ounce of her being to him with a sigh and an embrace.

His hand drifted to her hip, pressing her against him with an urgency that the gentle kiss belied. The hard length of him, the wedge of arousal, pressed against her softness, told her of desire, if not love. She wanted to rub herself against him, brand her soul and her body with his heat.

"Ah, Jill," he said, tearing his lips from hers and murmuring in her ear, "I've missed you. I was only half a man without you. Please say you forgive me."

"I'll always be here for you." *Ba'hono-mei. My love. My husband.* In her heart, he was *Ba'hono-mei,* even if he could never be so in reality. She held the important words inside, unwilling, or unable, to utter them.

"I wish I could believe that." His eyes darkened to a stormy hue, passion, and doubt clearly at war within him. "If I asked you to stay in Melesia, would you?"

"What exactly are you offering?"

"I don't know." Doubt won the war in his eyes. He eased his body away from hers and took her hand. "I only know that I am a better man with you, than without you. Come on, let me show you my home."

Jill nodded, her thoughts now as restless as the ocean surf pounding the shore in the distance. Was he offering her friendship? Lust? Love?

Whatever it was, she didn't dare hope he was offering her marriage. He'd been clear that his brother's marriage was arranged to "cement a political bond between the throne and a very influential old family." Now that his brother was abdicating, would the bond be broken? Would he feel it his duty to forge another one by his own marriage? Would he be required to do so to ease brewing political unrest?

Neither small town life in Ohio nor big city life in Chicago left her prepared for the only role he could offer her. That of mistress and behind-the-scenes consort to a king. As much as she loved him, such an arrangement would destroy her. Better to leave with her heart broken, than to stay and let her soul be destroyed.

Chapter 21

Constantine watched the play of the sunset on Jill's hair. Her dark tresses lit with warm gold and orange and burned with fiery red. Shoes in one hand, she walked barefoot in the surf, the wind molding her sundress to her every curve. Bless the wind—it didn't know which way to blow, so he was alternately treated to views of the lushness of her hips and the rounded perfection of her breasts.

Since the moment he'd stepped off the portico, leading her through the water gardens, he'd longed to pull her in his arms and explore those textures. He itched to see how much of her skin glowed golden from the sun, and how much of it was the pure alabaster he'd caressed in Chicago. To measure how much closer she was now to the light brown of his island heritage coloring. But they were never quite alone.

When she stopped by a pool containing a cluster of sting rays, she'd exclaimed over their graceful movements, watching, fascinated, as they swam in V formation, moving their fins like wings, flying through the water. He'd assured her they were gentle, and offered to let her feed them, but it was the student intern who fetched the food and showed her how to hold it steady as they sucked it delicately from her fingers.

The boy had simply been too enchanted with Jill to catch Constantine's subtle hints. Short of ordering the boy aside, he could only watch, jealous of both the young man who held Jill's attention and the bevy of rays that sucked at her fingertips, making her giggle with delight.

As they passed through each outdoor habitat, she'd stopped to greet the student workers. Without fail, boy or girl, the students lit up as she called each by name and asked about their studies. From each, he'd received a formal bow or curtsey accompanied by a polite nod and greeting. The smiles were reserved for her.

How, in such a short time had she managed to weave herself so deeply into the life of his subjects? *It doesn't matter to the people whether your bride comes from the house of Lyons, our most remote island, or the city of Chicago.* He was no longer sure whether it was Edmund's voice or his own that echoed that refrain nonstop in his brain. But judging from the workers' reactions, he was starting to believe it was true.

Yet when he'd asked her to stay with him, she'd evaded his question. A woman in love would have simply answered "yes," wouldn't she? Her body made its desire clear: she was soft and pliable in his arms. Her kisses held nothing back. But she hadn't answered his question. And he'd be damned if he'd force her, just to satisfy himself. If he was to be wed to an unwilling woman, it might as well be a political ally.

A shout of laughter drew his eyes back to Jill. "Come, join me," she called, dancing into water that surged past her knees. Like a legendary nymph, she tempted and teased him. A last ray of the setting sun caught the gem in her necklace and it flashed, bright as a beacon.

In that moment, he knew the truth.

She'd been sent to him.

She belonged to him.

She'd come from across the seas, wearing the royal talisman to mark her as bride to the monarch. His heart had responded. It didn't matter that she came by airplane not an arduous sea journey. It didn't matter that a thief, not an oracle or prophet had placed the insignia around her neck.

Fate decreed her to be his bride.

The people of Royal Island loved her, judging from the smiles she generated from everyone she passed. Alex and Helena loved her. Stephan loved her. Even little Ty loved her. It was a sign. All he had to do was convince her to love him. The rest—the pesky details of rank that set him apart from ordinary men—would fall into place.

Under the cover of twilight, Constantine threw protocol aside and allowed himself to be just a man. He kicked off his Italian leather shoes and waded into the ocean, not caring that his Armani pants would be soaked and ruined.

"What took you so long?" Jill asked when he joined her. "You looked so alone standing there on the beach."

"I was enjoying the view." He braced his legs wide apart and dug his heels into the sand. "A view which is about to get much better."

A wave crashed over them, higher and more forceful that the previous ones. He held her, kissing her senseless while the waves rolled. The tang of sea salt flavored her kisses, and the cool caress of the night sea left her shivering in the warm evening.

Or maybe it was his kisses. He nibbled a path down her neck then stepped arm's length away. Her dress, clinging and translucent from the dousing, revealed all the swells and hollows he longed to touch. "Very much better," he said.

Was it his imagination? Or did her nipples harden in response to his words? What his eyes couldn't see in the dusk, his fingers told him instead. His hand cupped the swell of her breast and his thumb teased the tip, a tip as hard as his imagination had hoped it would be.

Another wave crashed between them, cooling his skin, but flaming his desire. A desire that his wet clothing showed Jill just as clearly as her own attire showed him.

"I want you, Jill. Now." He scooped her in his arms and carried her to the beach, dropping to his knees in the wet sand. His body begged for release, ached to dive into her tight, wet embrace.

Instead, he took a moment to savor her strong, yet delicate beauty. She lay sprawled in the sand, eyes shining. His heart thumped painfully in his chest, suddenly as full and ready to burst as his body. She'd given so much, yet asked for nothing in return.

Unable to ignore the needs of his body any longer, he ground his hips against her, burying her deeper in the sand. The waves teased his feet and splashed against his buttocks like a thousand tiny fingers keeping him in a constant state of arousal. The wet, insistent driving matched his own need, the sea itself setting the cadence for their lovemaking. The urgent pounding of his heart joined the rhythm.

He rocked against her, and she moaned in response. The taste and feel of her wet body writhing beneath him intoxicated him. Each kiss was a sip of something heady and rich.

"Jill, let me make love to you. Here. Now."

She twined her arms around his neck and pulled him close for another lusty kiss. Words were meaningless.

He almost didn't hear the approaching people. But something, some well-honed sense, responded. He jerked to his feet and pulled Jill up after him. In moments, the voices he heard would turn into reporters, close enough to see them.

He motioned for Jill to remain silent and pulled her into a palm grove a stone's throw from the water's edge. With his back pressed to the smooth, ridged bark and Jill cradled in his arms, he strained to hear the voices.

At last he let out a sigh. "It's just standard media coverage of the island. They're gearing up for coverage of the coronation and all the associated festivities. I didn't expect them to be interested in the ocean view after dark."

"They'll be in for a surprise if they trip over our shoes."

He could hear the humor in her voice, even if he couldn't see her smile in the dark. "They'll be in for an even bigger surprise if we go back for them. Come on. I know a secret way to our rooms that will help us avoid being caught by the paparazzi."

He gave her a last, quick kiss, then tugged her hand and led her through the palm grove. Hidden near the inland edge of the grove was a thatched island shack that disguised a modern, state-of-the-art lab used for preparing and testing the water of the marine habitats.

The bubbling of aerators in the exotic fish tanks nearly covered the sound of Jill's soft gasp. She took in the surroundings, eyes round with interest. "Gracie would love to see this. It's a marine biologist's dream come true."

Guilt stabbed him when he remembered her sister. "Jill, I know you've been saving up to help with her education." Her forehead puckered in a frown, and he hurried on before she could remember that he'd had her investigated because he feared she was a thief. "I wanted to tell you that your sister, and any of your siblings are welcome to attend the Royal Academy, free of charge. I owe you that."

She stiffened and tugged her hand from his, her face pale in the artificial lab light. "Payment is not necessary, Your Highness."

"I'm pleased to hear it, Miss Bradley." He infused his voice with the same Arctic chill she'd used. "Because I wasn't offering payment. I was offering gratitude and thanks. I had hoped you would accept my gesture with good grace."

She whirled away and paced the short distance to a sterile white and chrome lab bench, her back stiff, her shoulders squared. When she turned to him again her face was blank, emotionless. "I don't need gratitude or thanks. And I don't need gifts that come with strings attached."

Her stiffness crumpled as soon as she spoke the words. In the silence, Constantine looked at her. Her rumpled, damp dress and swollen lips testified to their recent activities. Her cheeks flamed red as she studied her bare feet.

Damn. He was an idiot. He'd prided himself in his knowledge of women, but Jill threw everything he ever believed about himself into chaos. He raked a hand through his salt-encrusted hair. "I'm sorry."

She looked up, the vulnerability clear in her eyes.

"I'm not sorry about what we did on the beach," he continued. "I'm not sorry about kissing you or wanting you. I'm not even sorry about wanting to help your family. But I am sorry I was such a jerk these last weeks. And I'm sorry that I made my offer sound like a payment for… Well, for anything. I just wanted to do something that would make you smile."

She did smile, a wavering, almost invisible hint of a smile, but it was something. "It's been a long time since someone offered me a gift from the heart. I don't quite know how to accept it. I guess I'm a little out of practice."

"I'd like to change that." He'd given gifts to women before, but he'd never craved their acceptance so desperately. Maybe that's what love did to a person. It twisted him inside out and tied him in knots so that every word, every gesture, was a thousand times more important than it had ever been. Everything else—his duty, his family, his country—paled in comparison to the needs and emotions of this one woman.

And what she needed now was assurance that he wanted more than just her body. He longed to get down on one knee and beg her to marry him, but he couldn't. Not yet.

There were protocols to follow; he needed the blessing of the church, and the Monarchy. He needed the blessing of his brother. And though he could throw protocol to the wind as soon as he gained the crown, his sense of family and tradition wouldn't let him.

More than that, Jill's eventual acceptance by the people could depend on his adherence to customs. He couldn't jeopardize her future happiness just to meet his present needs. He would do this thing the right way. For both of their sakes.

He opened a door in the far wall. The cool air of the stone-lined underground service passageways seeped through the barred entrance. He pressed his code into the security keypad that unlocked the secret passages. The rarely used path would take them safely to the royal wing without alerting prying eyes.

"Come," he said, the words thick in his throat as he held his hand out to her. "Let me show you back to your rooms."

Chapter 22

*J*ill stared at the display before her, pretending interest in the array of gowns, shoes, jewelry and other items scattered through the palace rotunda that housed the queen's private shopping gallery. But her mind was on the cool stone labyrinth Constantine had led her through last night.

She shivered at the thought of the empty, unguarded passageways hidden throughout the palace. Passageways protected only by a key code that she'd watched Constantine punch in at half a dozen check points.

"Jill?" Helena's voice interrupted her aimless musings. "I thought you would enjoy shopping, but if you're tired, we can look for your ball gown tomorrow. The designers can make a gown so quickly it almost seems like magic."

"What? I hadn't planned on…"

"Nonsense. I expect you to attend the Coronation Eve Ball. Alex expects you to as well. And I'm certain Constantine expects you to be there." She paused, fingering a swatch of material and considering a gown draped on a mannequin. "This design is perfect for you. The neckline is low enough to be sexy, but tasteful, and the plunging back and side slit add a bit of daring to it."

Jill reluctantly let Helena position her beside the mannequin. A pair of shop owners brought a full-length mirror over and immediately began swathing Jill in fabric samples and bits of trim, looking to Helena and Jill for approval on each color and fabric.

She turned stiffly, letting them pose her like a plastic fashion doll, suddenly no more in control of her body than she was of her emotions. She felt out of place, more than a friend to Constantine, yet less than what she yearned to be. Jill Bradley didn't belong in a palace, or with a prince.

"I think the red satin provides the most dramatic effect. It looks beautiful with your skin and hair. Some beading and crystal accents will add just the right amount of sparkle. What do you think?"

Jill nodded, her mind more on her own chaotic thoughts than on Helena's thoughts about the gown. "Yes, it's lovely."

"What's the matter, Jill? Don't you want to go?"

"I...I don't know. Can we sit and talk for a minute? Please?" She longed to talk about something other than the ball. Besides, whenever she wasn't thinking about Constantine, she'd been buried in her research, trying to understand who would steal the Melesian Crown Jewels.

She'd learned from the security team that the remaining jewels were found meticulously wrapped and locked in the vault of a Melesian expatriate. No damage had been done. The expatriate had fled.

Something wasn't right, and it nagged at her. Last night, during a series of restless dreams, she'd been close to discovering an answer. But each time, she'd awoken, bathed in cold sweat, heart pounding with only the memory of being chased through the dark, secret passageways of the palace in her head. Passageways Constantine had led her safely through. What should have been safe turned into a dark menace at the hands of her subconscious.

"Helena," she said in a soft voice when the shopkeeper had drifted away, "I probably should have mentioned this earlier, but I think I have something that may belong to you."

They moved to a small table beside the central fountain and Helena called for cakes and tea. Once they were out of earshot of the knot of shop proprietors, she spoke carefully. "I don't understand. What could you have that belongs to me?"

Jill pulled the de Lyons signet ring out of her bag and handed it to Helena. "I found this in one of the small pieces of pottery I'd donated to my school. Constantine told me it was your family crest. He suggested I be the one to give it back to you."

Helena took the ring, her face composed, but puzzled. "I don't know what to say, Jill. It isn't quite appropriate to thank you."

Her heart sank as the smuggled ring cast a shadow between herself and the woman she'd begun to think of as a friend. She watched Helena twist the ring, examining it from every angle, wondering what to say.

"That is, I do thank you. For your thoughts, at least. This ring bears my family crest, but it isn't mine. I never owned a de Lyons signet ring." She looked at Jill, hurt and something else shimmering in her eyes as she hesitantly slipped the ring onto her finger. "To be honest, I don't particularly want to have it. But I'll send it to my father and let him see that it ends up where it belongs."

A server came with their tea. Jill poured, staring silently into her cup until the server was gone. "Helena, may I ask you a question?"

"Of course."

"You once said that the king wanted to right a perceived wrong with your marriage and that your father wanted you to be his political champion. Forgive my boldness, but what did you mean?"

Helena took a sip of tea and settled back in her chair. After a thoughtful silence, she answered in her soft, cultured voice. "Our history is riddled with feuds between the ruling family and those who dispute their claims to the throne.

"Like most countries, the struggle was bloody and brutal during ancient times. It has mellowed over the centuries, but feuds still exist between some members of the aristocracy. It is a little like your Democrats and Republicans or your Hatfields and McCoys."

"Or the D'Malias and the House of Lyons?" At the queen's startled look, she clarified. "I've been studying your newspaper archives since I arrived in Melesia."

Helena nodded. "Constantine told me you were clever. I'm surprised, then, that you don't know more about my father, Julian, Duke de Lyons. He has a reputation for being a recluse, but he fancies himself a kind of 'king maker.'

"He had long-cherished ambitions for the throne and hoped, through my union with the D'Malia family, to see a king of his bloodline sitting on the throne one day. With my marriage, he also hoped to elevate his level of influence within the government."

"And the former king? What of his wishes for your marriage?"

"He was influenced by my father. You see, when Alex's mother died, my aunt, Ophelia de Lyons, was next in line to be the king's bride."

"But that's barbaric." Jill lowered her voice as soon as she became aware of the stares her outburst sent their way. "Do you mean that the king has a waiting list of potential brides? Like the top applicants for a job?"

"It is exactly like that. At least, it was in the past. An ancient tradition dictated who was acceptable for the monarch's bride."

"But Constantine's mother was a commoner. Did the king break with tradition?"

"Not entirely. You see, in ancient times, the primary reason for arranging marriages was to forge peace and maintain ready allies. More recently, the concept of keeping the bloodlines pure was ingrained in the royal consciousness. King Tyronne Phillippe I believed he'd done his duty by marrying appropriately and producing an heir, Alex. He didn't feel the need to abide by the tradition for his second marriage."

"And now Constantine will reign instead of Alex. No wonder he feels pressure."

"Constantine has always struggled to do what he believes is right. To be fair, most people are not opposed to his ascension to the throne. A few, like my father, disapprove."

"And you?"

Helena's face tightened, her smile fading and a hint of anger creeping into her voice. "My father sees me as a political asset. There was never much fondness between us. There has been even less since my marriage. He lives in another century. It is all the nonsense about bloodline purity that bred weakness into Alex and his father.

"Alex's mother died of the same diseases and weaknesses he now suffers. Perhaps, if King Tyronne had made a love match the first time around, my husband would be as strong as his brother. And my son might not be in danger of suffering his father's fate."

"I'm sorry," Jill said, covering Helena's hand with her own. She didn't understand a world where children and parents weren't close. Fondness didn't even come close to describing the feelings she had for her parents, even her stepmother. The frozen look in Helena's eyes was as foreign to her as this island nation. "When I lost my father, it was sudden. I can't imagine the pain of seeing someone you love struggle with a slow, crippling illness."

"Actually, it is a great comfort to me that Alex is retiring to private life. It gives us a chance to be a family for as long as possible. I only hope Constantine doesn't let his sense of duty destroy his happiness. He should be rewarded for his sacrifice on our behalf, not strangled by ancient traditions."

She sent Jill a keen, searching look, nearly as perceptive as those of her husband. "Constantine's always been a rock to the family, but he can also be as unfeeling as marble. Since he met you, he's changed. He acts human for the first time ever. He's been alive, emotional, fierce, and passionate since returning from Chicago. He needs a woman like you at his side. Someone he loves and trusts, not someone from an impersonal bride list. Think about that."

After a moment of silence, Helena continued in a more playful tone. "Come, Jill. Let us find you a gown that will turn his head at the ball."

Even if what Helena said were true, it didn't mean she and Constantine had a life they could share. Not anymore. He'd accomplished what he needed to do in the United States. She'd helped him as she promised. Soon their association would be over.

Jill clamped her mouth shut on a response and followed Helena. Why ruin her friend's illusion that the ball would be the beginning of a wonderful romance, even though Jill knew it would be the end of her personal fairy tale.

Chapter 23

Constantine rose and walked to the sideboard to pour a glass of brandy for himself and his brother. It wouldn't do to stretch and fidget in front of the bevy of reporters crowding the private salon for an in-depth interview. The short walk restored his composure.

He pressed the drink into Alex's hands, noting the tightness around his brother's eyes and mouth, seeing the carefully concealed hints of exhaustion. The sooner the interview was over, the sooner he could rest. Constantine offered refreshment to the press then suggested that they prepare their final questions.

After a few more polite questions about the transition of the government and the king's health, a young woman in the back stood and identified herself as a reporter for a popular entertainment magazine. "Prince Constantine, you've enjoyed a reputation as a very eligible and amorous bachelor. How will your ascension to the throne change that? And should we expect to hear wedding bells anytime soon?"

He smiled at her and watched the microphone she held waver a bit. "I suppose I shall have to pass the title of Playboy Prince on to one of my younger brothers. Since Dimitri is barely fifteen, the honor will likely fall to Stephan. I can only hope he's prepared for the burden. As for wedding bells, I promise, you will be among the first to know. After the prospective bride, of course."

Laughter followed his comment, as he intended, and he used the disturbance to distract the rest of the reporters, thanking them for their attendance and dismissing them.

When the room was empty and silent, Alex sagged in his chair. "That went reasonably well. Although passing your playboy title on to Stephan is laughable."

"The press will have a hard time harassing him. There's not much tabloid-worthy news about a man who locks himself in a library."

"Don't forget his role as ambassador. He does travel quite frequently. He's also raised our reputation when it comes to our natural resources. The press will find something to interest them."

"Alex, the man has a traveling library. Even on diplomatic missions, he's squeaky clean. When he's home, he spends all his time on that yacht. Alone. The only girl he's likely to fall for is either a walking encyclopedia or a mermaid with fins and a tail."

"A Melesian mermaid might give us another boost in tourism," Alex mused. "Seriously, Stephan has been stepping up to take over a lot of support duties since we started planning my abdication. He'll be an asset to you."

"I know." Constantine gathered the glasses and returned them to the side table, running over the details of the next days in his mind. "All jokes aside, I trust his instincts on many things. He's a valuable advisor."

"Which leads me to my next point. You have a bastion of advisors. Don't ever think you have to do everything yourself. The public expects more than simply a competent ruler. They expect an icon." Alex paused, favoring Constantine with one of his eerily perceptive looks. "*Have* you thought of a wedding?" he asked quietly.

"I know my duty," Constantine replied, "but we should discuss this another time. Between the meeting with the Prime Minister and cabinet this morning, and this afternoon's press conference, it's been a full day. You should rest before tonight's reception with the Heads of State."

Alex rose, took a slow step toward the private corridor leading to his bedroom, then turned back. His eyes were clear and steely. "I must say one thing before I rest. Marriage is the most important decision you will ever make. I followed the proscribed paths, did the right thing, and got lucky. You needn't be bound by the same rules I followed. Your coronation will be the beginning of a new era.

"Being king is difficult. Having the right woman by your side makes all the difference. Consider which traditions are worth keeping and choose wisely, as both man and king."

His brother's cryptic words remained with him, long after Alex left. Whether he was advising Constantine to choose a bride for love, or for political necessity, Constantine wasn't sure. He still intended to marry Jill, but for the sake of family, peace and tradition, he hoped Alex would bless the marriage. The blessing of the church and the monarchy would cushion the break from the tradition of arranged marriages and help Jill be accepted by the people.

Throughout the rest of the afternoon, his thoughts returned again and again to her. He wouldn't tell her of his intentions until after he'd received Alex's official permission and blessing. Somewhere, after the coronation, during the many celebrations which followed it, he'd find a quiet spot and propose as soon as all was in place.

In the meantime, he dispatched Edmund to the vaults that housed the remaining family jewels. Buried there was a diamond and ruby ring, its ancient stones alive with the same vibrancy she'd brought to his life. When the time was right, he'd present it to her as an engagement ring.

Hours later, he was still thinking of her. The formal evening reception dragged on, Constantine, Alex, and Helena circulating among dignitaries from countries around the world, exchanging pleasantries and building the relationships that would serve him in the future.

Jill should be here. With her gift for diplomacy and languages, she would shine in this setting. It was another reason why she was the right choice for his queen.

But she wasn't here, and without her, every minute was a lifetime. At last, a suitable amount of time after Alex and Helena retired for the night, he said his good nights and slipped away.

Minutes later he knocked softly at Jill's door. She opened it and let out a breathy, startled sigh. He leaned against the door frame and smiled, slowly tracing the creamy lace that edged the deep V of her ivory satin nightgown and wrapper with his eyes. "I'm a poor refugee, recently escaped from an intolerably dry and boring state dinner. Will you rescue me and give me shelter?"

She stepped back allowing him into the suite. "You look handsome tonight." Her voice held a tinge of awe as she raked her gaze over his formal white shirt and black tails.

"So is that a yes?"

"*Aaya*, yes. You can hide in my suite for as long as you like. I'll give you whatever you need."

"I need *you*." He reached out and cupped a hand around her neck. The warm skin beneath his palm and the silky brush of her hair against his knuckles was familiar yet enticing. He stepped into the inviting curves of her body, feeling the rasp of his starched cotton against her satin smoothness.

His gaze was locked on hers as she tilted her head to keep him in view. Her brown eyes were like the deep pools nestled in ancient volcanic craters, full of mystery, likely to bubble over with passion, and irresistible. He was drowning in those pools;

his only hope for survival was to steal the breath from her parted lips.

He kissed her, intending to be gentle, but the soft brush of her lips tore his barriers asunder. He needed her. Like a starving, parched refugee offered food and drink, he feasted on her lips without restraint. Her arms snaked up beneath his formal tails and pressed against his back, urging him closer, giving him permission, answering with her own passion. He shrugged his free arm out of his jacket, his other hand never leaving her nape.

She tugged his shirt free and tunneled under it. The small, warm, insistent pressure of her hands made him feel nurtured, wanted and safe. In moments, he'd be under her power and unable to speak, or think clearly. He pulled away while he still could. His jacket, free at last when he released her nape, slithered to the floor.

"Jill, before this goes further we have to talk. If I wait, I'm not sure I'll be able to say what I need to. Worse, if I wait, you might not believe me."

Her hands toyed with the belt of her robe and her face paled. Damn his ponderous, diplomatic need to ramble, tonight of all nights. He wouldn't have many stolen moments with her until after the coronation. He needed to tell her tonight. How hard could it be to just say it?

He framed her face with his hands and tilted it up. She seemed fragile, her smooth golden skin surrounded by his large, sun-darkened hands. "Don't look so distressed, *Ba'hona-mei*, I only meant to say I..." He took a deep breath and was surprised to find he was quivering inside, more rattled and discomposed than he'd ever been.

Emotionally naked and completely subjugated to the whim of this one unpredictable, courageous, beautiful woman. He forced the words out in a rush before he lost his courage again.

"I love you, Jill. I have for a long time. I was just too much of a fool to admit it. I want you in my life, somehow, someway, and I'll take whatever you're willing to give me." He trailed one hand down her neck till it rested on her collarbone, his thumb on the necklace. The temptation to ask her to marry him now, before another minute passed, was strong.

He'd called her *Ba'hona-mei*, my beloved, my spouse, and he meant it. But he wondered if her knowledge of the language picked up on the subtle difference between *Ba'hona-mei*, a soul mate and *Er'hona-mei*, a desirable one.

The desires of his heart wrestled with the duty of a lifetime. In the end, he held his tongue for her sake. She would be more easily accepted if she became his bride with the weight of tradition behind her, not in opposition to her. It could wait for a few more hours.

"I love you too," she said into the silence. "I'm not naïve, *Ba'hono-mei*. I know you aren't a free man. You have duties and responsibilities."

So she did know the difference, even to the detail of choosing the appropriate gender for her words. She was everything that he'd ever hoped for, and more. *Ba'hona-mei* and *Ba'hono-mei*. They belonged together.

"Thank you." He crushed her to his chest, smothering whatever else she intended to say. "Thank you for not asking me to throw tradition to the wind. I would, if you asked, but it's better this way."

"You would be torn apart." She tipped her face up to him. Her eyes glistened, like a misty island morning. "You wouldn't be the man I loved if you could give up on your family and your responsibilities so easily."

"Then let's make the most of tonight. Tomorrow, the madness begins, and it will be a long time before I can have you alone in my arms again."

He captured her mouth, seeking the solace that had been denied him for days. At the nudging of his tongue, she opened to him, accepting his exploration and initiating one of her own. She rubbed against his groin and suddenly his formal trousers felt too tight, too confining. Even his skin felt too tight and confining.

Jill worked her fingers between their closely pressed bodies and popped the studs on his shirt front. The warm touch of her palm on his bare skin both soothed and aroused, like a fiery corner of heaven. She skimmed her hands over his torso, parting his shirt.

The ping of a dozen tiny studs against the stone floor roared in his ears as she eased a fraction of an inch away. But the pounding of his blood was louder still. She teased his nipples with a small, wicked hand, tweaking them and scoring him with her nails.

He shrugged out of his shirt and reached for the tie of her robe, but she backed away. He followed, but then, what choice did he have? With each dancing step away from him, she teased, reaching for the buttons on his trousers. Like a clever hunter luring him into ambush, she led him to her bed.

Like a clever man, he let her. A breeze from the curtained windows fluttered into the room, ruffling the thin satin of her night clothes and clearly outlining the peaked tip of a nipple pressing against the cloth.

She wasn't as unaffected as she'd been pretending. He brushed his fingers over the peak and drank in the harsh breath and moan that was her response.

He pushed the satin and lace of the gown aside and cupped the golden flesh. The nipple strained, a dark coral temptation. He took her in his mouth, his lips surrounding the puckered pink mound. Against his seeking tongue, her nipple rasped, hard and cool, setting loose sparks of desire within him.

Jill's fingers were at work, too, unfastening his trousers and pushing them away. He reluctantly released her nipple as she sank to her knees, stripping him. He kicked off his shoes and socks and stepped out of his trousers to stand naked before her.

Instead of standing herself, she cupped his buttocks and dropped light, teasing kisses on his thighs. He tensed at the scrape of her nails, pleasure coursing through his body. Each kiss brought another shudder of anticipation. There was no denying her effect on him, it was hardening and quivering before her eyes, reacting to each touch of her lips with a pulse, begging her to come closer.

She eased his torture with a long, slow lick. He tensed at the warm wetness, but the pleasure was over quickly, leaving him cooling in the breeze, longing for more of her heat.

Another lick, another tease. Then, she took him in her mouth, and the warm, slippery pleasure surrounded him.

He groaned. His hands fisted in her hair as each sucking stroke robbed him of more willpower.

"Jill. Stop."

When she refused to listen, he dragged her to her feet and pressed his throbbing shaft into the satin cradle of her thighs. "I want more."

He crushed his mouth to hers, savoring the salty taste of passion on her tongue. His itching palms found the curve of her backside and fitted themselves around it. He raked his nails across her, the same teasing motion she'd used on him. She sagged against him, as if her knees no longer held her steady.

When he released her, she leaned against the high bed, clutching its down-filled mattress for support. "I'm curious," he said, brushing his hands over her breasts with their straining nipples and moving until he reached the tie at her waist. He flicked it open with practiced fingers and gathered a fistful of the flimsy material.

"About what?"

"You were pale when we arrived. Now you're golden. Exactly where are your tan lines?" Without giving her a chance to answer, he swept the gown and wrapper over her head, baring her in a flash. A shiver of gooseflesh covered her, and he stepped in to warm her with his own body.

Constantine kissed her ear lobe, nibbling it until she moaned. "I'm going to start here, and not stop until I find those tan lines." The skin on her neck was golden, her shoulder, the curve of her breast, likewise. In the wavering light of her bedside lamp, he found a faint outline of white, a strip barely covering those tempting nipples.

He traced it with his tongue, indulging in a lick across her tight peak. "I'm glad to see you left something to the imagination. Although, not much." The valley between her breasts was as golden as their slopes.

"I was very care—Oh."

He chuckled at her reaction as his searching fingers slid along her intimate flesh. He nestled his hand deeper in the warm curls at her thighs. A second, slick stroke across her swollen, moist cleft brought another exclamation. More passionate and less surprised.

"So," he continued, striving for a dispassionate tone, even though he knew she could hear the falseness of it, "you shamelessly bare your breasts to the sun."

"I was in a private—Oh."

"No excuses," he chided, laughter slipping out with the words. He rubbed his fingers along her slick path while she writhed against the bed where she was propped, struggling to stay upright. "Understand?"

Her incoherent, panting response, was all he'd hoped for. He kissed his way from her rib cage to her stomach, dipping into her belly button and delighting in each tense contraction he produced.

His search yielded only the thinnest possible line of white shielding her private assets from the sun. Jealousy ripped through him, white-hot and sharp.

What if she'd been seen? He guessed she'd used the private beaches and balconies for her advanced tanning, but still someone with a high zoom lens could see. And he was determined that he'd be the only one, ever, to see those tan lines again. There would be great stretches of white from her breasts to her thighs if he had the choice.

But he didn't have the choice or the right. Not yet. Maybe never in this day and age. But the urge to mark her, to make her his own, was too primitive to ignore.

He grasped her about the waist and lifted her to the platform bed then pushed her thighs apart. At last he saw the pale smoothness he craved. Nestled among the dark curls was a glistening pink invitation.

He buried his head in the musky moistness and flicked his tongue along the cleft his fingers previously caressed. The slick, sweet wetness was like honey in his mouth. A river of honey with a tiny succulent treasure buried within. He teased the hard tip, delighting in the feel of it. Like her nipple, it rasped and probed along his tongue, a magic spot with a taste all its own.

Beyond the pleasure of his own exploration, he felt Jill, her thighs clamping against his hands, her body bucking. With one last lick, he reluctantly eased away, teasing her lightly with his fingers. A sheen of sweat covered her body. Her face flushed deep pink, and her breath came in gasps. He stroked her gently, watching as the eruption of passion cooled to a simmer.

His own need, simmering until now, seemed to take the heat from her and demand release. He climbed onto the bed, tumbling beside her in the feathered nest. "Jill, you are beautiful, inside and out. You are everything—Oh."

Her fingers clamped around him, rubbing his hardness, sending a tingling jolt from his groin to the tips of his toes.

"No more talking," she said, mocking his stern tone. Her palm slid along him once more until her thumb teased his aching, moist tip. "Understand?"

Mutely, he nodded and buried his face in the hollow where her shoulder joined her neck. He nuzzled the soft spot, and she twisted beneath him, her grip tightening until it was too much. Gently, he twined his fingers around hers and pulled them away.

She opened her thighs in invitation, and he eased into her wet heat. For the first time, he touched her without barriers. Nothing would keep him from claiming her now. Both as lover and as bride.

It was both torture and pleasure. Though her hands on his backside urged him to hurry, he sank in slowly, savoring each tight inch as it milked him with a sizzling slickness. By the time he was buried within her, he was covered in a sheen of sweat himself. He eased out again, slowly, the tingle and pulse of anticipation almost too much. He couldn't help it. The rhythm picked up, the friction built, the slow pleasure became a frenzied race.

Jill dug her fingers into his back, urging him on. When she cupped him and squeezed his most tender flesh, he knew he had only seconds more.

He bit her nipple.

Forced a finger between them to caress her intimately.

Then he cried out, unable to stop the explosion. Light splintered before his eyes, lightning shot from his groin to every extremity in his body, the tingle singeing his fingers, his toes, and the roots of his hair.

Jill cried out too. The tremors of her body caressed him, teased him, and drew from his body and soul an explosion of tenderness unlike anything he'd ever experienced with a woman. He gathered her in his arms. "I love you," he whispered into her hair. "I love you more than words can express."

"I love you too." Her words were thick and choked with passion.

As he slid into sleep, cuddled against the woman he loved, an unfamiliar prickle behind his eyes threatened to spill over. He'd heard women talk of tears of happiness; he'd just never expected to feel happy enough, and vulnerable enough to experience it. He closed his eyes against the unmanly impulse and contented himself with the warm trickle of happy tears that Jill cried for them both.

Chapter 24

*J*ill wandered from her bath into the sitting room and curled up on the couch, hugging a pillow. The magic of last night wove around her in a bittersweet cloud of memory. Constantine, devastatingly handsome in his formal wear, stole her breath. But he'd also broken her heart. In plain clothes he'd been attractive. In Armani, he'd appeared merely rich, but last night he'd been breathtaking. Regal. Far above what she'd been accustomed to. More like the prince he was.

Every fiber in her being ached with love for him. She treasured the words of love and the unconscious endearments he'd murmured to her, hugging them to her heart the way she hugged the pillow to her chest. He'd promised to throw away tradition if she asked. To throw away his bride list and choose her. She didn't doubt the sincerity of his tone, but she couldn't ask him to give up his duty to his family, any more than she was prepared to sacrifice her own.

And even though it was right, it had hurt when he breathed a sigh of relief and thanked her for allowing him to follow tradition. *It's better this way.* His words echoed in her mind, firm and resolute. She wished he'd been at least a little unwilling or unhappy to utter them. Instead he'd seemed relieved.

Would he really be satisfied with her as a girlfriend or a mistress until he chose a bride? Would she? Would she be able to leave him when the time came? The questions attacked her too quickly, demanding an answer where there was only a mass of unfulfilled desires and tarnished dreams.

If she thought about it any longer, she'd go mad. Worse, she'd give in to the tears that threatened. Before him, she'd never cried. Not once after her father's funeral. She'd locked away both her tears and her passions. Until she'd met him.

Now she fought tears on a daily basis. If this was love, it was a messy, painful affair. She wished she could just not love him. Too bad she didn't have a choice. She could only choose how long she would stay with him before she left. A broken heart delayed was a heart still broken.

She stood and paced the room, determined to wipe her mind clear of morbid thoughts. She didn't want a look of misery on her face to be the last thing he saw. Last night's tears had been bad enough. Thank goodness he'd fallen asleep before they came.

Tonight, she'd smile and give him a good memory to keep after she left. Tomorrow, in the bustle and confusion of the coronation, she'd slip away and learn to live without him.

A knock at the door drew her from her musings. Alia answered it and brought her a heavy book and a note, sealed with the royal crest. Her stomach knotted at the memory of the last note she'd received with the royal seal. She dismissed Alia and sat, her legs too wobbly to stand. She broke the seal.

My Dear Jill,

You asked me once about my father. I fear you will meet him tonight at the ball. He is not kindly disposed to those whose bloodlines he considers inferior. His disapproval is usually veiled, however, in light of topics that Constantine and Alex discussed this morning, he may give you a rather poor welcome. Please do not allow him to distress you. A recent state photo is in this book. It may help you to avoid him.

Rest assured that you are most welcome by those who matter.
Sincerely,
Helena

Jill opened the book, steeled against the sneering face she expected to find there. Instead she saw the smile of her one-time mentor, Mr. Dimas. The thief. And possibly a murderer.

Without effort all the pieces fell together in her mind. The questions she'd pondered since her arrival all made perfect sense, now. Constantine had told her that the monarch's signature on the gold of the crown was an essential part of the coronation process. It was a private ceremony with the Melesian aristocracy as witnesses. Without the crown, no transfer of power had ever taken place.

Bloodlines. Julian, Duke de Lyons, head of the family who rivaled the D'Malias for the throne, was concerned about bloodlines. He'd settled the feud, a generation later than he'd hoped, by marrying his daughter to the crown prince. At his death, Ty, a product of both D'Malia and de Lyons blood would rule.

Disease and abdication robbed him of that long-cherished goal. King Alexander's decision to abdicate on behalf of himself and his son assured that an heir of de Lyons blood would never rule the kingdom. And Constantine was an essential part of that plan. So de Lyons had tried to prevent the abdication by stealing the Crown Jewels and thereby invalidating Constantine's upcoming coronation.

How many years would he need to delay Alex's abdication before Ty could ascend to the throne? What was the age the child prince was no longer covered by the decisions and actions of his parents? She couldn't remember what Constantine had told her. And nothing in her research had outlined the details governing all the possible lines of succession.

But they'd effectively overcome that obstacle when they returned the Crown Jewels. Yet Jill was sure Julian de Lyons would have a backup plan. How else could he prevent the abdications? She forced herself to breathe deeply and think rationally.

What if Alex were to die before he announced his formal abdication? Would Ty then automatically inherit the throne?

Would the Duke stoop to poisoning Alex? Or worse? With only hours to go before the formal abdication announcement and security at an all-time high, she doubted de Lyons would find success with that plan.

What next? He could try to injure Constantine, but again, security for the event made that a remote possibility.

What if Constantine was simply judged unfit or unable to rule the country? Had a complaint even now been lodged against him? Could it delay the coronation? Invalidate it? Who decided these things?

She shook her head. Everything Constantine had done in the past weeks—during his whole life for that matter—proved his dedication to his country. Surely, they couldn't make a case against him. Unless…

Could de Lyons and his sympathizers deem him unfit because he'd consorted with a woman suspected of stealing the Crown Jewels? Would they try to deny him his position if he refused to marry someone on the official bride list?

Ugly as it sounded, it was plausible. She'd seen enough political smear campaigns in her own country to know how effective the technique could be. And an effective spin doctor could easily twist her past to resemble something salacious.

She refused to be the downfall of the man she loved.

Fear slithered up her spine. To the rest of the royal family, de Lyons was nothing more than a political opponent. Jill touched the necklace at her throat. He'd passed it to her under the pretense of affection.

She saw it now for what it was. A goad, a prod, a flick of the finger at Constantine. She wanted to tear it from her throat, but she wouldn't give the scheming old man the satisfaction.

Instead, she penned a hasty note to Constantine identifying de Lyons and raising her fears of possible assignation attempts. She left out her own private fears. Jill summoned a page, impressing on him that the note concerned a matter of national security. Once assured he would follow her orders and put it directly into the prince's or Edmund's hands, she turned back to her room.

Surely, there would be no need to appease the House of Lyons by choosing a bride from their ranks now. Not when the head of the house betrayed the monarchy. If there was any reason to throw the bride list to the winds, this was it.

A glimmer of hope worked its way through her gloom. If they could get through this night without incident, there might be a way to be together. After all, de Lyons couldn't mount a campaign against Constantine from prison.

She considered the scarlet gown with its glittering accents and matching beaded shoes and accessories. She breathed a sigh of thanks that Helena had insisted on ordering it. Tonight, when she stepped into the ball, Jill would do so with her head held high, ready to stand at her prince's side, should he ask.

Jill spent the afternoon treated to the most extensive spa experience she'd ever heard of. A full body massage, special facial cleansing and moisturizing, manicure, pedicure, and a bevy of beauticians fussing over her made her feel like royalty herself. She hid a smile as they bustled about, complimenting her on her flawless skin and hair.

Her normal routine consisted of drug store products and home remedies—not fancy but apparently effective. Still, she enjoyed the pampering. If only something in their bag of tricks could have calmed the flutter in her stomach.

When Alia came to help her into the ball gown, Jill took a deep breath and tried to steady her nerves. Tonight, she thought as the satin and crystal gown slithered down her body, might be her last night with Constantine. Or it might be the beginning of something deeper. It all depended on his reaction to her note.

Alia slid the zipper up to a point just below the small of her back. Turning in front of the mirror Jill saw how the deep V-cut of the gown bared most of her back with only a few strands of beaded "laces" crisscrossing the expanse and giving the illusion of coverage. A short train swept behind her.

In front, the dress skimmed her shoulders and dropped to a scooped neckline, showcasing her neck and revealing the royal insignia. More red crystal beading and rhinestones formed a delicate pattern that sprinkled across the dress from her right breast cutting diagonally to the slit high on her left thigh. The beading followed the length of the slit and meandered around the hem of the gown. The overall effect was glittering, faintly suggestive, but not overly daring.

"Prince Constantine will love this gown, Jill. He won't be able to take his eyes off you." Alia stepped behind her and tucked a few more pins into her upswept hair.

"Are you sure the color isn't too dramatic?"

"It's perfect. Here, let me help you with the gloves."

Jill had never worn gloves, much less ones that reached to the middle of her upper arms. The effect increased the drama but somehow left her feeling like a child playing dress up. As she sat to slip into her shoes, there was a knock at the door.

For a wild moment, she hoped it would be him, but her heart settled back into its normal rhythm when she saw Alia returning with a small box.

"For you." She thrust the box into Jill's hands.

Jill opened the engraved card, her fingers trembling. *Please wear your necklace for me tonight. I regret that I was not the one to give it to you. In the meantime, these trinkets are a token of my devotion. C.*

Warmth flooded her at the note. In all the preparations, he'd remembered her. Hope fluttered to life as she looked at the strong, fluid writing on the note.

"Aren't you going to open the box?"

Jill sent a bemused glance toward Alia. It's not the gift, but the giver. A wise friend taught her that. Jill hadn't believed her friend, not even when Claire had fallen in love with a billionaire entrepreneur in disguise.

But a happy marriage with passion that showed no sign of dimming had gone a long way to convince Jill. Then, she'd met Constantine. Now she understood her friend's message. Someday Alia would understand too. Smiling, she opened the package.

Inside the box, a diamond and ruby bracelet sparkled against green velvet. A matching pair of drop earrings, set in silver with a fine filigree pattern, lay displayed there as well. Jill put on the earrings and let Alia fasten the bracelet over her gloved wrist. She hugged the girl and then lifted her train with a concealed loop to keep it from dragging and left to make her way to the ballroom.

Jill declined the assistance of the student page who offered to escort her. She needed a few quiet moments to herself. Exiting the royal apartments, she stepped off the portico and wandered along the outside paths.

Torchlight blazed, reflecting in the quiet pools that littered her path. The air smelled of the sea, the tang of oil and smoke, and a subtle perfume from the island flowers. Overhead, the sky was clear, the moon bright, and a few stars visible in the velvet blackness.

The churn and hiss of the surf mingled with the crackling of the torches and the chirp of small night insects to weave enchantment over the island. It was a night of magic, and Jill dared to dream for her wishes to come true.

She walked along the paths, skirting the edge of the palace and avoiding the crowds that came through the main entrance. In the gardens nearer to the ballroom, she guessed there would be clusters of guests, fleeing the heat and drinking in the beauty of Melesia. But here, nearer to the royal apartments, all was still, except for the occasional, silent guard melting into the background.

The meandering paths eventually led her to the ballroom. Narrow paths and deep stone steps led up to the mullioned windows of the ballroom which stretched three stories high forming an eight-sided semicircle of glass around the massive room. The ballroom itself jutted out like a grand peninsula overlooking a still, glittering lagoon that led to the open ocean.

The paths were empty, all the guests cocooned inside the ballroom. From her perch outside the windows, Jill let her eyes roam the room. Elegant gowns and sparkling gems flashed in a sea of color. With a shock, she recognized world leaders, the Prime Minister of England, the U.S. Secretary of State, and a dozen other members of the elite whose origins she could only guess.

At the opposite side of the room, facing the windows a wide, winding staircase filled one wall. Guests glided down the stairs in pairs or small groups, each being announced by a man dressed in Royal Livery.

As she watched, a slender blonde woman in a voluminous, white skirt of lace and chiffon eased down the stairs with the grace of one born to wealth and status. Like Cinderella at the ball, she drew all eyes to her. And when the prince offered her his arm, she floated along beside him, mingling with the international dignitaries as easily as Jill mingled with her high school classmates. A perfect match.

Jill clenched her jaw against the conflicting emotions churning in her gut. She loved Constantine, but was she a fool to think she could live in this world? The woman in white belonged here, not the blatant imposter in red.

A blaze of torchlight glinted off her wrist when she would have turned to leave. The bracelet flashed and sparked, circling her wrist as surely as her love for Constantine circled her heart. It gave her courage. He wanted her there. He expected her there. She closed her eyes and gathered her resolve, preparing to slip in the back doors.

A man stepped from the shadows. "Miss Bradley?" She recognized one of the student workers she'd befriended. "May I escort you to the ballroom entrance?"

"I'd prefer to slip in the back, Seth, if you don't mind."

His smile flashed in the dark. "I don't mind, Miss Bradley, but I'm afraid Their Majesties would. Protocol demands the guests be announced. It's not far to the grand staircase." He offered his arm.

Chapter 25

*P*rotocol. Tradition. Every time she thought she under-stood, some new protocol popped up to complicate her life. If she couldn't even slip in the back door of the party, how could she expect to slip into the life of a prince? Before she could ponder it further, Seth deposited her at the official entryway.

"Enjoy the party tonight, Miss Bradley. If I may say so, you have a beautiful smile. It will dazzle everyone here."

"Thank you, Seth." Bolstered by his compliment, she smoothed her hands over her gown, dropping the train back into place and turning to the head of the stairs. They stretched, a dizzying array of white marble, descending into a swirling, unfamiliar world of wealth and privilege.

"Announcing Miss Jillian Louise Bradley, of the United States."

At the sound of her name the crowd stilled. Jill stiffened her spine, smiled her best smile and walked carefully down the stairs. Flash photos blinded her, crinoline skirts rustled, and whispers scuttled across the ballroom floor.

Jill kept her eyes ahead of her but was aware of the crowds shifting below. Near the foot of the stairs she glanced down and her breath caught in her throat. Constantine waited, one hand behind his back, the other extended formally toward her, his eyes simmering with warmth.

A smile played on his lips, welcoming and teasing at the same time. Intimate. She shivered at the memory of the last time they'd touched.

She'd thought him regal in his tuxedo and tails last night. How wrong her impression had been. Tonight he was royal in both dress and manner. He stood, hand outstretched, motionless, waiting for her.

His formal white jacket with its high collar and double row of gold buttons was accented by a royal banner in green and gold draped across his body from shoulder to hip. Medals of office and commendation glinted against the green background, winking in the candlelit hall. Dark trousers hugged his thighs and his high boots shone with a military gloss.

He was every inch a prince, looking like he stepped from the pages of a storybook, radiating an aura of undeniable command. She stood frozen, trapped in the magic of the moment, afraid to move, lest it shatter.

"Jill?" His query was soft, meant only for her. The twinkle in his eyes coaxed her down the last steps until her gloved fingertips touched his. Heat from their joined hands shot through her, melting the icy calm she'd managed to surround herself with.

A flood of emotions, fear, desire, anxiety, uncertainty, anticipation, all washed through her, but when she looked into his eyes, her love for him made all the other emotions insignificant. She kept her gaze locked on those eyes, using them as her anchor in this swirling world of fantasy. Letting love push all negative emotions aside.

"Dance with me?" A hint of uncertainty threaded through the quiet query, as if he, too, were spellbound in the moment.

"I would love to." A warm glow wrapped around her, and she knew her smile held nothing back.

As he led her to the center of the room, the crowds parted for them. Not one of the faces that lined their path, smiling or frowning, could touch the happiness that surrounded her like a cocoon. She floated with the music. Twirled in his arms. Danced as if she had no cares in her life.

He pulled her as close as the confines of the dance and propriety allowed, but despite the restraint, desire filled the space between them. "You are the most beautiful woman I have ever seen. You mesmerize me. Enchant me. I wish I could spend all of my time with you tonight, and every night," he whispered.

"But duty calls?"

Relief shone in his eyes at her easy acceptance of his duty. "I received your note. I've notified security. You'll be safe." He flashed her a brief smile before becoming serious again. "Later, I must speak with you on a matter of importance. Alone. Will you meet me?"

"Any time. Any place." The music slowed, and she knew the magical moment was near its end.

"Good," he said, his voice dropping to a whisper. A photographer appeared on the dance floor, rapidly approaching them. Constantine's features shifted into the polite, bland mask of a diplomat as he raised her gloved hand to his lips in farewell. The kiss covered his low murmur. "Until then, *mi'hona*."

Sweetheart. No longer beloved one. Nor even desirable one. Neither was appropriate on a ballroom floor, but still, something in his voice seemed amiss. She didn't need his private farewell later to make her place clear.

As he eased away to his duty, all the warmth of the enchanted evening went with him. The admiring glances she received from the crowd turned away to the next woman who graced his arm, and Jill was alone in a world where she didn't belong.

She accepted a glass of champagne from a passing waiter and moved to the windows where it would be easy to slip out the back and make her way to her suite. He would know where to find her.

Below her, the ball continued in full force. Prince Stephan chatted with the American Secretary of State while Queen Helena danced with the British Prime Minister. It was a world she'd never imagined.

"It is a beautiful party, isn't it?" A shiver slithered down her spine at the sound of that voice. A voice she'd once trusted.

"You." She turned and faced the man she'd known as Mr. Dimas. The man who was, in truth, Julian, Duke de Lyons, the thief and murderer who had betrayed his country. "What are you doing here?"

"Surely, you can't be that surprised to see me, Jill. You must have expected I'd be here."

"But…you…I sent a note…" Her mind was whirling, her voice running ahead of her chaotic thoughts. Constantine had seen her note, implied he'd taken care of everything. Why wasn't the Duke de Lyons in custody? Did justice work differently within royal circles? Or had her note been intercepted and tampered with? Suddenly, nothing was clear. She felt numb.

"My dear, I think you've indulged in too much champagne." He took the glass from her limp fingers and dropped it on the tray of a passing waiter. "It wouldn't do to make a spectacle of yourself. More than you already have, that is.

"Did you really think it would matter if you discovered my identity? I assume from your surprise that you've turned me in, pointed the finger of guilt at me, and as you can see, nothing has happened. Did you accuse me of theft? Murder? Treason? I've committed all of these crimes. With impunity." His voice projected a confidence that was beyond arrogance. He truly believed he was above the law.

"Did you really think your word would stand against mine? That you could harm me with your petty accusations?

Melesian justice requires more than the word of a common foreigner to accuse a member of the nobility."

Julian raised his eyes heavenward and smiled a sickly smile. "Even if that were not true, my own dear, departed wife's signet ring was found among the smuggled items. As were many pieces of de Lyons family jewelry. That alone proves that we were victims as surely as the king. No court would believe otherwise. Especially not on the word of a woman so desperate to be in the prince's bed."

He raked a gaze over her that left her feeling slimy. She suppressed the urge to shiver, refusing to give him the satisfaction.

"I'm one of them, Jill," he continued coldly. "I belong to the aristocracy. You, despite your obvious charm, will never belong. It's a pity Prince Constantine didn't choose to stay in the United States with you.

"Things could have been so much more pleasant if he hadn't insisted on doing his duty by his country. I had so hoped his taste for debauchery would prove stronger than his misbegotten sense of duty. Too bad he didn't take the bait I left for him."

"Bait?" Jill's insides quaked, a mixture of anger and something else. Duke de Lyons's aloofness clung to her like cold sludge.

"Yes, bait. You're a pretty little bit of distraction. I'd rather hoped once he discovered you, he would give up this mad scheme. King Alexander may not be well, but his blood is the most pure of the D'Malia clan. My grandson would have been king one day, but for this madness. It would have been the first step to cleansing the stain from the monarchy."

"Your talk of bloodlines sounds like a neo-Nazi creed. Would you really sacrifice the king's happiness and health for the sake of a pure bloodline?"

"I don't expect a commoner to understand. He doesn't even understand." Julian nodded in the direction of Constantine who was dancing with the Cinderella in white. "But his unexpected loyalty to family, tradition, and duty will still be useful to me."

He gripped her elbow to prevent her from leaving. "Do you see the woman he'd dancing with? That's my niece, Sophia of the House of Lyons. She's been promised to him since birth."

"Since birth?" An icy chill crept down Jill's spine, and the blood drained from her face, even as she remembered the bride list. And with de Lyons free, he would use every tool at his disposal to make sure Constantine chose to marry Sophia.

"Surely, you didn't think he would throw away everything for you, did you, my dear? The security of the country is at stake. Her political stability is on the line. Prince Constantine has proven to us all that he knows his duty.

"He'll marry Sophia as tradition decrees and give me another child of my blood line to rule Melesia. You had your chance, but he chose the crown over a future with you. Now, you'll never be anything but an embarrassing footnote in the history of our country."

"It's not true," Jill said faintly, but the malice of his words buried themselves deep in her heart. Last night, Constantine had thanked her for allowing him to adhere to tradition. Not even Julian's treason would stand in the way of tradition. As she would have left, Julian gripped her arm more tightly and nodded toward the dais at the front of the room.

"You know him. When has he ever put pleasure above duty? Do you think he would sacrifice everything for you? At best, you'll be a dirty little secret he hides from his wife and from the cameras." For a second, he looked almost kindly. His voice softened. "Is that all you want, Jill? To be mistress to the king? Go home. Find someone else. Forget Melesia and be happy."

The music stopped and silence fell over the waiting ball-room. Then, on cue, the national anthem began to play and King Alexander Augustus Tyronne D'Malia walked to the center of the platform.

"It is with a mixture of great sadness and great joy, that I formally announce my abdication of the Throne of Melesia in favor of my brother, Prince Constantine Phillippe Ramon D'Malia.

"Sadness, because *Melesia is always in the heart*, and in my heart. Now I must leave her for other hands to guide. Joy, because I am confident that my brother will lead her to even greater glory than I could. But there is more reason for joy." He paused, and the crowd seemed to hold its breath in anticipation.

"As head of the Church of Melesia, I am pleased to announce that tonight I have given my blessing to Prince Constantine and his choice of a bride. He has chosen wisely.

"Although he wishes to keep the decision private between his intended and himself until after the coronation, he petitioned for my blessing before I relinquished my duties to church and state. Rest assured that his bride will cherish and honor the people and traditions of Melesia."

His speech continued, but the bottom dropped out of Jill's world. Constantine had already chosen a woman to be his queen. One who would be a political asset rather than a potential liability.

A woman who, at this moment, watched him with the knowledge of their secret engagement locked away in her heart. And despite his whispered words of love last night, the honor hadn't gone to her.

Half an hour ago, she'd believed love was enough. Now, she faced the impossible. Beside her, Julian loosened his grip and cast a deathly cold smile her way. He'd won.

Julian's words spread like poison through her thoughts. The diamond and ruby bracelet—Constantine's sign of devotion—glinted in the dim light. Perhaps devotion meant something different to a prince than to a farm girl from Ohio. The kind of devotion she needed called for a diamond solitaire and a plain gold band.

She slipped from the room before the speech was over. Her eyes, blurred with tears and blinded by memories, didn't adjust well to the dark, but she hurried along the path, not caring where she went as long as it was away from the crowd.

The night closed in on her and she swallowed a sense of growing panic. Her heel caught in the cobblestones of the path, wrenching her ankle as she struggled for balance.

She ripped the shoes off, gathered the train of her dress and clamored barefoot along the rough path. The uneven flagstones, bordered by crushed shells tore at her stockings and cut her feet, but the throb of her ankle and the sting on her feet couldn't compare with the pain in her heart.

From the ballroom, she heard the faint sounds of the national anthem strike up again. People would be streaming out the doors soon, crowding the water gardens and pathways. She glanced over her shoulder and rushed ahead.

Her swollen ankle twisted again on the rough path and she fought for breath. Like the restless dreams of being chased through the secret palace passageways, she imagined evil a single step behind. Then, reality and nightmare collided. Someone pushed her and she tumbled off the path.

She lost her footing in a slide of crushed shells, gravel and sand. The world whirled out of focus, like it had on the dance floor not so long ago. Only this time, there was no strong arm to lean on, no one to catch her. She pitched sideways down a steep incline, the rock border of a decorative pond obscuring her vision.

A sharp pain pierced her temple and as she slid into the gaping blackness, she imagined the triumphant laugh of Julian, Duke de Lyons, bidding her farewell.

Chapter 26

Constantine scanned the room as Alex made his way to center stage. A cold foreboding snaked down his spine at the sight of Jill standing beside the Duke de Lyons, the traitor's hand wrapped around her elbow.

To one side, his guards waited, watching the Duke's every move. Constantine prayed that Jill trusted him, despite whatever venom de Lyons spewed. She had to. They were so close to having it all.

With his brother's blessing, he was free to marry Jill—if she'd have him. He wished he'd had the chance to ask her before the announcement, but tonight was the last opportunity Alex would have to give his blessing as monarch and head of the church. The crush of the dance floor wasn't the place to propose to the woman he loved. It was better to announce the blessing, and keep the bride's identity a secret, than to rush the most important question he'd ever ask.

He planned to speak to her, to ask for her hand, before the ball, but her letter implicating Julian in the theft of the Crown Jewels and possible assignation plots required immediate attention. Theft, treason, and murder were—at his discretion as king—punishable by death, exile, imprisonment or worse. No one was above the law.

A sharp pain pierced his temple, and Constantine forced his jaw to relax. Forced his lips to smile, despite the turmoil in his gut. Julian de Lyons' presence at the coronation ball appeared to support the transition of power from Alex to Constantine, stabilizing the government during a vulnerable time. Moreover, it kept the eyes of the media on the coronation eve activities, not on the duke's impending arrest.

Later, the security teams would quietly make their move. Even now, de Lyons was under surveillance by Constantine's staff. More of them would be waiting to escort the unsuspecting duke from the ballroom. He wouldn't realize he wasn't returning to his luxurious apartments until it was too late. His sympathizers would be closely watched for signs of treachery.

Still, Constantine regretted not being able to prepare Jill for the evening. Her nervous tension as she entered the room slammed into his gut and lodged there. The wide-eyed look of astonishment, bordering on terror, followed him, chastising him throughout the evening. He'd forgotten how intimidating a royal ball could be. And there wasn't a thing he could do about it, because he, in his imposing role as Crown Prince, was part of the problem.

For a moment, they'd reclaimed the magic between them, until the ever-present press had forced him to put aside any appearance of favoritism toward her. She'd have enough to deal with once news of their engagement was made public. She didn't need to deal with speculation and rumors before then.

Maybe he should dig out the faded blue sweater he'd worn in his guise as Phillip Raymond when he sought her out later. It would be sweltering here on the island, but if it reminded her that he was the same man who'd made unforgettable, passionate love to her in Chicago, it would be worth it.

A move on the dais caught his attention. Alex stepped down and motioned for him to give his speech. He jerked back to reality and scanned the room for Jill. She wasn't there. After a few remarks, he signaled the musicians and the national anthem began again.

He and Alex left the stage, Alex to retire for the evening with Helena on his arm, and he to mingle with the crowd and speak his farewells.

A security officer dressed as a waiter slipped beside him. "Your Highness, there's something that needs your attention. If you would make your way to the back doors, someone will fill you in. The staff will see that the crowd gives you some privacy."

For a heartbeat, he thought Jill had sent for him. That she was waiting in the dark beyond the ballroom to welcome him. But a glance in the officer's eyes killed the hope. He hurried to the windows as fast as he could without raising alarm.

The warm, humid air pressed on him as he exited the ballroom and moved onto the dark, torch lit pathway. Around a bend, out of sight of the windows, a cluster of security guards surrounded a small, rock lined pool. One of the guards stepped forward.

"Your Highness, we saw Miss Bradley leave the ballroom during the king's speech. Then, on a routine sweep of the grounds a few minutes ago, we found her body on this path. We believe she stumbled and struck her head. She was unconscious and we have reason to believe she may have suffered a head trauma. We don't know the extent of her injuries, but there was blood. We had her rushed to the palace infirmary and sent for your personal physician."

"How long ago?"

"She was moved right before we summoned you. We worried that your presence would attract media attention. I assumed you wanted to avoid that, Your Highness."

He nodded, only half listening to the man. The world stopped for a moment. His gut clenched as he tried to hold back the surge of anger. Anger at himself, because he hadn't protected her, anger at Duke Julian, with his obsession over bloodlines, and anger at the duty that tormented him and kept him from declaring his intentions before the ball.

He scanned the ground, wishing he could turn back time. The stones beside the pool glistened in the torchlight, whether from water, or from her blood, he couldn't tell. Half buried beneath a thorny shrub at the water's edge, something else flashed and glittered in the wavering light.

A red high heeled shoe lay abandoned in the sandy soil. He picked it up and rubbed a thumb over the delicate beading that covered it. Jill had worn red the first day they met. She'd worn red tonight. The color suited her. It was as vibrant and full of life as she was. It flashed with the spark and fire that she'd kindled in the cold places of his heart.

He had to see her…to reassure her. To reassure himself.

He ordered the security guard to take him to the infirmary then clamped his jaw shut, locking every bit of feeling inside, hiding his fears behind the mask of the king.

Jill slumped in a plush armchair, grateful for the thick, soft nightgown they'd found for her after they bathed and bandaged her wounds. The tiny flowered print and cotton lace trim reminded her of home. Until she looked around. The private room of the palace infirmary could have passed for a luxury hotel suite, except for her torn and blood-spattered ball gown crumpled in a corner.

She tried to forget the ghastly sight she'd seen in the mirror on the way in. The dirty, matted hair could be washed, the torn dress mended or replaced, but the garish purple bruise covering half of her swollen face wouldn't disappear soon.

When reality intruded into her dream world, it did so in a big way. Eventually everything would heal, but the bruising would mark the rest of her stay in Melesia, reminding her that the fairy tale was now officially over.

The brief glimpse in the mirror taunted her, contrasting with her prince's glowing words of praise. *You are the most beautiful woman I have ever seen. You mesmerize me. Enchant me.* The magical words, on which she'd built impossible hopes, replayed themselves in her mind, their irony throbbing in time with the pain in her head. If only he could see her now.

Prince Constantine's private physician. Dr. 'Oodsoon bustled into the room, breaking her out of the despondent thoughts. "You took quite a tumble, young lady." The doctor's words were brisk, but her touch was gentle as she tucked another pillow under Jill's foot where it rested on an ottoman. "I've brought you an ice pack that should help the swelling, but there won't be much dancing in your immediate future. Keep that ankle elevated and as still as you can."

The doctor handed her a couple of pain killers then rested her hand on Jill's forehead in an old-fashioned, comforting gesture that reminded Jill of her childhood.

"You'll be wanting to sleep, and that's good, but I'll be checking you throughout the night to make sure you don't have a concussion."

Jill nodded, accepting the doctor's words, but then winced as the doctor lifted her eyelid and a sliver of light from a penlight bombarded her eyes. After a minute or two, the doctor seemed satisfied.

She handed Jill another ice pack. "This will soothe your face and help with the swelling. Don't worry. You'll heal. I've taken care of a generation of young royal patients, and every one of them survived to adulthood. You just rest here for a minute, and then we'll get you tucked in for the night."

As soon as the doctor left, Jill sank into the chair, giving in to the dizzy sleepiness that dogged her. All too soon the doctor interrupted her again.

"Miss Bradley?" Jill pried her groggy eyes open. "Prince Constantine is here. I've told him you are resting comfortably, but he insists on seeing you." The doctor grinned, her teeth gleaming white in the darkened room. "I can send him away if you want. Those boys don't tell Dr. 'Oodsoon what to do."

"Thank you, Doctor. Please send him away. I don't want anyone to see me. I...I'm very tired."

The doctor patted Jill's hand and left the room.

Jill closed her eyes and sank back into the dim recesses of the chair, exhausted. Her wrenched ankle ached. Her temple throbbed, despite the cool ice pack, and her eye felt thick, swollen shut. At least no one but the doctor could see her.

Her weeks of enchantment were over, the final magical night gone in a haze of pain. Tomorrow, she would pack up her dreams and go back to being Jill Bradley, responsible sister and stepdaughter. No more dreams of princely grandeur. No more shared confidences or secret smiles with the most handsome man in the world. He belonged to someone else now. Her body would heal within weeks, but her heart would never be the same again.

The doctor walked back into the room and came to her side, probably to be sure she was awake. All she wanted to do was sink into a dreamless sleep, but even that escape was denied to her.

"Jill?" Not the doctor. She should have known he'd barge in despite her wishes and the doctor's orders. "*Ba'hona-mei*, I'm sorry to disturb you, but I had to know if you were all right. Please, look at me."

She let the ice pack fall and turned to him, braced for his reaction to her ugliness. But it wasn't dismay, it was tenderness filling his eyes. He tucked a wayward strand of hair behind her ear so gently that she barely felt his touch. Then he lowered himself to one knee, crouching beside her chair so he could look in her eyes.

"Oh *Ba'hona-mei*. Doctor 'Oodsoon told me you would be all right, but she didn't indicate how badly you were injured. I insisted on seeing you despite her attempts to keep me away. Does it hurt?" He raised her hand to his lips and pressed a kiss to it. "I'd try to kiss away the rest of the pain, but I'm afraid it would hurt you."

It would only hurt her heart, but he didn't need to know that. She held onto his hand a second longer, savoring the warmth she'd never feel again, then she slipped her hand from his. She might be his *Ba'hona-mei* in private, but she would never be so in public. "Why are you here? You have important guests to attend to. Your people depend on you."

"No one is more important than you, right now. No one ever has been. Besides," he flashed a wicked grin that turned her insides to jelly, "there's an ancient tradition I have to carry out. You left my party early when I was expecting you to wait for me."

"I had to leave. Julian explained everything to me. I won't stand in the way of what you have to do for the country, but I couldn't stay and listen to you—"

"Don't pay attention to anything he has to say. He is a traitor who betrayed us all."

Jill shrank back. Neither the scowl on his brow and lips nor the anger flashing in his eyes was muted by his unfeeling public mask. They were etched on his face in harsh, merciless lines. It wasn't a look she ever wanted directed at her. But the ferocity faded back to tenderness when he captured her hand again. This time there was no pulling away.

"I promise I will do everything in my power to keep him from hurting you again. He's already been escorted to prison and his known associates are being watched. So put him from your mind, *Ba'hona-mei*. As I said, you left my party instead of waiting for me. I was devastated. I had to find you."

He reached beside the chair and dangled her ruined pump in front of her. "I found this in the gardens. I believe, according to tradition, this is where I return it to you and ask you to marry me. Jill, I love you. Will you marry me?"

Her eyes filled with tears, blurring the red, rhinestone studded satin of the shoe. If only he was free to follow through on his gallant gesture without risking the nation's security. If only she was a woman capable of becoming a princess. But reality was as far from that romantic vision as her bruised face was from her former beauty.

He was destined for another. The announcement had been made at the ball. He couldn't change the past. And even if he could, she wouldn't let him give up his destiny for her.

"Jill?"

She took the shoe from his hand, letting the tears fall. Her voice was thick and forced, as if her throat, too, was swollen shut. "You are the most wonderful person I've ever met. I love you with all my heart. If I could... You have your duties. You don't need a wife, you need a queen.

"Someone who belongs to your world, your class. Someone I can never be. You don't need a small-town transplant who grew up surrounded by corn fields and destined to be a farmer's wife."

She rubbed the toe of the shoe with her thumb and forced herself to look away from the hurt in his eyes. "Besides, my handsome prince, you've got your fairy tales mixed up. Your princess should be dressed in white with glass slippers, like the lovely Sophia who's been promised to you from birth. These shoes are red. Everyone knows the ruby slippers take you home. There's no place like home," she intoned softly, lulled by the childhood mantra.

"Jill, I need you. *You.* I know that now, and I think you know it too."

"No. You need your tradition. You said so yourself. Things need to be done the right way. Marry Sophia. Make heirs for the Melesian crown."

"Jill, I—"

"Your Highness, your time is up." The lilting Melesian accent carried a firm undertone. "Miss Bradley needs to rest." The doctor moved beside her and thrust her hands on her hips as she pinned Constantine with a glare. "This agitation isn't good for her. You can visit again tomorrow evening. After the coronation," she added with emphasis.

A flash of anger sparked in Constantine's eyes then faded to acceptance. He nodded to the doctor. His gaze traveled between them, smooth and courteous, but with a hint of steel. "Of course, Doctor 'Oodsoon. We both want what is best for Miss Bradley. Jill, this isn't over. We will discuss it tomorrow."

Jill nodded and watched him leave the room. He didn't know, but there would be no tomorrow for them. By the time his coronation was official, she'd be on her way out of his life. He would be free to find the queen he needed. She wouldn't let him sacrifice his future out of guilt or misplaced gallantry. She absently fingered the shoe she still clutched. *There's no place like home.*

Chapter 27

Constantine allowed the tailor to poke and prod him, making final adjustments to his uniform in the minutes before the ceremony. Images of Jill flashed through his mind as they had all night.

He'd left the infirmary, hoping that her refusal stemmed from the bruises and the loss of confidence she suffered when her stunning beauty was dimmed. But her words stayed with him, a throbbing litany that even now pounded in his head. *Tradition. Sophia. Tradition. You said so yourself. Sophia. Tradition. Duty. Since birth.*

"Ouch." He bit back the expletive when a pin from the tailor pricked him.

"I'm sorry, Your Highness. Please, hold still for a moment longer while I make a final adjustment."

Tradition, as tight and molded to himself as his formal coat, was the reason for Jill's refusal. In a flash he understood. She'd misread the confessions he'd whispered into her pillows on their last night together, believing his insistence on tradition to mean a traditional, arranged marriage. If only she hadn't been sleeping off the effects of pain medications when he'd tried to visit her suite this morning, he could have cleared up her misconceptions.

The tailor finished and Constantine turned to the mirror. He saw a prince, soon-to-be king, standing erect, formal and imposing. How few people truly understood that inside the prince beat the heart of a man.

"Your Highness, it's time to leave." Edmund's voice broke into his thoughts and pulled him back to the present.

"Edmund, I need you to check on some final arrangements for me. After the coronation, I have pressing private business to attend to." He bombarded Edmund with a rapid-fire list of instructions as he made his way from the palace to his waiting carriage.

The procession gained momentum with each step, adding bodyguards and dignitaries as centuries of duty and tradition drove him toward his coronation. Despite it all, Constantine knew now what he had to do before this day was over. And no duty would keep him from it.

Jill looked around her room one last time, committing each nuance to memory. Her gaze lingered on the bed where she'd made love with Constantine. Her beach tote, packed with a few of the items she'd brought from home, lay ready by the door.

She'd send for the rest of her things later. She refused to take the gifts he'd lavished on her. Not the clothes, not the jewels. Nothing but the simple sundress she was wearing, and only that because she needed the matching hat to help hide her bruises.

One last thing remained to be done. Her fingers shook as she unclasped the royal insignia necklace from her throat. Once her good luck charm, it now reminded her that she'd been used to wreak havoc on the royal family and the country of Melesia.

She arranged it on the dressing table and lovingly traced the intricate pattern with a shaking fingertip. The design was intended for a royal bride. Of course, this necklace was fake, just like she was fake, but the memories it held were real. She longed to snatch it back, to carry home a tangible reminder of this place. But the memories themselves would have to suffice.

She made a final adjustment to the angle of her hat and headed to the door. As promised, the friends she'd made from among the student staff had everything arranged. A short car ride took her from Royal Island, past the gatehouse and across the bridge. Everywhere, the streets were decorated and lined with people hoping for a good view of the coronation and parade. Proceedings were due to start within the hour.

Standing on the curb of the public airport, she watched the car pull away. Unlike the private airport where she'd arrived with the prince just weeks ago, this structure was designed for tourists, streamlined and functional. And empty.

Inside, a lone ticket agent informed her that, due to the coronation and increased security, the first flight to leave the country would be late tonight. She bought a ticket, walked through security and customs and settled into a hard, plastic and chrome chair.

TV monitors, tuned to channels around the world, flashed pictures of the parade route, the cathedral, and the palace. Reporters covered the coronation in half a dozen languages from around the globe.

Restless, Jill wandered around the waiting area. She bought a cheese sandwich and a soda from a vending machine, watching the last of her Melesian coins slide away, just like her moments of happiness on the island. Then, having exhausted all of her options, she settled down to watch the ceremony.

Was her life destined to be like this? Spent alone, watching the world go by? Remembering the love she'd let slip through her fingers?

Constantine appeared on screen, his entourage making its way from the palace to the cathedral in regal formality. Even on the tiny screen, his image blurred by dust and grime, he made her heart stop and her breath come in painful gasps.

She wondered how he would look, silver threading through his dark hair, laugh lines etched into his handsome face. She heard his laughter, imagined it coming from children, and wondered if his sons and daughters would be dark, like him, or golden, like Sophia.

Jill's heart ached at the thought that he would love another but broke over the thought that he would live without love for the rest of his life.

As the afternoon shadows lengthened and dusk crept over the runways, a few people straggled into the airport. One or two news crews—looking exhausted—lounged about, chatting and planning follow up stories. More than once she heard speculation over the royal bride. She moved to a remote corner, wishing for the silent emptiness she'd had earlier.

When the floodlights pierced the darkness and the whir of cameras started up, she turned, desperate to keep her swollen face out of the light. She headed to the gate agent, ready to ask when her flight would board, but a uniformed security guard intercepted her.

"Miss Jillian Bradley?"

"Yes." It seemed as if the cameras all turned toward her.

"Would you accompany me, please," he asked in a low voice. "The customs agents need to discuss a few irregularities with you."

Her heart dropped to her stomach. Constantine had arranged for her passport and paperwork. Surely, she didn't need special permission to leave the country. Did she? The guard's face was impassive as he led her away, cameras recording every step.

Maybe it was the trauma of last night. Or maybe it was the long, empty day of eerie silence. Whatever the cause, her nerves were stretched to the limit and playing tricks on her. She followed him, like a criminal on the way to her execution. They passed into a dim hallway. At least, the execution would be private.

He opened the door to a small, windowless room with a table and single chair and motioned her in. Instead of accompanying her, he shut the door and a lock clicked into place.

"I couldn't let you leave without seeing you again."

Jill whirled at the sound of the deep, familiar voice, her heart thumping in glad anticipation even as her common sense tried to still her reaction. She'd never thought she would hear his voice again, except in her imagination.

Constantine stood in a shadowed corner of the room. He pushed away from the wall and moved into the glare of the single, bare light bulb dangling from the ceiling. Only he didn't look like Constantine, King of Melesia.

He looked like Phillip Raymond, the disguise he'd worn in Chicago. Faded jeans hugged his hips and the blue crew neck sweater that she'd once peeled, soaking wet, from his body hung loosely on his frame. Perspiration dotted his upper lip, but otherwise he was the same.

"What are you doing here?"

He took a step forward and gently took her hat off, tossing it on the desk. "I think that should be obvious."

She couldn't pull her gaze away from the deep, sparkling blue of his eyes. When he threaded his fingers gently through her hair and kissed her, the last of her reserves—and her knees—gave out. She wrapped her arms around his waist, palms caressing the moist skin under his sweater. She wanted this man, this last good-bye.

His lips pulled away, leaving her unsatisfied, longing for more. He slipped easily from her grasp and passed an arm across his brow.

"Why on earth are you dressed that way? It must be sweltering outside."

He smiled, a teasing, little lift of his lips. "I wore it to help you remember."

It had worked. The image of his rain-soaked body caused her body to heat. "Remember what?" she asked in a shaky voice.

"All the reasons why we should be together. All the things that happened between us when I was just a man and you were just a woman. Remember, Jill." He cupped her cheek with a touch so light she barely felt it against her bruised skin. "You are the most wonderful thing that has ever happened to me. The best part of my life. I don't want to go on without you."

Her throat tightened. She hoped her gaze spoke for her because there were no words to describe the emotions tumbling through her. His gaze, his kiss, his touch, the memories. Everything was ragged, raw and aching, longing for an impossible solution. He looked as if he might kiss her again, but he spoke instead.

"I can't make you love me. I can't make you marry me. But I can, and I will, keep you from leaving on that flight tonight. Give me one good reason why we should deny ourselves the thing we want, and I'll let you go. Or tell me that you don't love me. But don't leave for the wrong reasons."

"What about tradition? Your marriage?" The words burned in her throat, but they had to be said.

"Jill, you're wrong about the bride list. Yes, Sophia was one of a select few with royal bloodlines, but no binding promises were made. No one will question my right to choose my own bride. Despite what you might think, Melesia doesn't live in the dark ages."

"But you said—"

"When I spoke of tradition, I meant the tradition of asking for the monarch's blessing. It was right to have Alex bless my intentions before he stepped down. My father didn't have a blessing on the marriage to the woman he loved. That was part of the reason my mother had to fight so hard for acceptance. I didn't want that for you."

"What of Sophia?"

"She's young, Jill. A child who's never had a life of her own. She doesn't love me. And she'd never have the spunk to tell me off or throw a book at my head when I was in the wrong.

"Alex and Helena were against a union with her. Helena wanted her cousin to have a chance at life, and maybe a chance to fall in love. Julian never gave her that. She's like a sister to me, but I could never love her. Not the way I love you."

"And Julian?"

"Don't think his treason will be ignored. Despite what he may have told you, I've had him watched. He will pay for his crimes. He'll never threaten anyone or anything I love again. Thanks to you, I can sleep easier knowing the crown is safe. That was a good bit of detective work on your part."

His smile threatened to rob her of what little sense she had left. "I was just lucky."

"*Laddos,*" he cursed in Melesian. "If I have to spend the rest of my life convincing you to value yourself for more than your beauty, I will. You are an accomplished diplomat, a genius with languages and cultures, a woman any man would be proud to have at his side."

He kissed her then, lightly, his lips teasing rather than tasting. Her doubts were fleeing, all thoughts of being noble and self-sacrificing burning up in the flames of desire he awakened in her.

He stepped back and regarded her, the sparkle in his eyes and the quirk of his lips giving lie to the stern expression he tried to adopt. "Now, I'm going to ask you an important question, and I want you to consider your answer carefully."

"I already know—"

He held a hand up to still her. "Here's a hint. The answer is either *yes* or *I don't love you.*"

His jaw tensed and all teasing dropped from his face. But his eyes blazed with hope, uncertainty, and most of all love. Jill took a deep breath and made her choice.

"I do love you."

"Then will you marry me?"

"*Aaya.* Yes. I'll marry you." Her heart beat faster and the look he sent her caused the heat to curl in her stomach.

He dug in his pocket and pulled out a diamond and ruby ring. Without waiting for her to admire it, he slipped it onto her finger, then took her in his arms and leaned close. "You've made a very wise choice," he murmured against her lips. "We'll be married as soon as tradition allows. I'll have a real bride's necklace commissioned for you to declare to the world that you are my *Ba'hona-mei.*"

Everything she'd ever wanted was here in this room. Love. Romance. A man—who just happened to be a king—offering her his heart. It was strange, and wonderful, the way happiness eclipsed all the pain of the past days.

Constantine's brow crinkled, and a look of mischief twinkled in his ocean-blue eyes.

"As I said, you made a wise choice by accepting my proposal, because I've discovered the ancient penalties for an attack on a royal person—such as throwing a book at his head, for instance—can be rather severe."

"Dare I throw myself on your mercy and hope for leniency?" she teased, nipping at the corner of his lips.

"Too late. You're already committed for a life sentence. Besides, *Ba'hona-mei*, I'm sure you can make me forget it ever happened." He claimed her lips at last, one strong arm drifting down to cup her buttocks and press them into the waiting hardness of his hips.

This time, the kiss sizzled. Fire raced from his lips arcing through her body and turning her core to molten desire. Already she ached with the torment of desire denied, even as his lips and tongue played with her mouth, bringing her to a fever pitch of unfulfilled longing.

It was a sweet torment at the hands of the man she loved. She wound her hand around his neck, plunged her fingers into his hair and held on, giving as good as she got. With Constantine, King of Melesia and man of her dreams, one lifetime was never going to be enough.

Epilogue

June, one year later

Jill stared out into the night, the sound of the surf and the velvet blackness of the sky soothing her pre-wedding jitters. In the short, blissful months between Constantine's proposal and their official engagement, and the long arduous ones after, Melesia had become her home.

During the flurry of activity over the last weeks—wedding gown fittings, official portrait sittings, her formal oath of citizenship, endless interviews, and a parade of royal relatives—she'd been able to push her fears aside.

Tonight they came flooding back. Despite the intensive year-long study of politics and protocols, despite being surrounded by top-notch advisors and a loyal staff, she wasn't sure she was ready to be a queen.

Instead, she closed her eyes and focused on Constantine. Duties and obligations were part of the package—a part she would willingly accept—for the sake of the man she loved. Tomorrow, surrounded by friends and family, she would take her vows with confidence.

Only one thing was missing. "Daddy, I wish you were here with me," she whispered into the darkness. She longed for her father's strong presence during her walk down the aisle tomorrow, yet knew that as she leaned on her brother Geoff's arm, a piece of her father would be there too.

A quiet knock pulled her from her thoughts. She opened the door to find her stepmother. "How are you holding up, honey?" The question held a hint of uncertainty.

Jill wrapped her in a hug and ushered her into the room. "I'm fine, Mom. Just a little nervous."

"Nerves are as traditional as white gowns and wedding cake. You're going to be a beautiful bride, Jill. I just wish…" Her mom took a deep breath and perched on the sofa. "I wanted to be the one to make my daughters' wedding gowns and bake their cakes. And here you are with a professional wedding staff and an entourage of attendants from who-knows-where, and…"

"You still have Gracie, Amber and Char. There'll be plenty of wedding gowns for you to sew," Jill said gently.

"The gown isn't really the point, Jill." She took Jill's hands in her own. "Years ago, I would never have believed that I could love another woman's child as much as I love you. I know I'm not your real mother, but I—"

"You're real, Mom. In all the ways that count." Jill swallowed past the lump in her throat. "I love you too."

Her mother smiled although her eyes remained misty. "Before we came to Melesia, I found the wedding bands your father and mother wore as well as some small pieces of her jewelry. I had them made into something you can keep with you always. Something you can wear even when you're draped in gems fit for a queen."

Jill opened the small box. Inside a slender gold cuff bracelet lay on a bed of burgundy velvet.

"I hope you don't mind, but there wasn't quite enough gold in the rings, so I used some of my own jewelry too."

The tears Jill had held back until now spilled over as she slipped it onto her arm. The slim gold band was a reminder of her family, her roots, and the people she loved. It bound her to the past like her wedding band would bind her to her future. "It's perfect. Thank you."

"They would have been proud of the woman you've become. So am I. Your happiness is all we've ever wanted." With a final hug, her stepmother said good night, and Jill went to her bed, wrapped in warm memories of the three people who'd raised her.

Music from the grand organ in the Royal Cathedral filled the private anteroom as Jill's attendants slipped out, leaving her alone with her family. Many of the attendants were distant royal cousins—people she barely knew yet felt compelled to include. But here, in this room, were the ones she wanted. Amber and Char crowded around her, while Gracie, Geoff, and mom hovered nearby.

"We made this for you to carry." Char pushed a package into her hands, barely able to contain herself while Jill unwrapped the antique white handkerchief. "I sewed the lace on it."

"And I added the pearls," Amber said.

"I salvaged the material from your mother's wedding dress," her stepmother said quietly.

"Something old, something new, something borrowed, something blue," Char recited. "Mama embroidered each of our names in white on the corners and we each added a design of our own. Mine is the blue flower." She pointed to a small cluster of blue dots forming a forget-me-not.

Amber had stitched a gold star, and Gracie a small silver fish. Even Geoff had stitched a clumsy row of Xs and Os.

"Thank you, everyone." Jill gathered Amber and Char in a hug. "Now all I need is something borrowed."

"Here." Gracie stepped forward and pushed something into her hand. "Daddy gave me this locket. You can borrow it for today."

Jill hugged Gracie and whispered her thanks, but her sister muttered an embarrassed "I love you" and wiggled out of the embrace as soon as possible.

"I'll get everyone lined up for the processional. You just enjoy your wedding day." Gracie hurried the girls and Geoff out of the room.

Jill watched her sister leave then turned to her mom. "Gracie seems so alone."

"Don't worry, honey, she's going to be fine. Strong emotions are difficult for her. But she's getting better. And I think starting school here in the fall will be the best thing for her."

"I don't like the way she's going about it. Not telling the world she's my sister seems so…" Jill fidgeted with the locket. "I'd rather help her than sit back and watch her flounder."

"I understand. But Gracie has to do this on her own. Or at least have the illusion that she's on her own. Don't push too hard. She'll come to you when she's ready. Now," she kissed both of Jill's cheeks, "do as she says and enjoy your wedding day."

Moments later, Jill stood at the back of the cathedral, clutching Geoff's arm. She could barely make out the end of the long aisle, seeing instead a thousand faces looking expectantly at her.

One step. Then another. She smiled automatically, making her way past the crowds, trying to forget that cameras from around the globe followed her procession. Her hand trembled as she clutched the exotic bouquet of white lilies, lush greens, and ornate bird-of-paradise.

Then she saw him and nothing else mattered. Constantine stood, tall and regal, at the front of the cathedral. The heated look in his eyes and the curve of his lips melted the last of her nerves and warmed her own smile.

She paused and turned, executing a formal curtsey showing her respect to the King and Queen Emeritus who sat in the front row. She turned again, showing the same respect for her king and husband-to-be.

Then, with a single step forward, it was no longer a royal wedding couched in protocols and formalities surrounded by strangers.

It was her wedding.

To the man she loved.

Surrounded by family and friends.

And with words of promise, symbols of love both ancient and new, and a kiss of passion, Jill and Constantine began their own happily ever after.

Reluctantly Royal

Excerpt

Chapter 1

June, the royal wedding of Constantine Phillippe Ramon D'Malia

Gracie tightened her fist around the locket as her gilded carriage wove its way through the streets of the island kingdom of Melesia. The familiar shape soothed her frazzled nerves and provided a tiny piece of home amid the foreign finery.

Today's fairy-tale regalia was nothing more than an illusion, broadcast via satellite to every cable channel in the world. She straightened her shoulders and ignored shouts from reporters, cameramen, and film crews along the parade route, focusing instead on the coach at the head of the parade where her sister and new brother-in-law rode in regal splendor.

Her sister, Jill, made a radiant bride. She would have anyway, even if it had been a regular wedding, rather than a royal wedding to Constantine D'Malia, king of an important Caribbean archipelago.

Thank goodness Gracie's official part in the festivities was over. She rubbed her thumb along the worn gold of the locket that she'd let her sister carry during the wedding ceremony. The chatter of the strangers in the coach beside her faded into insignificance. Their smiling faces and crowd-pleasing waves blurred before her eyes.

Twelve years rewound themselves in her memory, taking her back to the year she turned eight. To the week her father gave her the locket. When he was still alive. When she and Jill giggled and shared secrets.

Now, all she had of her father was a faded photo. And her sister was a distant stranger. Despite occasional strained words of affection, Gracie wasn't sure they even liked each other anymore.

The carriage bumped to a halt, bringing Gracie back to the present and landing her smack dab in the middle of reality. The bizarre reality of a royal wedding. A footman helped her down the single step and into the media frenzy below.

Her chest tightened, the beat of her pulse pounding the air from her lungs as they closed in, scraping away her defenses like piranhas peeling flesh from a victim. She forced her lips to curve, shielding her raw, private emotions from exposure. She'd never let someone record her vulnerability again. She breathed, relaxing the tightness as she sailed forward, head high.

The wedding party wound its way through the Grand Hall, past the Queen's Gallery, and toward the ballroom. Gracie's steps slowed. Royal cousins and Melesian nobility swept past her and up the stairs to the balcony, following the bride and groom.

Gracie clutched the locket and kept her smile in place. A few more seconds and she'd be out of media range. A minute after that, she'd be plain Gracie Bradley of Ohio again, not the royal bride's half-sister. An hour from now, she'd be immersed in a book and the morning would be an uncomfortable memory.

She eased toward an exit leading away from the ballroom. A few more seconds…

"Miss Bradley?"

Gracie turned. She cast a longing glance at her almost-escape route then braced herself as a reporter headed her way, cameraman in tow. The king's younger brother and presumptive heir, Crown Prince Stephan, intercepted them. Flicking her a dismissive glance, he edged between her and the reporters.

His assessment stung. Apparently not even professional makeup, hairstyling, and designer gowns made her acceptable. Gracie bristled at his high-handed treatment, but his words brought her to her senses.

"Ladies and Gentlemen, if you have a moment, I'd like to introduce you to the bride's sister." Gracie's younger sister, Amber, stood by his side, glowing with all the innocent enthusiasm of a seventeen-year-old charmer. The press, from the looks of it, loved her.

Gracie slipped out of sight until a masculine laugh drew her attention back to the ballroom. A handful of reporters converged on Prince Stephan as if drawn by his elegant gestures and easy smiles. *Like bees to honey.*

He laughed again, and Gracie took an unconscious step forward before she forced herself back into the shadows. *Intelligent women did not fall prey to dashing princes. She was immune. Curiosity caused her rapid heartbeat. Nothing else.*

She studied him, mentally cataloguing and analyzing each detail like a scientist observing a specimen.

His quick smile should have made him less imposing than the rest of the royal family, but instead, it accented the subtle authority that radiated from him. He demanded attention. He personified flawlessness. Polished shoes gleamed. A sharply pressed military uniform outlined his broad shoulders and lean torso. Not a single golden hair fell out of place.

As he chatted with the gathering crowd, expressions—humorous, interested, intrigued, concerned—flitted across his face, each fading away leaving his smooth honey-gold skin unmarked by emotion.

Until he turned in her direction.

A sharp, irritated frown puckered his brow, and his lips tightened. The full force of his disapproval hit Gracie in an instant, even as he turned away, his features resuming their normal composure.

A rush of heat, fueled by anger and embarrassment, washed down her body, leaving her lightheaded in its wake. How dare he judge her as unsuitable? His polished perfection embodied the royal image, but she was a woman of substance, not image.

In the world outside the glass bubble of the monarchy, her intelligence would trump his sophisticated smoothness every time.

Gracie turned and took two firm strides down the hallway and out of sight before kicking off her shoes and allowing her shoulders to slump in relief. The anger seeped from her body, leaving her disgusted with herself for staring at him like a starstruck teenager. She took a deep breath to calm her racing pulse and restore her analytical world view.

With luck, she could avoid any further encounters with the overbearing prince during her short stay on Melesia. And when she returned in the fall, she'd be nothing more than another transfer student, finishing her degree, awaiting graduate school, and best of all, living in the dorms far from the influence of the royal D'Malia family.

Stephan risked another glance toward the marble archway and breathed an internal sigh of relief when he saw it was empty. Gracie, Jill's painfully shy sister had—finally—made her escape. He'd spent every ounce of charm he could muster to keep the press focused on him while she lingered near the edges of the ballroom. A few more seconds and he wouldn't have been able to protect her from their zeal.

Having solved the problem of Gracie's privacy, he turned to other issues, smoothly directing the press to the outdoor gardens and returning Amber to her mother.

Those lingering in the ballroom consisted only of a few high-ranking Melesian citizens, the American family and friends of the new queen, and palace staff. He headed to the stairs to join the bride and groom, only to be cut off when Lady Ophelia de Lyons hurried forward and grabbed his arm. Her husband followed, an apologetic yet slightly weary look etched on his face.

Once the epitome of Melesian aristocracy, Ophelia barely resembled the beauty she'd been as a young woman. Bitterness, more than circumstance or age, had etched fine lines into the corners of her eyes and mouth.

"Prince Stephan." Ophelia gave him a cool smile. "What a pleasure to see our king happy with his love match! Just as my dear Gregor and I are. We couldn't be more pleased."

Stephan murmured in agreement, not challenging her obvious lie. Ophelia's ambitions outstripped any love she felt for the baron she'd married. "Always a pleasure to see you, as well."

"If I might have a moment of your time, Your Highness." Her vise-like grip contrasted with the forced deference in her tone.

"My time is always at your disposal." Stephan turned to them, carefully disengaging her hand and placing a polite kiss on her knuckles before guiding it to her husband's arm.

Her smile dimmed a bit. "Despite today's joy, my brother's disgraceful behavior toward our king distresses me. Treason. Murder plots." She shuddered. "The king was right to strip him of his title. However, Gregor and I fear for my niece Sophia."

She drew her husband closer to her side. "With her guardian imprisoned and her..." Ophelia paused meaningfully, "marriage prospects gone, we were hoping to petition the king for a favor."

"The royal family holds Sophia in the highest regard." Stephan waited, knowing Ophelia had more on her mind than the king's opinion of Sophia.

"That is a comfort. Now with the king married and soon—we hope—with an heir on the way, we wondered if he might consider something more substantial."

Stephan spared Gregor a sympathetic glance. Ophelia had a gleam in her eye that caused tension to grip his gut every bit as tightly as she'd gripped him earlier. He crossed his arms and raised an eyebrow, silently inviting her to finish her petition—quickly.

"As I was saying, Sophia's uncle is in jail. Her father—may he rest in peace—would have been next in line for the de Lyons title. With no male heirs remaining, might the king consider giving the title and lands to Sophia?"

Stephan hid his surprise, smiling blandly. A woman trained to the position could rule a duchy or even a country. But Sophia? Would she want the burden? Could she handle it?

"Your concern for Sophia is admirable, Lady Ophelia. I will convey your request to the king. At an appropriate time." He glanced pointedly at the hall, decorated in celebration of the royal wedding. "For now, please enjoy the festivities."

With that, Stephan turned and climbed the stairs, pondering the situation. Ophelia and her deposed brother were as alike as twins when it came to political machinations and lust for power. Sophia had never been more than a political pawn to either of them.

Before he counseled his brother on any moves in the game they were playing, he'd make damn sure he understood the role of every player on the chessboard. And he'd do everything in his power to protect the players—king, queen, and pawn alike—no matter what it took.

Chapter 2

racie crept down a deserted corridor, shoes still dangling from her fingers, and slipped into a reception room far from the cameras and microphones. The thick, luxurious carpet soothed her bare feet as effectively as the quiet room soothed her nerves.

"Someone else seeking refuge from the crowds."

Gracie's gaze flew to Lady Sophia de Lyons, who sat in a wing back chair, serene and thoughtful. Although they were similar in age, size and coloring, Lady Sophia radiated elegance and poise.

Caught by another royal. This time, Gracie couldn't summon her anger as a defense. Beside Sophia, she felt more like an awkward, gangly child playing dress-up than a twenty-year-old woman.

You're the smart sister. Her mother's voice echoed in her memory. Smart enough to know when it was time to leave. She turned to the door.

"I envy you." Lady Sophia's voice carried a hint of inbred authority and eloquence that Gracie envied, in spite of her own egalitarian principles.

Gracie hesitated. "Why? You belong here. I'm just the bride's sister, dressed up and trying not to embarrass her."

"Exactly. Soon the press will forget you. They'll hound me for weeks, prying to see if my wounded heart is mended." A faint edge of bitterness crept into her voice.

Gracie eased herself onto a sofa, arranging the unfamiliar layers of formal skirts around her. "Was your heart really broken? Were you in love with Constantine?" The uncensored words popped out and hung in the air, muffled by the thick carpet and brocaded wall hangings. The sound of the ocean, faint from beyond the windows, somehow magnified the silence in the room.

"Love was never part of the picture for us." Sophia rose and walked to the French doors, beckoning Gracie to follow. "I envy him too. He broke the rules and found love. Alex and Helena are also in love," she said, referring to the ailing King Emeritus who'd abdicated in favor of his half-brother. "I'm just the spare bride who's now out of a job."

"I don't understand."

"How could you?" Sophia stepped onto a shallow patio with a view of the balcony where Jill and Constantine stood surrounded by the royal family, smiling at the cheering crowds below.

"Look." Sophia pointed to them. "A royal wedding is a fairy tale come true. If I'd been on the balcony instead of your sister, the fairy tale would have unfolded in exactly the same way. Except the looks in their eyes are real. They love each other. He and I would have been pretending.

"I'm very good at pretending. From the moment I came to live with the Duke de Lyons, he's prepared me to be the spare bride. He fed the press with enough romantic nonsense to fuel the illusion. I played along."

Sophia's words stirred uncomfortable memories of a time when Gracie's life had been defined by a newspaper story and a lie too.

"What do you mean—the spare bride?" she asked, distracting herself from her own memories.

"Royal sons are *the heir and the spare.* Alex was the heir. Helena was raised to be his bride. Constantine was the spare. I was the spare bride. At least that's what the duke planned."

"It must have been awful." Gracie knew the Duke de Lyons—dubbed the Disgraced Duke by the press—had been involved in a plot to control the government. The plot, which implicated her sister for theft and treason, had nearly gotten Jill killed.

Sophia was another pawn in the duke's quest for power, locked in a role chosen for her at birth. No matter how beautiful the island paradise, Gracie could never be at home in a place where birth determined more than worth.

She prayed Sophia was right about Jill's marriage, but the emotional chasm between the sisters was too wide for her to know. The older sister she'd once adored had disappeared the night their father died. In her place was a stranger. The nine-year age difference between them might as well have been a generation. Gracie no longer knew if Jill was the kind of woman to marry for love—or something else.

"It makes a great story." Sophia's cultured voice lured Gracie back to the present. "'Lady Sophia, Foster Daughter of The Disgraced Duke, Jilted by the Prince Who Broke Her Heart.' The tabloids will adore it."

Damn. Sophia's words transported Gracie back to the days surrounding her father's funeral. *Such a beautiful child,* the mayor murmured, staring at the photo of Gracie and Daddy. *Too bad about her father.* He'd used her photo and story in the local newspapers to campaign for everything from new road construction to improved driver safety classes.

The articles twisted her memories until Gracie hated the beautiful, fatherless child they described. The papers soon forgot her, but Gracie never forgot their power over her.

She swallowed and tried for a light tone as she answered Sophia. "If your tabloids are anything like ours, they'll have you engaged to someone else within a week."

"Of course. When Alex abdicated in favor of Constantine, I suppose Stephan became the next spare. One brother should be as good as another. But I don't wish to be bounced from prince to prince until the public gets its next big romance."

She sighed. "I'm tired of being controlled by the papers. And by my family. And even by the king. I want a life of my own."

A sparkle of light snapped Sophia out of her wistful mood. She moved inside, ushering Gracie into a cool shaded corner. "Photographers. Tabloids. We're this week's entertainment."

"I see why you envy me." Gracie thought back to the way Prince Stephan had unwittingly deflected the press' attention from her. His arrogance became her blessing. Even today, she was nothing more than a blip on the media radar screen. "No one cares about the bride's brainy half-sister."

Gracie chewed her lip, remembering the peace she'd found when she finally slipped from the public eye. Everyone deserved a chance at that peace. Even a member of the Melesian aristocracy. "Do you ever want to just disappear?"

"All the time," Sophia replied, a hint of sadness shadowing her voice. "I've made plans to spend a year abroad with Princess Lydia at her home in Europe. After that, I'll join a Melesian goodwill tour scheduled to visit Europe and the Americas.

"The press will speculate I'm nursing my broken heart. If I'm lucky, I can stay away until the next heir to the throne is born. When your sister becomes pregnant, I'll have a measure of peace. I will never have the freedom that you do."

Gracie's mind raced and she considered ways to help Sophia. "What if you could be someone other than Lady Sophia for a few days? Someone like me?"

A flicker of interest lit Sophia's eyes.

"You said the goodwill tour is scheduled to visit the Americas eventually," Gracie continued. "If you could get away from the entourage while you're in the U.S., I could buy you a few days of freedom."

"Tell me." Sophia leaned forward, her attention riveted on Gracie.

"I'll be transferring to the Melesian Royal Academy for the fall semester," she began, grateful that her family and the school administrators had agreed to let her register under her mother's maiden name instead of the name Bradley, which she shared with her now famous sister. "I won't be making many trips back home."

Hours later, Grace Susan Bradley handed Sophia her driver's license and a detailed plan for escaping the goodwill tour for a day or two of freedom. Now all Gracie had to do was fade into the background, focus on her studies, and hope the world forgot her.

Again.

AUTHOR'S NOTE

The story line of a hero-in-disguise has always fascinated me. Run away princes, reclusive billionaires, and super heroes all come to mind when I think of the troupe. Part of the enjoyment, at least for me, is the push-pull of wondering if and when they will be unmasked. And will the unmasking lead to happiness or disaster?

Creating a new, fictional kingdom as a setting for Royally Scandalized was a pleasure. Here are some tidbits about my kingdom, its culture, and its creation.

- The archipelago's name, Melesia (pronounced Mel-ee-see-ah) was inspired from the Greek word for honey (meli), which is fitting since my fictional kingdom was founded by exiled Greek rulers.
- In addition to blending Greek and Caribbean cultures, I was influenced by Polynesian culture as well. One day, I'll need to introduce a legend to explain these influences.
- In searching for a term of endearment that could have variations ranging from "sweetheart" to "soul mate" I contacted writer friends who were fluent in multiple languages. When that avenue stalled, by husband stepped in, laughing as he played around with twisting some of his own terms of endearment for me into "foreign" sounding phrases. I credit him with the creation of the various forms of hona/hono. If you are interested in the Melesian language—stay tuned. I actually created more rudimentary aspects of the language for Reluctantly Royal (book 3 of the series).

- Speaking of creating a culture, check my website. A talented musician is creating a national anthem for the Kingdom of Melesia. Another is creating a map of the area. When these tidbits are ready, you'll find them on the website!

As always I appreciate you taking the time to enter my world. I hope you enjoyed the Kingdom of Melesia and its royal family.

While you are waiting for the next installment, can I ask for your help?

Reviews and word-of-mouth are critical for authors when it comes to finding new readers. Please consider leaving a review or even just a rating of the book at Amazon, Barnes & Noble, Good Reads, Book Bub, or wherever you go to find new books. Then tell two friends about the book and ask them to do the same!

Thank you from the bottom of my heart!

ABOUT THE AUTHOR

Kelle Z. Riley, writer, speaker, global traveler, Ph.D. chemist, and safety/martial arts expert has been featured in public forums that range from local Newspapers to National television. In addition to her works of fiction, a personal story was included in "Chicken Soup for the Soul: Living with Alzheimer's and Other Dementias."

Her fiction publications include cozy mysteries and contemporary romance.

In the Undercover Cat Mysteries a cupcake baking scientist turns sleuth—an much more. *The Cupcake Caper, Shaken, Not Purred, The Tiger's Tale,* and *Studying Scarlett the Grey,* as well as free short stories set in the Undercover Cat world are available on Amazon or wherever books are sold.

In the *Riches and Royals* series, modern career women fall for princes-in-disguise, only to discover that *"happily ever after"* isn't guaranteed. Can love turn their cautionary tale into a glittering fairy tale, or will their hearts shatter like glass slippers?

A former Golden Heart Finalist, Kelle resides in Chattanooga, TN. She is the past program chair and popular speaker for the Chattanooga Writer's Guild, a member of Sisters in Crime, Romance Writers' of America and various local chapters. When not writing, she can be found pursuing passions such as being a self-defense instructor, a Master Gardener, and a full time chemist with numerous professional publications and U.S. patents.

To learn more about the Riches & Royals world, as well as Kelle's other works, visit www.kellezriley.net or scan the code below.

Book one of Riches & Royals: Read My Lips
Book two of Riches & Royals: Royally Scandalized
Book three of Riches & Royals: Reluctantly Royal
Book four of Riches & Royals: Counterfeit Commoner

Join Kelle's newsletter list to get announcements for FREE short stories, upcoming releases, deleted scenes, and inside information on how the Kingdom of Melesia was born!

 www.kellezriley.net

 www.facebook.com/kellezriley

 www.twitter.com/kellezriley